Outstanding praise for th

MAXIE MAINWARING

"Clever and campy . . .
—*Publishers Weekly*

"This fluffy whodunit, this marshmallow mystery, is entertaining . . . perfectly made for summertime reading."
—*Dallas Voice*

BOBBY BLANCHARD, LESBIAN GYM TEACHER

"Shamelessly campy!"
—*Instinct Magazine*

"Nolan's pell-mell pastiche of varied genres is great fun."
—*Pittsburgh's Out*

"If you're looking for silly, satiric fun, Bobby will show you a good time."
—*Edge Magazine*

"A fun, fresh, and feminist satire on pulp fiction of the fifties and sixties."
—*Orange County Blade*

LOIS LENZ, LESBIAN SECRETARY

"Unabashedly campy and titillating, Nolan's debut novel is a tale of 1950s lesbian career girls loose in the big city . . ."
—*Publishers Weekly*

"Nolan squeezes her kicky premise for plenty of juice, leaving the pulp in *Lois Lenz, Lesbian Secretary* deliciously intact."
—*Entertainment Weekly*

"Monica Nolan's first novel, *Lois Lenz, Lesbian Secretary*, is a delicious contemporary homage to queer pulp novels . . ."
—*Bay Times*

"In her second book, Monica Nolan gives us what we really want—a campy pulp filled with gratuitous lesbian sex, communism, reefer madness, and ruthless dictation . . ."
—*Curve Magazine*

"The 1950s. Virginal young women. Small-town values. Repressed deviant desires. Big-city temptations. No, it's not lurid new fiction from lesbian pulp pioneers like Ann Bannon or Paula Christian—though Nolan's campy novel is an exhilarating homage to their lusty novels of yore . . ."
—*Bookmarks*

Books by Monica Nolan

LOIS LENZ, LESBIAN SECRETARY

BOBBY BLANCHARD, LESBIAN GYM TEACHER

MAXIE MAINWARING, LESBIAN DILETTANTE

DOLLY DINGLE, LESBIAN LANDLADY

THE BIG BOOK OF LESBIAN HORSE STORIES
(with Alisa Surkis)

Published by Kensington Publishing Corporation

Dolly Dingle, Lesbian Landlady

MONICA NOLAN

KENSINGTON BOOKS

www.kensingtonbooks.com

KENSINGTON BOOKS are published by

Kensington Publishing Corp.
119 West 40th Street
New York, NY 10018

All Kensington titles, imprints, and distributed lines are available at special quantity discounts for bulk purchases for sales promotion, premiums, fund-raising, educational, or institutional use.

Special book excerpts or customized printings can also be created to fit specific needs. For details, write or phone the office of the Kensington Special Sales Manager: Attn. Special Sales Department. Kensington Publishing Corp., 119 West 40th Street, New York, NY 10018. Phone: 1-800-221-2647.

Kensington and the K logo Reg. U.S. Pat. & TM Off.

eISBN-13: 978-0-7582-8832-5
eISBN-10: 0-7582-8832-8
First Kensington Electronic Edition: October 2014

ISBN-13: 978-0-7582-8831-8
ISBN-10: 0-7582-8831-X
First Kensington Trade Paperback Printing: October 2014

10 9 8 7 6 5 4 3 2 1

Printed in the United States of America

For J. A.
and for Sean, in memory of all those
holiday movies we watched,
over and over and over and over

Chapter 1

In the Wee Hours

"Ho, ho, ho," chortled the girl in the corridor, like a female Santa Claus.

Dolly startled awake from an uneasy sleep. She'd been dreaming she was in bed with a naked woman who wouldn't stop kissing her. In the dream she'd been torn between lust and a lassitude that made her eyes close, despite the affectionate attentions of her naked friend.

She stared blearily into the dimness of her room on the fifth floor of the Magdalena Arms and wondered what time it was and who was making that racket. But when she lifted her head to take a gander at the clock, the room spun dizzyingly around her.

Dolly let her head fall back on the pillow with a groan. She'd had quite a bit to drink at the farewell party for Lon, earlier that evening.

Her pajamas were twisted uncomfortably around her midriff. Dolly tried to straighten them and discovered she was wearing her girdle, and nothing else. She put a hand on the soft flesh under her jaw. Good lord, she must have been far gone when she fell into bed! She hadn't even put on her chin guard.

The girl in the corridor giggled again, and the sound

went through Dolly's head like a chainsaw through an old hickory stump. "Don't make me laugh," said Dolly's unseen tormentor. "I have the hiccups!"

Was she one of Netta's students? The girls who roomed on the fifth floor of the Magdalena Arms were quiet types—Dolly excepted. This rowdy character in the corridor must be some delinquent protégée the dedicated teacher across the hall had brought home from her job at the Eleanor Roosevelt School for Troubled Girls.

A bass voice responded to the giggling girl, murmuring something unintelligible that made her laugh even harder. *Why of all the*—Dolly sucked in her breath in indignant astonishment. Netta's protégée had a man out there! A man on the fifth floor! Hadn't Netta told her troubled teenage friend that men were off-limits at the Magdalena Arms Residence for Women? Noise was one thing, but a man—

The hungover girl struggled to sit up, feeling for the clock on the bedside table.

But there was no bedside table, with its clock and clutter of bobby pins, reading glasses, and throat lozenges—only air. Dolly's flailing hand struck the brass rails of the bed's headboard—which was confusing, since she didn't have a brass bed. She peered into the darkness, dazed.

This wasn't her room on the fifth floor of the Magdalena Arms! Where was she?

She collapsed back onto the strange bed, cudgeling her aching head for clues. She didn't even notice when the giggling finally receded down the corridor.

Maybe that naked woman hadn't been a dream after all!

Tentatively, she felt through the tangle of sheets and blankets until her exploring hand encountered a soft, warm body. Fragments of memory came back to her, like the flickering pictures of an old movie. Someone was unbuttoning her shirt—she was sitting on the edge of the bed, kissing someone—someone pushed her playfully down on the bed—someone's voluptuous breasts swayed just above her face...she remembered a voice too: "Don't fall asleep on me, Dolly!"

But who was the other actor in this half-remembered drama? That cute brunette she'd bought a drink for, after Lon and the gang departed? The serious blonde who'd told Dolly all about her dog-walking business later, when everything began to blur?

Damn that bouillon and celery diet she'd been following! Damn Jerry, her agent, for insisting that if she reduced she'd get better roles! This was what came of drinking on an empty stomach: waking up in a strange room with your head hammering and a mouth like cotton wool.

Dolly sat up, swung her legs over the side of the bed, and pushed herself to her unsteady feet. Stumbling a little, she bumped into a lamp and groped for the switch. Light flooded the room, and Dolly blinked as she took in the bed, its other occupant buried under blankets, the bureau, the cheap landscape on the wall, the fire exit diagram on the door. *I'm in a hotel room*, she deduced, pleased with her acumen.

There was a murmur from the blankets. The shape under the covers turned over, and a disheveled head emerged. "Dolly, honey," said a sleepy voice. "What are you doing?"

"Sylvia," breathed Dolly. *Oh, cripes!* She wished she could hide under the covers and pretend she was still unconscious. She'd much rather have found herself in bed with a stranger than playing this intimate scene opposite Francine's perennial barfly!

It wasn't that the woman, sitting up in bed now and lighting a cigarette, wasn't attractive. The black lace negligee she wore showed off her well-preserved curves and even after an evening of steady drinking, with her makeup smeared and her hair tousled, she exuded a certain louche charm.

But Sylvia had been a fixture at Francine's for almost a decade, coming in once or twice a month, escaping from her dreary life in the suburbs for a weekend and parking herself at the ladies-only watering hole. How many times had Dolly passed Sylvia, leaning moodily on Francine's jukebox, listening to some out-of-date song? How many times had she watched this perennial visitor to the twilight world try out her unhappy housewife story on any girl who hadn't heard it before, until she landed a playmate for the length of her stay? Why, Sylvia was practically a rite of passage at Francine's! Dolly herself had spent a weekend with the hot-to-trot housewife back in '58.

But a repeat performance—that was strictly from hunger!

The dismayed girl spotted her clothes, tossed untidily over a chair, and reached for them. She had to escape this stuffy hotel room—it must be the Prescott, which was where Sylvia always stayed—into the fresh air of the street.

Sylvia blinked as Dolly pulled on her gray slacks. "Where are you going? It's the middle of the night, and I have the babysitter until noon tomorrow! We could spend the whole morning in bed."

Dolly tried to conceal her instinctive recoil at the prospect of an entire morning with the mixed-up mother. Had she truly gone with Sylvia to this room at the Prescott of her own free will? She couldn't think of a tactful way to frame the question.

"Does your daughter still need a babysitter?" she asked instead, as she fastened her bra and pulled on her orange turtleneck. She looked around for her socks. "Isn't she in high school now?"

"She's only twelve." Sylvia looked offended as she stubbed out her cigarette.

"Sure, twelve, I remember now. Well, gosh, I'd love to do breakfast in bed," Dolly fibbed, "but I've got to be at the studio very, very early." She buttoned a brown and yellow Pendleton plaid over her turtleneck. Where on earth were her socks? Her feet would freeze in just her loafers. Ah! There they were, coiled like two brown snakes, halfway under the bed.

"The studio?" Sylvia furrowed her brow. "Oh, your television show, *The Jarvises*. I'll have to tell the girls in my bridge club I spent the evening with Julie Jarvis. Of course, I won't tell them what we were up to!" She winked.

"*Meet the Jarvises*," corrected Dolly. "I was *Judy* Jarvis. But it's been off the air—"

"Judy Jarvis!" Sylvia said. "You were always having trouble with your steady Fred. 'Nice girls don't pet!' " she trilled in a falsetto, then ruined her impersonation of teenage Judy with a phlegm-filled cough.

Dolly was used to girls imitating Judy Jarvis, the wholesome, apple-cheeked, all-American teenager she'd played for five years. "But, Daddy, I'm almost sixteen!" a pickup might mock-squeal before tossing back her drink at whatever dimly lit bar Dolly found herself in. Or, "Mother, you simply don't understand," a forty-year-old executive would murmur as she led Dolly to the bedroom. Some girls could quote whole scenes between Judy and her boyfriend Fred, especially the "I don't pet" episode. "I'll be Fred," more than one eager girl had told Dolly, as they slid under the covers, imitating the teenage boy to wheedle, "Then why do you have to be nice?" Thus cued, Dolly would oblige with a shocked, "Why, Fred!"

But those faithful fans who knew the show by heart were a thing of the past, and the number of girls who still recognized Dolly as a one-time television star had dwindled considerably, ever since reruns had gone off the air. Dolly eyed Sylvia in the bureau mirror as she ran a comb through her mussed hair. Even the middle-aged housewife seemed hazy on the details.

"I'm on a new show," she said, wondering who she was trying to impress. "*A Single Candle.*"

"Really!" Sylvia perked up when Dolly named the popular daytime drama. "Why, I love that show. I watch it every day. Who do you play?"

"Nurse Hamilton."

"Nurse Hamilton?" Sylvia looked puzzled.

"The night nurse," Dolly helped. "Remember the scene where Linda is brought to the hospital after Steve crashes the car just as they're eloping? I'm the nurse who said, 'She's still unconscious, doctor.'" She watched Sylvia hopefully, but no sign of recognition lit the unhappy homemaker's face. A little cast down, Dolly shrugged on her camel-hair coat.

"Wait," Sylvia begged, but she no longer cared about extending their tryst. "You've got to tell me, *when* is Linda going to come out of her coma?"

"I'm not allowed to say," said Dolly. She didn't tell Sylvia she didn't know anyway. She slipped her feet into her loafers and picked up her handbag. "I've got to run, Sylvia. Thanks for—everything."

She hesitated a minute. Should she kiss Sylvia goodbye? But the fence-jumping femme was already flipping through a black address book she'd fished out of her purse. Dolly left, closing the door softly behind her.

Her relief at extricating herself from the awkward scene dissolved into a wave of melancholy as she made her way down the deserted hotel corridor. Who was she to be snooty about Sylvia? She wasn't so different. They'd both been kicking around Bay City's sapphic scene far too long. If they were cartons of milk, they'd be past their sell-by date—positively curdled!

She hurried through the lobby past the dozing night clerk and pushed open the door to the street.

Hunching her shoulders against the bitter November cold, Dolly realized she'd left her wool scarf behind. She turned up her collar and plunged her hands deep into her pockets—she certainly wasn't going back to Sylvia's hotel room to hunt around for it while Sylvia phoned her next conquest!

Time, which had stood still all those years she'd played a fifteen-year-old, had suddenly sped up. In the two years since the Jarvises had left the airwaves, Dolly felt like she'd aged twenty years at least. She was thirty-five now, and whenever she opened a magazine, some beauty columnist was warning women her age to stay away from short skirts or long hair—"if you're over thirty-five, these styles are too young for you!" the magazines said sternly.

Where had the years gone, and what did she have to show for them? The over-the-hill actress frowned, as she reviewed her pitiful résumé since *The Jarvises*. Some radio work. A girly calendar. A guest spot here and there. Even her once-thriving, fetish-photography modeling career had petered out. All she had was a job plumping pillows as the forgettable Nurse Hamilton.

And wasn't it a little sad that while so many of her friends paired up and moved out of the Magdalena Arms into their own apartments, Dolly had stayed on, the perpetual single girl, roaming the half-empty halls of her old rooming house, looking for a Ping-Pong partner?

And now this—a one-night stand with someone she wasn't even attracted to!

The actress passed Francine's, shuttered and dark, the

blue and pink neon sign with the down-pointed arrow switched off. She frowned at the scene of her recent blunder—the misplaced, alcohol-infused friendliness that had landed her in Sylvia's bed. If only she'd gone home at a reasonable hour, like the rest of her friends.

The gang got together so rarely these days that Dolly had wanted to make the most of the occasion. Yet it seemed like they'd scarcely sat down before the departures began. Netta had said her "bon voyage" to Lon first, claiming she had some cause-y meeting to attend. Rhoda and Janet left next—they were still in the honeymoon phase; everhelpful Phyllis departed with Lon, the guest of honor, explaining, "I promised to help Lon pack." Lon at least had an excuse: She was catching an early flight to Paris this morning. Pam and Lois had stayed a little longer, but gregarious Dolly had grown bored with their conversation, dominated as it was by domestic problems, and had gone looking for new friends. She'd been dancing with a darkhaired girl when Lois tapped her on the shoulder to say that she and Pam were going home.

That left Dolly, keeping the party going in a bar full of girls who looked younger than Judy Jarvis.

It's time for a makeover, Dolly resolved. She was going to start acting her age. No more late nights at Francine's. No more breaking her diet with Swedish pancakes at Swenson's. No more going home with strange—or not so strange—women when she was tipsy. From now on she would be mature, serious-minded, career-focused.

The cold air was invigorating. It cleared the hungover girl's head like a plunge in an icy mountain creek. Dolly's natural optimism reasserted itself as she walked briskly through the dark, deserted streets. Thirty-five wasn't *so* old. She could still make that comeback she'd been working on. First order of business: Persuade the soap's producer to build up her part. That meant sticking to this awful diet until she slimmed down into the shapely sort of nurse television viewers expected. Then her stalled career would start moving again—bringing bigger parts, game show appearances, maybe even her own show!

And as soon as the money started flowing, she'd move into her own apartment, maybe in a doorman building in Lakeside. She shivered. It sounded kind of lonely—after all, she'd lived at the Arms for fifteen years and she was used to the camaraderie and company of two dozen other girls.

But she wouldn't be alone, Dolly reminded herself. She'd get a steady girlfriend, maybe someone in showbiz, who could help her climb the ladder. Look at the way advertising executive Lois and sportswear-buyer Pamela kept each other current with the latest trends. And wasn't corrections administrator Rhoda in the perfect position to provide clients for her lawyer girlfriend Janet?

I can certainly do better than Sylvia, Dolly told herself firmly.

Her step took on a jaunty swing as she thought back to last week's shoot. Hadn't there been hints on the set that she was due for a juicy scene? Oh, nothing definite, but she felt it in her bones, as surely as she smelled snow in the air. It was the way the wardrobe mistress had measured her so carefully for a new uniform, and the fact that the producer herself had appeared to watch that unimportant bit last week, where Nurse Hamilton plumped the comatose Linda's pillow. To clinch it, she'd overheard the director and his assistant talking about the difficulties of a scene where someone's uniform was ripped—"we want a little skin, but we can't overdo it," the director had mused.

Dolly turned the corner, her mind filled with rosy pictures of Nurse Hamilton being attacked by a lustful patient or doctor. Maybe even troubled Dr. Dwight!

A frightened cry drove the soap opera's plot twists out

of her head. Dolly stiffened as she spotted two figures struggling on a stoop at the end of the block, the street-light casting sinister, swaying shadows. A girl's voice said, "Let me go! Let me go or I'll scream!"

As Dolly quickened her pace, the girl opened her mouth and made good her threat.

Chapter 2

Jackie

Dolly broke into a run, racing toward the struggling couple like a nurse toward an ambulance. The thug had managed to clap a hand over the girl's mouth, stifling her cries for help, when Dolly came up behind him and swung her purse with all the force of her solidly built five feet and eleven inches.

She caught the mugger squarely on the back of his head, and he yelped as he half turned to face this new onslaught. His captive took advantage of his distraction to bite his hand, and he gave a grunt of pain and released her. But he only backed away a few feet, the breathing space to pull a switchblade from his pocket and flick it open. "Don't give me no more trouble," he began.

"Trouble is my maiden name!" Twirling her purse as adeptly as a Roman gladiator with a mace, Dolly knocked the blade from the astonished attacker's hand. Meanwhile, his erstwhile victim aimed a series of kicks in the direction of his shins. The miscreant turned and ran, stumbling in his haste to escape.

For an instant the only sounds in the deserted street were the two girls panting and the receding footsteps of the fleeing criminal. Dolly's voice was shaky as she asked, "Are you all right?" She bent to scoop up the switchblade, then turned to the girl she'd rescued, getting a good look at her for the first time.

Short, dark hair fell in attractive wisps about an elfin face; her dark eyes were wide with shock, fear, and excitement. She wore jeans and a leather jacket—inadequate protection against the Bay City cold, judging by the way she shivered. "I guess so," she said, dazed.

A typical Riverside waif, Dolly diagnosed, sweeping the girl from head to toe with one comprehensive glance. One of the flood of would-be bohemians that had invaded Bay City this past year. *She couldn't be more than twenty,* the older actress thought with a kind of envious pity.

The girl patted herself as if to make sure she was still there, and then dug into her pocket. "And I've still got my tips!" The money seemed to reassure her. She bent down and retrieved a black wool cap that had evidently been knocked off in the struggle, pulling it down over her ears with trembling fingers. She was still in shock, Dolly decided.

"Are you on your way home? Why don't I walk you? Where do you live?"

"I live here." The girl pointed to the apartment building they were standing in front of. "But my—my friend locked me out. I was just trying to think what to do when that jerk asked me for a light and then jumped me when I went to get my matches. Gosh . . ." She seemed to really see Dolly for the first time. "I don't know what would have happened if you hadn't come along! I don't think I'd have been able to fight him off all on my own!"

"Think nothing of it." Dolly waved away the girl's gratitude modestly. "Sometimes it's handy, being such a big girl. But what kind of 'friend' locks you out? That's no way to behave!"

"Well, we—we haven't been getting along lately." The Riverside waif was evasive.

Love trouble, Dolly diagnosed. She decided to be blunt; it was too cold to keep pussyfooting around what she suspected was a shared sapphic secret. "Let me guess—your girlfriend found someone new?"

"Why—how did you know?" The naive girl's big eyes widened even more.

"Lucky guess." Dolly summed up years of experience and intuition with a shrug. This new generation seemed to think they'd invented sapphic romance!

Now that Dolly had mentioned the love that dare not speak its name, the younger girl turned talkative. "Cynthia's been on my back to move out, but I didn't think she'd do something this drastic!"

"You'd better come home with me," the actress told her kindly. "There are plenty of spare rooms at the Magdalena Arms. Let's get going before we freeze to death or that fellow comes back with a friend."

"I'm Jackie," said the girl as they set out. "And I can't thank you enough for coming to my rescue. You're like my knight in shining armor, no kidding!"

Dolly couldn't help preening at the girl's admiration. "I'm Dorian Dingle, but call me Dolly." She felt Jackie casting sidelong glances at her, probing, curious looks.

"You seem so familiar," murmured the bohemian girl. "Like I've seen you before. Maybe in the neighborhood? No . . ."

Dolly helped her out. "I was in a show on TV," she began.

"That's it!" Jackie interrupted. "Nurse Hamilton on *A Single Candle*! I'm a big fan of yours!"

"You are?" Dolly was torn between astonishment and pleasure.

"Everyone else on that show is busy chewing the scenery and you just quietly *emote*. You make it look so easy—always present, always still—not *acting*, but *being*. I know how hard that is. You see"—Jackie's voice betrayed her self-consciousness—"I'm an actress too. At least, I will be someday."

As they walked through the wintry night, the younger girl told Dolly her life's story. She'd been attending college in a little town called Appleton, majoring in English literature, when she fell hard for a senior named Cynthia. "We played opposite each other in *Twelfth Night*," Jackie confided. "Every rehearsal, when I said the line, 'Most radiant, exquisite and unmatchable beauty,' I felt it *here*." She put her hand on her breast.

The love-struck sophomore had dropped out of college that spring, when Cynthia graduated, following her beloved to Bay City to live with her and study acting. "I've never been the conventional type," she told Dolly, rather proudly. Jackie seemed unfazed by the fact that the romance part of this plan had apparently failed. She'd been in the city for six months, working at a dinette in Dockside and studying at the Actor's Academy with famed teacher, Sidney Meier.

"He cast me as Laura in the academy's production of *The Glass Menagerie*," the aspiring actress boasted. "Even if things didn't work out between Cynthia and me, studying the Meier Method with Sidney has changed my life, literally! Where did you study? Do you use the Meier Method, or are you a strict Stanislavski kind of girl?"

Dolly was spared the difficulty of explaining the Jarvis Method to the serious thespian by their arrival at the Arms. "This is where I hang my hat," she told Jackie.

"Oh, *this* place." Jackie looked at the old building curiously. "I've always wondered who lived here."

The Magdalena Arms had a certain grandeur that set it apart from its neighbors. The big square building had old-fashioned, gracious proportions; instead of being flush with the sidewalk, it was bordered by a fringe of lawn and shrubbery. Three marble steps led the way to double glass doors covered with a brass grille.

But it was a shabby grandeur. The hedge was stunted, with gaps like missing teeth. The marble steps they climbed were chipped and cracked; the elaborate brass grille on the door Dolly unlocked was tarnished. As the long-time tenant led Jackie inside, the younger girl exclaimed, "Wow! It's like something out of Poe!"

Dolly was no English major like Jackie—she only knew Poe from those Vincent Price movies—but this didn't sound like a compliment. She looked around, seeing the lobby of her home through Jackie's eyes.

The Arms had been sliding slowly downhill for years, but now the evidence of its decline glared at Dolly from every side. The chandelier had been broken forever—couldn't Mrs. DeWitt have found a better substitute than that bare lightbulb over the abandoned front desk? The paint on the ceiling was buckling and unpeeling in swaths as wide as Dolly's fist, and tile squares were missing from the mosaic *M* in the center of the marble floor. Jackie was right—the place only needed cobwebs hanging from the doorways to play the part of a haunted house!

"What's that sound?" Jackie clutched Dolly's arm in sudden alarm.

"That's just Mrs. DeWitt, snoring," Dolly reassured the frightened girl as the ominous rumbling filled the hall. "She's our housemother, or landlady, I guess you'd

say." How to explain to this girl from the "now" generation that the Magdalena Arms had been established in an
era when nice girls were not permitted to live in Bay City
unchaperoned?

"Come on," she said instead, leading the way to the
wide, curving staircase. "The elevator's out."

Mrs. DeWitt too had descended into decrepitude over
the years, Dolly realized sadly, as they climbed. The
housemother seemed particularly frail of late, drifting
about the first floor, sipping gin while sorting the mail, or
murmuring melancholy bits of verse as she presided over
the breakfast that was included in the rent. She'd always
mangled her tenants' names, but lately her memory had
become so faulty she forgot them completely.

"Mrs. DeWitt used to be an actress too," she felt com-
pelled to inform Jackie. "She's performed all over—from
cabarets in Berlin to the Orpheum here in Bay City. She
played opposite Edgar Villiers once!"

"Who's that?"

"Another actor—he was famous for his Iago in the
thirties."

"Oh." Jackie was busy peering down the dim hallways
of each floor they climbed past. "Who else lives here? I
mean, what kind of people?"

"Well . . ." The question was hard to answer these
days. The long-time tenants Dolly knew best had mostly
left (or been taken away, in one sad case) and the fresh-
faced girls who replaced them all looked alike to the
older actress. These new tenants never stayed long anyway—to them, the Magdalena Arms was a way station, a
place to pause while they got their bearings in Bay City.
Besides Netta, Maxie, and Phyllis on the fifth floor, the
only old-timer still around was Kay, the clarinetist on
four.

Now Dolly told Jackie: "We used to have mainly actresses and other theatrical types, but now there're all sorts—secretaries, teachers, nurses, statisticians. All kinds of girls."

"You mean, there aren't any men?" Jackie's eyes widened.

"That's right. It's a women-only boardinghouse."

"Wild! Like my old dorm!"

They'd reached the fifth floor by this time, and both girls were breathing hard from the climb. Dolly felt a little dizzy—she was still a bit blitzed. Glancing at her new friend, she wondered if this was another tipsy mistake, bringing a stranger back to the Arms. The last thing the tenants needed was another light-fingered girl, like that sharpie Mrs. DeWitt had evicted last month after she was caught rummaging in her neighbor's jewelry box.

I couldn't leave a homeless girl out on the street! she reasoned.

Dolly unlocked room 505 with the spare key Maxie had left her. "You can sleep here," she told Jackie. "Maxie won't mind."

"Where's Maxie?"

"She's in France, looking for manuscripts. She's a successful businesswoman—runs her own publishing company and has quite a few other interests."

Thinking of Maxie lifted Dolly's spirits. After all, if her next-door neighbor had gone from being broke and unemployed to running not one, but two successful businesses, and acquiring not one, but two girlfriends in the process, surely Dolly could manage a few minor improvements!

"Looking for manuscripts in France? I don't get it."

"She and her friend Stella plan to visit Tangier, where there's a bunch of English and American writers," Dolly explained. She could still hear Maxie planning gleefully, "Those drug-addled expats will sell us salacious stories cheap, and I can write this vacation off as business!"

"Her other friend, Lon, is flying to Paris to join them tomorrow, or I guess I mean today. That's why I happened to be out so late. I was at Lon's bon voyage party."

Jackie wasn't listening. She was examining Maxie's bookcase. "*Mob Girl: Inside the Lindqvist Gang*," she read out loud. "*The Coral Reef: The Truth about the Twisted Sisters in Our Midst.*"

"She published both of those," Dolly told her proudly. Jackie plucked a book off the bottom shelf.

"*Boarding School Hussies*! This is for me." She laughed. "Can you feature it? 'Their sins snowball into an avalanche of depravity that threatens the whole school!' What a hoot!"

"I'll be next door, in 503," said Dolly, glad her new friend was so easily entertained. "The bathroom's at the end of the hall on the left. I'll rustle up an extra towel, and there's always a supply of new toothbrushes in the medicine cabinet." At least the fifth floor is still prepared for unexpected overnight guests, Dolly consoled herself. The place hadn't gone completely to the dogs!

"Dolly, you're wonderful," said Jackie earnestly. "You're like a fairy godmother, bringing me here, to this crazy place! I didn't know that people still lived like this."

Dolly guessed that Jackie meant that as a compliment to the Magdalena Arms. As she undid her girdle with a sigh of relief, she decided she *hadn't* made a mistake, bringing Jackie here. Anyone who appreciated the Magdalena Arms's special qualities had to be okay.

Dolly slid into bed and turned out her light. A second later she switched it on again. She'd almost forgotten to put on her chin guard.

Chapter 3

Plumbing Problems

Dolly was woken by the usual Saturday morning sounds: the twittering of birds in the spindly elm tree out back, the opening and closing of doors along the corridor, the sound of running water and muffled chatter.

She winced as she sat up and undid her chin guard. She must have strained a muscle in her back, flailing at Jackie's attacker. Or was it from passing out in Sylvia's sagging hotel bed? The hungover girl banished the unpleasant memory from her mind. That was yesterday. Today belonged to the new, improved Dolly. Pulling on her terrycloth bathrobe, she made her way to the washroom at the end of the hall.

Phyllis was at the sink, splashing her face. Netta, already dressed in faded blue slacks and a heavy pullover, was combing her hair. "Howdy, gals," Dolly greeted them breezily.

"Good morning, Dolly." Phyllis turned off the faucet and picked up a towel. "What time did you get home last night? I was listening for you, but I must have fallen asleep."

Frizzy-haired Phyllis, with earnest eyes of washed-out blue behind newly acquired gold-rimmed glasses, was the conscientious one of the gang. She worked as a statistician in the Bay City Planning Department and divided her life between pushing utopian schemes for subsidized housing and pining after her former supervisor, Miss Ware, now director of Bay City's Department of Human Services.

"I'm glad I didn't wake you." Dolly evaded the question. She was fond of Phyllis, but the staid statistician would never understand finding yourself in a strange bed with no memory of how you got there. "That was fun last night, wasn't it?"

Phyllis agreed. "It was wonderful to get the whole gang together."

"That's what I thought!" Dolly turned to Netta, now wiping her tortoiseshell glasses. "You left too early."

Without her thick-lensed glasses, the progressive schoolteacher was a rather attractive girl. But as soon as she settled them on her nose, she turned into the serious-minded crusader, who spent all her free time attending meetings and organizing campaigns to remake the world according to her stringent specifications.

"There was an emergency meeting of the Union of Concerned Teachers for Nuclear Accountability," she said now. "Why, what did I miss?"

Dolly filled her in on the latest gossip. "Did you hear that Lois and Pamela are moving to a bigger place, since Pam got promoted again?"

Netta grunted. "Quite the conformist couple!" She hung her towel tidily on its hook.

Oh dear. Dolly kept forgetting how Netta disapproved of Pam and Lois and their pursuit of conventional success. Netta blamed Pamela, of course. "Lois didn't use to be so materialistic," she told anyone who would listen. "She knew what mattered when she was with *me*."

It was crystal clear to everyone but Netta that jealousy

was behind her high-minded criticism. Dolly didn't get it—Netta was the one who'd broken off with Lois the summer before last, after all. Did she want her ex-girlfriend back? Or was it just that she didn't want her to be quite so happy?

It had to sting a little, having the girl you'd dumped settle down in domestic bliss, however square that made her, while your own forward-thinking flames fizzled out. Netta was currently single.

For an instant, Dolly studied her neighbors, pondering the strange twist of fate that had made the three of them, despite their differences, close friends. If Mrs. DeWitt hadn't placed them on the same floor so many years ago, the struggling actress might never have met the radical schoolteacher or the oddly innocent statistician. Each year they stayed on, while other tenants came and went, had strengthened their bond.

They did have one thing in common, Dolly thought dolefully: None of them, at least lately, had had a romantic attachment that lasted any length of time. Abruptly, as if looking in a funhouse mirror, Dolly saw reflected in the glass above the sink not three old friends, but a trio of pathetic spinsters, or maybe eccentric old maids, abandoned by time on the fifth floor of this deteriorating boardinghouse.

"Good morning!" Jackie's greeting dissolved Dolly's disturbing illusion. The fresh-faced girl paused on the threshold, beaming. "There you are, Dolly! I just knocked on your door—at least, I hope it was your door."

Phyllis and Netta were examining the bohemian girl curiously, and Dolly hurried to make introductions. "This is Jackie—we met last night—"

"I was getting mugged, and Dolly here charged to the rescue!" Jackie interrupted.

"And since she was locked out of her place and it was

four a.m., I brought her back here and put her in Maxie's room."

"Four a.m.?" Phyllis knit her brow, and Dolly saw that the sharp-minded statistician was computing the difference between Francine's two a.m. closing time and the hour of Jackie's rescue.

"So you all share this bathroom?" Jackie looked around in wonder. "Oh look, you have little labeled shelves for your toiletries! How cute! I feel like I'm in that boarding school book I was reading."

The older tenants made space for her at the long sink counter.

"Gosh, the water's a little icy!" The young girl tested the water with her hand and looked up in alarm. "You do have hot water here, don't you?"

"Of course we do," said Netta, a touch impatiently. "Or at least"—she turned on the water in her basin— "we're supposed to." She sighed. "Another plumbing problem for you, Dolly!"

Dolly tried the third basin. No hot water. "Hmmm!"

"Maybe something needs a patch, like the kitchen sink last week," Phyllis suggested hopefully.

Dolly shook her head. "A leak wouldn't turn the water cold. I'll bet it's the pilot light on the water heater."

"Let's get breakfast and tell Mrs. DeWitt," said Netta. "She might have to call a plumber this time, instead of relying on you."

"Oh, no." Dolly was all assurance. "All you need to do is relight it. I can do that."

During Dolly's various periods of unemployment, the elderly landlady had come to rely on her tenant's self-taught repair skills and native resourcefulness—not to mention her size and strength. Time and again, Mrs. De-Witt had turned to Dolly and said, "Dolly, my dear, it makes no sense to call some upstart mechanic who will only overcharge when you can do the job just as well." Dolly had been happy to help, particularly since Mrs. DeWitt was nice about waiting for the rent during those lean times when Nurse Hamilton's nursing skills were not needed on the soap opera.

Now the girls all trooped down the hall after Netta. At the head of the stairs, the fifth floor's last tenant was emerging from her room. Netta made the introductions this time: "Beverly, this is Jackie, who's staying in Maxie's room. Jackie, this is Beverly Butler."

Dolly hoped Jackie wouldn't blurt out, "I didn't realize such an old-fashioned place would be integrated!"

The aloof young Negro girl had arrived that fall from Mississippi. She'd belonged to one of the youth groups Netta had helped organize during her summer stint registering voters. When Netta learned that Beverly's dream of becoming a nurse was stymied by Mississippi's segregated educational system, she'd arranged for one of her progressive groups to sponsor Beverly's move to Bay City and further education.

If Jackie was surprised to find a girl of another race at the out-of-date boardinghouse, she kept it to herself. "Hello, Beverly," she said with her wide smile, while Dolly explained again the circumstances that had brought Jackie to the Arms.

"Bay City's dangerous—not like home," Beverly said as the girls descended the stairs. Then she rephrased it. "I mean, in a different way from home."

Soon Jackie and Beverly were swapping stories about their new lives in the big city. Dolly listened in astonishment as the student nurse actually laughed at Jackie's account of getting on the wrong bus and ending up at the county jail instead of Gruneman's department store. She'd considered the new girl a little stuck-up, but now she wondered if maybe Beverly was just lonely. *After all,*

Dolly reminded herself, *in Beverly's eyes, Netta and Phyllis and I probably look as old as an aunt!* Jackie was the nurse's own age.

The aspiring young actress turned around to tell Dolly enthusiastically, "I bet Beverly could give you lots of help with your interpretation of Nurse Hamilton—stuff you can use when you're creating your objectives!"

"I haven't had a chance to watch Dolly's show," said Beverly politely. "But I'd surely be happy to help, if I can."

On the fourth-floor landing, a lanky girl almost as tall as Dolly joined them. "No hot water," she reported.

"So it's unanimous." Dolly realized that if Kay on the fourth floor was affected, the whole building must be. She repeated her reassurance: "It's just the pilot light—fixing it will be easy as pie. Meanwhile, meet your new neighbor Jackie. Jackie, this is Kay Coutts."

Kay shook Jackie's hand. "What room are you in? 505? I'm right underneath you then. I hope you like the clarinet!"

Kay taught musical enrichment part-time, traveling around the Bay City's public school system, but her heart was in the all-woman combo she played with, the Sisterhood of Swing. Like the rest of the old-timers, the musician stayed at the Arms because it was cheap; and like Dolly she was still hoping for that big break—a tour, a recording deal, a permanent gig.

Outgoing Jackie was already asking about the ins and outs of the clarinet. As they reached the first floor, the bohemian girl turned to Dolly and exclaimed, "This place is crazy, but completely! It's like an art commune, or something!"

Netta snorted.

"Well, sure, we're pretty artistic, I guess," Dolly said to make up for the sourpuss teacher. Quickly she changed the topic. "Is that coffee I smell?"

The reassuring scent of coffee greeted them as they descended the narrow flight of stairs to the basement dining room. "A cafeteria in your own home!" Dolly heard Jackie exclaim. "Wild!"

It wasn't really a cafeteria. Breakfast these days was served buffet style, with everyone helping herself from the old mahogany sideboard, which held the coffee urn, pitchers of orange juice, cartons of milk, and dry cereal. This morning the sideboard also held a chafing dish of scrambled eggs, which Dolly knew from experience would be overcooked and rubbery. The coffee cake next to the eggs, still in its white pasteboard box, would be slightly stale, because Mrs. DeWitt got it day-old, at a discount, from a bakery on 48th Street.

As Dolly drew a cup of coffee from the urn, she remembered the days when plump cinnamon rolls, warm from the oven and glistening with melted butter and brown sugar, were a regular feature on the sideboard; next to them might be a pan of poached eggs with hollandaise sauce and a platter piled high with crisp bacon. Her mouth watered at the memory.

In those days, the Arms could still afford a cook-housekeeper. Now Mrs. DeWitt manned the kitchen herself, leaning heavily on store-bought food.

Better for my diet. The actress sipped her black coffee and tried to erase the vivid picture of pastries from days gone by. *I will be svelte!* She attempted to imagine herself, slender as Audrey Hepburn only taller, struggling in the arms of the tormented Dr. Dwight.

A girl from the second floor—Sue something—appealed to Dolly, "When's the hot water going to be fixed? I asked Mrs. DeWitt, but it was like she didn't hear me."

"I'll find out." Dolly set down her coffee and went into the kitchen.

The Magdalena Arms housemother stood at the sink,

washing a frying pan and reciting a poem. Mrs. DeWitt had studied elocution in her youth and could reel off reams of verse at the drop of a hat. All the Arms girls had gained a nodding acquaintance with Tennyson, her favorite poet. Odd bits of "The Lady of Shalott" were permanently lodged in Dolly's head.

It wasn't Tennyson today. The old actress recited in a low, somber voice:

> *" 'Perhaps in this neglected spot is laid*
> *Some heart once pregnant with celestial fire;*
> *Hands, that the rod of empire might have swayed,*
> *Or waked to ecstasy the living lyre,' "*

Dolly began, "Good morning, Mrs. DeWitt—"
Mrs. DeWitt peered around vaguely. "Good morning, my dear," she said, before continuing,

> *" 'But knowledge to their eyes her ample page,*
> *Rich with the spoils of time did ne'er unroll;*
> *Chill penury repressed their noble rage,*
> *and froze the genial current of the soul.' "*

Dolly wondered if this was one of Mrs. DeWitt's bad days, when the cloud of gin that hung around her thickened into an impenetrable curtain. The landlady's gray hair was piled atop her head in a haphazard pompadour. She wore the red plaid bathrobe the tenants had chipped in to purchase last Christmas. Below the hem, an ancient pair of lavender satin lounging pajamas peeked out. Her old-fashioned carpet slippers were dark and stained. Water stains, Dolly realized. Mrs. DeWitt was splashing water out of the sink and onto the kitchen floor each time she turned the pan over.

"Mrs. DeWitt, you're standing in a puddle of water," Dolly told her.

Mrs. DeWitt glanced down at her feet in surprise. "Why, so I am!" She turned to Dolly, a sudden glimmer of intelligence in her eye. "That reminds me, Dolly, I meant to ask you where the hot water has gone to. You're so clever about these things—"

She started to take a step toward Dolly and then turned back to the sink to put the frying pan down. Perhaps it was the weight of the big frying pan or trying to move in two directions at once, but whatever the cause, Mrs. DeWitt lost her balance. The slick soles of her soaked slippers flew out from under her, and the old actress landed on the wet linoleum with a sickening crash.

Chapter 4

In the Sub-basement Storeroom

The girls came running from their breakfasts at the sound of Mrs. DeWitt's fall. Beverly pushed her way through the crowd. She knelt by her landlady's side, ignoring the puddle of water, which soaked her nylons and the skirt of her white uniform. The old woman was groaning incoherently, as Beverly felt her over gently.

"I believe she's broken her hip." She spoke matter-of-factly, but her eyes were worried.

"I'll call an ambulance." Netta vanished from the kitchen.

Mrs. DeWitt clutched at Dolly's arm. The alarmed tenant was crouched on the old landlady's other side. "I can't leave my girls," she moaned.

"Don't worry, Mrs. DeWitt, I'll look after things here at the Arms," Dolly tried to reassure the prone woman. It was as if a mighty oak that had stood forever in a city park had suddenly toppled.

"The keys—" Mrs. DeWitt lifted her hand and stopped as a grimace of agony contorted her face.

"I'll get them, lie still." Gingerly, Dolly fished the big ring of keys from the plaid pocket. Mrs. DeWitt's eyes closed and then fluttered open again. "There's something I'm forgetting—"

"Take it easy. Don't worry about a thing," Dolly tried to reassure her.

It seemed ages before Jackie called, "The ambulance men are here!" and ran in, showing the way to two burly men in white coats. Beverly outlined the situation as they laid the stretcher next to Mrs. DeWitt and then rolled her on her side while they slipped it under her. Despite their quick efficiency, the old woman gasped and groaned. It was terrible—and strangely fascinating—to see their histrionic landlady, who was given to dramatizing the smallest emotion, in actual pain. As the men lifted the stretcher, Mrs. DeWitt grasped Dolly again. Her grip was like iron.

"The trustees' meeting! You go—explain—tell them— just a minor fall—" Her eyes were wide with anxiety. "It's vitally important!"

"I'll go, I'll explain everything. Don't worry!" Dolly hastened to soothe her landlady. Mrs. DeWitt's eyes closed in relief. They all followed the stretcher up the stairs and out the front door. "Monday, at Mrs. Putney-Potter's," Mrs. DeWitt croaked, as they slid her into the ambulance.

Beverly climbed in after her. "I'll telephone as soon as I've heard what the doctor says," she called to the anxious group before the ambulance doors closed.

Slowly the girls filtered back downstairs to the dining room, to pick uncertainly at their lukewarm breakfasts. Dolly looked around at the discombobulated tenants. She felt the weight of the key ring in her bathrobe pocket, and the even greater weight of responsibility. "Take care of my girls," Mrs. DeWitt had as much as said. It was Dolly's duty to pep up the shaken tenants.

"I'm going to brew up a fresh pot of coffee," Dolly declared. "And who feels like waffles?"

Faces brightened. Everyone felt like waffles. Dolly pulled down the battered waffle iron from its place in the pantry and tripled the recipe from the *Woman's Companion Cookbook*. In no time at all, the iron was steaming and the stack of hot fluffy waffles was growing. The girls fell on the treat as if they were starving, and a buzz of animated chatter filled the room. It was worth using up the last of the eggs and milk, Dolly decided, pleased.

"Do we pay our rent to you now?" Sue from the second floor posed the question as she held out her plate for thirds.

"Rent's not due until December first. Mrs. DeWitt will probably be back by then." Dolly scraped the last of the batter into the waffle iron.

"If we can eat like this, I hope that Mrs. DeWitt takes her time recovering," Sue's friend muttered to her. Dolly glared at the girl, and the two hastily took their waffles to the far corner of the dining room.

"How long does it take someone to recover from a broken hip, if that's what Mrs. DeWitt's got?" Dolly asked, sitting down at the table with the other fifth-floor girls. She poured syrup liberally over her own plate of waffles. *You need extra energy in an emergency*, she excused herself.

Netta and Phyllis looked at each other dubiously. "Six weeks?" hazarded Netta. "That's how long Roseanne was in a cast after she broke her arm in a gang fight."

Then possibly she *would* be collecting December rent, Dolly realized. Or would the trustees find someone to take over until Mrs. DeWitt recovered? It would be odd, having a stranger in charge of the Arms.

Jackie spoke up. "My great-aunt broke her hip and went to the hospital and never came out," she said solemnly. "She just never healed properly, and then she got pneumonia and died."

The other girls looked at her askance. "She was ninety-two, of course," Jackie added hastily. "Much older than Mrs. DeWitt."

They sipped their coffee in silence. Then Phyllis said what they were all thinking: "Of course, Mrs. DeWitt isn't a fourteen-year-old girl like Roseanne. Her recovery may take longer. And even after she comes back from the hospital . . ." Her voice trailed off.

The younger tenants were dispersing, but the old-timers sat worrying and speculating. Kay brought her cup of coffee over to the fifth-floor table and sat down. "Shouldn't Beverly have called by now? I wish there was something to do while we wait."

"There's plenty to do," Dolly declared, pushing her chair back. "And we'll all feel better if we keep busy. I'm going to find out what happened to that hot water—want to help?"

"Sure," agreed Kay. "I don't know much about water heaters, but I can at least make sure you don't slip in any puddles."

"We need to do the dishes, and one of us should listen for Beverly's call," Dolly ticked off the tasks.

"We'll take charge of breakfast cleanup," Phyllis volunteered. "Right, Netta?"

Netta looked at her watch before assenting. "My Democratic Teachers group isn't meeting until two."

"And I'll cover the phone," Jackie said. "Can I move in, Dolly? It will be so much more fun living here with lots of girls than sharing an apartment with just one!"

Jackie's undiminished enthusiasm was like a tonic to the anxious actress. "That's a terrific idea," she assured her new friend. "Why don't I telegraph Maxie? You can sublet her room for now—I know she won't mind. When

Mrs. DeWitt..." Her voice trailed off and then she rallied. "We'll get you set up with a regular room of your own, once the dust settles."

With new energy, the girls scattered to perform their tasks. As Kay and Dolly climbed the stairs to change into old clothes, Dolly confided to Kay, "I bet if I had the time to tinker, I could get that elevator working. Maybe after we relight the pilot light!"

"That's not a bad idea," said Kay. "If Mrs. DeWitt... well, she may not be able to manage stairs for a while."

Dolly winced at the picture of Mrs. DeWitt picking her way down the narrow flight to the basement on a pair of crutches. "If I can't fix it, the trustees will have to hire it done," she declared.

"We're lucky you have such a useful hobby," Kay said. She paused to take a breath on the third-floor landing. "I used to wish Mrs. DeWitt had put me on the fifth floor, but now the fourth floor seems plenty high." She grinned at Dolly. "The stairs are good for building my wind and improving my playing—at least that's what I keep telling myself!"

Dolly had been trying to convince herself that the broken elevator was good for her waistline. "Why on earth did you want to room on the fifth floor?" she panted.

"You and the other girls seemed to have more fun than the rest of us, back in the old days. Remember Ramona? She kept everything lively!"

Dolly left Kay at the fourth floor, and as she climbed the final flight, she thought about Ramona, who had left the Arms so abruptly seven years ago. Of all the members of the fifth-floor gang, Dolly had felt closest to the adventurous girl, who'd abandoned the librarian career she'd trained for to pursue a series of risky moneymaking schemes. Had she too settled down somewhere, with an apartment, girlfriend, and career? She'd sent the occasional postcard—from New York, Rapid City, Las Vegas—but no one had heard from her in years.

Ramona liked a good time as much as me, the actress thought nostalgically as she shed her bathrobe and striped pajamas and pulled on an old pair of pants and a sweater with a hole in the elbow. Then she scolded herself: *I've got to stop dwelling in the past!* What was that poem Mrs. DeWitt recited sometimes?

> *O memory, thou fond deceiver,*
> *Still whatchamacallit and vain,*
> *To former joys recurring ever,*
> *And turning all the past to pain.*

Putting the halcyon days of the Arms's heyday out of her head, Dolly picked up *Do It Yourself: One Thousand and One Ways to Save Money on Home Repair* from her nightstand. After all, reminiscing about past parties wasn't going to get the present plumbing problem fixed.

She rejoined Kay, all business. "After we relight the pilot light and fix the elevator, what say we flush the radiators? Get everything shipshape for Mrs. DeWitt's return!" Dolly had read about this simple procedure for maintaining the heating system efficiency and been itching to try it.

"Okay by me," said Kay agreeably. The musician was a comfortable, easygoing sort of girl. She'd told Dolly once that her calm was characteristic of clarinet players. "We're not a bit like trumpeters," she'd said with a mock shudder. "Those prima donnas!"

Jackie was at her post behind the front desk, where the Arms' lone phone lived. The mail had come, and she was sorting it into the labeled pigeonholes on the wall behind her. "No call yet," she reported. "I thought I'd play post office while I waited."

"That's the Magdalena Arms spirit!" Dolly approved.

She and Kay descended to the basement. In the kitchen, Netta and Phyllis had heated a big pot of hot water to rinse the dishes. "It's hygienic," explained Phyllis, who had once taught a class in home economics at a Dockside settlement house. She dipped a pitcher into the pot and poured the steaming water over the dishes in the strainer.

Netta was drying the rinsed dishes and putting them away. "Beverly hasn't called yet," she reported.

"Jackie told us." Dolly took out the ring of keys and unlocked the door in the far corner of the kitchen.

"I've never been down here," Kay said, as they started down the narrow, cobwebbed flight of wooden stairs that led to the sub-basement storeroom. It was like descending into a cold, damp cave.

"There's just a lot of junk old tenants have left behind," Dolly told her. "And of course the furnace, the water heater, the fuse box, the shutoff valve for the water main . . ."

Her voice trailed away as they reached the bottom of the steps. "Lordy day!" said Kay behind her.

Water filled the storeroom. It lapped at the sides of an old brass-cornered trunk Dolly recognized as Ramona's. It had soaked through the bottom cardboard boxes of the many stacks that lined the walls. A push broom floated in the middle of the room.

There was a faint burble, like the sound of a spring. Water was still coming in from somewhere. Heedless of her shoes, Dolly plunged in and sloshed across the floor to the shutoff valve. She grunted as she tugged at the rusty knob, pulling with all her force. Slowly it turned, and the burbling sound faded away. Dolly sloshed around in a semicircle, surveying the damage with disbelieving eyes. Kay was standing on the bottom step, her mouth agape.

Automatically, the actress leafed through the pages of *Do It Yourself.* "The water heater's copper bottom must have busted," she said as she scanned a section titled: "Your Plumbing: Staying Out of Hot Water."

Dolly prided herself on her all-around handiness, whether it meant mixing up a Pimm's cup, pecan pie, or some plaster of paris to patch the hole above the sideboard, but now she looked up at Kay in dismay. "I don't think I can fix this!"

Chapter 5

Linda Comes Out of Her Coma

When the elevator opened on the twelfth floor of the KBAY building Monday morning, Dolly hurried out, heart pounding. It wasn't just the too-tight girdle she wore under her best dark wool day dress (dark colors were so slimming) that made her heart race and her breath come fast. It was the call last night from the assistant director, asking her to be at the studio half an hour early.

"What's up, Frank? More lines? A story change? Give!" Dolly had begged the AD, but all she'd gotten was a tight-lipped, "Be there at eight thirty."

She skirted the hospital room set, where technicians were adjusting lights, and went down the corridor to the tiny dressing room she shared with two other actresses. It was good to be back in the familiar world of make-believe, after a weekend of housework, plumbing repairs, and worry about Mrs. DeWitt. Dolly wondered if her landlady's hospital room looked like their set and if the nurses plumped her pillows the way Dolly did on the show.

Mrs. DeWitt had suffered a fractured hip. "She'll need surgery," Beverly reported, "and they'll probably keep her here three weeks or more, but she should recover just fine." Netta and Phyllis had been to see her yesterday, while Dolly stayed home to supervise the arrival and installation of the new water heater. "How was she?" she'd asked the two girls anxiously when they returned.

"She's bearing up wonderfully," Phyllis had assured her.

"But she's pretty weak," Netta had added. "I never realized how *old* she's gotten."

Dolly's feelings must have shown on her face because Phyllis tried to cheer her: "She was awfully happy when we told her about your waffle breakfast."

Dolly sat down at her dressing table. She took off her hat and fluffed out her blond waves. She'd set her hair last night, with Jackie's help, and touched up her roots. She turned her head, appraising herself in the mirror. Big blue eyes, a turned-up nose, toothy smile (oh, those braces!), and apple cheeks. Still the all-American girl, just a little blurred around the edges, her dimples less distinguishable from laugh lines with every passing year. She raised her chin a notch. No softness now—if only she didn't have to look down so much at actors lying on hospital beds!

Neither of the other actresses who shared the dressing room had been called today, thank heavens. Dolly felt all aquiver with nerves, like a girl stepping into the spotlight for the first time. She unscrewed her foundation cream. Nurse Hamilton. She would think about the trouble at the Arms later. Now, she had to concentrate on Nurse Hamilton, night duty nurse at Evergreen General Hospital.

Jackie had asked her last night what Nurse Hamilton's first name was, and Dolly had confessed that she didn't know if Nurse Hamilton had a first name. The Meier Method actress had been shocked. "You ought to give her one. Otherwise, how can you hope to really understand *who* she *is*?"

Hedwig Hamilton, Hannah Hamilton, Harriet Hamilton . . . Dolly's thoughts slid back to Mrs. DeWitt. Her first name was Harriet. It was funny to think about Mrs. DeWitt having a first name. Last night, when she'd phoned the invalid, the hospital operator had asked her, "DeWitt, Harriet C.?"

Poor Mrs. DeWitt! She'd seemed quite low in spirits. "Vital spark of heavenly flame!" she'd recited mournfully. "Quit, o quit this mortal frame!"

"Now, Mrs. DeWitt, that's no way to talk!" Dolly had scolded.

Mrs. DeWitt had returned to the topic that dominated her thoughts. "The trustees' meeting—did I tell you it's at four thirty? At the Putney-Potter house on Linden Lane? You can explain the situation better than anyone! You won't forget, will you?"

"Of course, Mrs. DeWitt, you can count on me," Dolly had repeated patiently.

She hoped the trustees would be quick about hiring a substitute Mrs. DeWitt. It would be a relief to turn over the breakfast preparation and the mess in the sub-basement storeroom to someone else. Dolly and Kay had unclogged the drain in the floor and swept the dirty water down it, but the water-damaged detritus of decades of Magdalena Arms girls was still piled in disorderly heaps.

Dolly picked up her sides, and resolutely shut out the Arms and its problems. She was a nurse, not a housekeeper. Looking into the mirror, she tried for Beverly's cool, aloof expression and was disappointed when she just looked blank. She studied the script.

DR. DWIGHT: This is a delicate job. She
may not know where she is, or even who she
is at first.

NURSE HAMILTON: I understand, doctor.

She tried it with a little hauteur: "I understand, doctor," lifting her chin. Were the producers finally bringing
Linda out of her months-long coma or was it just another
tease? Dolly turned the page.

NIGHT. NURSE HAMILTON SITS BY
LINDA'S BED. LINDA'S EYELIDS
FLUTTER. NURSE HAMILTON DOESN'T
NOTICE. LINDA MOVES AND MAKES A
SMALL SOUND. NURSE HAMILTON
GETS UP AND BENDS OVER HER
PATIENT. SHE FROWNS.

Dolly counted her sides. Four whole pages! This *must*
be the juicy scene she'd hoped for.

There was a knock at the door. An assistant poked his
head in. "Mr. Halloran wants you for blocking, Miss
Dingle."

"Thanks." Dolly gathered up her sides and went to the
set. Avery Halloran, a newish director, was talking to the
camera operators. Danielle Stevens, the winsome brunette
who played Linda, was sitting on the edge of the hospital
bed, still in her street clothes, a tweed skirt and sweater.

"Wakey-wakey!" Dolly hailed her.

"Finally." Danielle heaved a sigh. "I was practically
developing bedsores!" They smiled at each other with
identical, excited anticipation for the upcoming scene.
Later they would be vying for the best camera angle, but
right now they were united in delight.

"Okay, girls," the director began briskly. "Danielle, dear, you're in bed." Danielle lay down obediently. "Dolly, you're here." He placed Dolly, and his assistant crouched down to mark Nurse Hamilton's position with an X of tape. "Right. Time to rise and shine. Sit up, dear. Nurse, you're taking her pulse." Danielle sat up, and Dolly picked up her wrist. "You don't recognize this woman— where are you? Who is this person holding your arm?" Danielle gaped blankly at Dolly. "You pull away. Nurse, you try to make her lie down." Danielle pettishly yanked her hand away, and Dolly shoved her back on the pillow. "But Linda is too strong for you, Nurse—"

"I'm too strong for Nurse Hamilton?" Danielle interrupted. She looked dubiously up at Dolly.

"Dear, you're delirious. You have superhuman strength. The research department said it was plausible."

"I've heard of that," interjected Dolly. Sure, she was a little husky, but she was playing a hospital nurse, not some crime drama heavy! She fell back dramatically, as Danielle gave her a tentative push.

"That's right," the director encouraged. "Nurse tries again to restrain you, but you put your hands on her neck. She breaks your grip. You claw at her—this is where the uniform rips. Joe, we want camera three on a tight shot here. Nurse, you're trying to cover yourself— that's right—and Linda, you go for her neck again—yes— why don't you sort of slide out of bed—Nurse, you're on your knees. Can you scrunch down any, Nurse? Squeeze, Linda—squeeze this stranger attacking you. Yes—and, Nurse, you try to break her hold, but you can't—you're growing weaker—you can't breathe—your eyes close— you go limp. Perfect. It's over. Linda, you look at the nurse and then you stare at your hands. What have you done? You're a killer now. Cheat left, Linda—"

"I'm dead?"

"I'm a killer?"

Both actresses erupted simultaneously. The director looked taken aback. "Well—yes. Didn't you know? I mean, I figured the morning of—" He studied the sheaf of papers in his hand as if hoping to find an answer there.

"Dead—you mean like a doornail? Or just dead to the world?" Dolly climbed to her feet. "If I'm really dead"— she tried and failed to take it in—"if I'm really dead—I'm off the show!"

One minute she was rehearsing the best scene she'd had on this show and the next minute she was dead and unemployed!

Danielle had forgotten her own concerns about her murderous character and put her arm around Dolly in sympathy. "You can't kill off Nurse Hamilton! Isn't there a way to revive her?"

There was a flurry of movement behind the cameras, and then Madeleine "Mad" Morganstern, the producer, swooped onto the set. Dolly saw, with a sick feeling, that her agent, Jerry, was right behind.

"You ass!" the television executive lambasted the flustered director. "Do you think we make up the schedules for your leisure reading? What are you doing rehearsing this scene before the read-through?"

"I was just trying to be efficient," the director stammered. "I didn't realize . . ."

Mad Morganstern cut him off with a freezing look and turned to Dolly. "I apologize, Dolly, that you had to find out this way."

It was the final nail in the coffin. Dolly felt her last shred of hope die as surely as the strangled Nurse Hamilton.

Jerry reached up to pat the dazed actress consolingly.

"Don't you worry about a thing, Dolly. I've got something lined up for you already."

The short, balding man had done Dolly's deals since she was sixteen. Now, when Dolly looked down, she noticed that the shiny spot of bare scalp showing was bigger. *Everybody's getting old*, she thought despairingly.

Jerry tugged her down to his level and whispered, "I wanted to tell you sooner, but Mad Morganstern said she'd have my head if I breathed a word to you. It's their big television moment, and they don't want anything should spoil it!"

"I was going to tell you this morning, privately, in my office," Mad was explaining on Dolly's other side. "That's why Frank asked you to come early. But I had a contract dispute to settle and—well, you don't need to hear any more excuses. I just can't apologize enough."

"Don't worry, Mad. I'm an old hand. I know how it is," the actress choked out.

Dolly should have been hardened by now to the rejection and abrupt end to employment that was part of her profession, but she'd always disliked it, from the time she'd lost the Shirley Temple look-alike contest at age four because her dimples weren't deep enough.

She'd had such high hopes for *A Single Candle*! When Mad Morganstern hired Dolly, after seeing a photograph of the actress wearing a leopard-skin bikini and holding a trident aloft, the old trouper felt like at last she'd found something stable. Sure, Nurse Hamilton didn't even have a first name, but who would have thought she'd fall prey to a fatal plot twist so soon?

"Why me?" Dolly couldn't help asking. "Why not one of the other nurses?" *Like wooden Nurse Wilson*, Dolly thought resentfully. *She is the more expendable member of the Evergreen General Hospital staff!*

"Oh, we couldn't use just any nurse! We needed an actress who could make it memorable!" Mad seemed to be sincere. "I know you won't believe this, but it's a huge compliment to you as a performer."

Dolly knew Mad was a fan of her fetish photographs, one of a coterie of powerful executives who collected them like teenage boys with baseball cards. She examined the anxious executive. Maybe Mad really believed she was doing Dolly a favor. The actress's exit from Evergreen General Hospital would certainly attract attention.

"And besides." Mad was choosing her words carefully now. "Your—your unusual physique makes the murder more interesting, more attention-getting, than your run-of-the-mill, temporary-insanity killing."

There it was again! Dolly was too large for the small screen. *Mad might as well just come right out and call me a big oaf!* the actress couldn't help thinking.

It had been like this ever since that growth spurt her second season as Judy Jarvis. She'd been popular enough by then that the producers had worked around her height, stacking apple boxes under Freddy and playing with angles to conceal the fact that Dolly dwarfed her teenage sweetheart. It was even worse now, when petite, twiggy girls were all the rage.

The cast and crew of *A Single Candle* were milling around the set now, gossiping about this latest backstage drama. Mad muttered something to Frank, who clapped his hands for attention. "Let's get to work, everyone! Read through in room five for Nurse Hamilton, Linda, and Dr. Dwight!"

Mad squeezed Dolly's arm a trifle too long. "I'll see you before you leave," she assured the actress.

Jerry instructed, "Meet me at Le Cheval when you've

wrapped and we'll talk what's next." He gave Dolly a final, encouraging pat. "Knock 'em dead!"

Dolly squared her shoulders. *I'll make them sorry they knocked me off,* she vowed. *I'll give Evergreen General Hospital a strangling they'll never forget!*

Chapter 6

Dolly Goes Off Her Diet

"Sorry I'm late." Dolly slipped into the chair opposite Jerry. "They put together a little farewell thing at the last minute."

Barbara Babcock, who played matriarch Olivia Kane on the show, had arranged the impromptu party. "We'll miss you, Dolly!" she'd said. "We couldn't let you leave without some sort of festivity, after all the get-togethers you've organized!"

It was true, the gregarious girl was always the first to put together a cocktail party for an expectant mother or bring cake and ice cream for the prop boy's birthday. It had been nice to know her efforts had been appreciated.

Mad Morganstern had presented the departing actress with a gold charm in the shape of a candle, a tiny stone set in the flame. Dolly hoped she wouldn't have to hock it.

Jerry waved at the waiter, saying, "You're here now. We'll make this fast. I've got an appointment at four."

"You said you had something lined up—" Dolly stopped and stared as the waiter deposited a steak sandwich with french-fried potatoes in front of her, then set down a saucer of creamed spinach and a martini.

"I ordered for you." Jerry smiled. "No more diet! Eat! Eat!"

No more diet? Dolly didn't wait to be told twice. "What gives?" she asked, picking up the steak sandwich eagerly.

"We're moving you into mother roles," Jerry laid it out. "You've outgrown the ingenue. We'll change your look—new hairstyle, give you a darker rinse, then head shots, new audition material, maybe a stage role or two to warm you up—"

Mothers. Dolly chewed thoughtfully. She didn't have much experience with mothers. She hadn't seen her own since Jerry had aided her to legally emancipate herself after they discovered that Mom Dingle had gambled away Dolly's salary from her first radio serial, instead of putting it in a bank account like she was supposed to.

"What do I live on while I remake myself as mama?" Dolly asked.

Jerry took a sip of his drink. "I've lined up a spot on *General Jiggs and Friends.*"

"The kiddie show?" Dolly was dubious.

"They're looking for a new Honey Bear—you wear a whole bear suit, so it doesn't matter what you look like. And they're asking for someone tall. How's your voice? You need to sing."

Dolly ate a french-fried potato. "Gee, Jerry, isn't there anything else? Those animal costumes can be awfully hot and stuffy."

"Well, there's the reunion show . . ."

"Reunion with who?" Dolly was suspicious.

"They've got Buddy Harmon committed."

"You mean—Fred?" Dolly was more doubtful than ever. The actor who'd played opposite her on *The Jarvises* had fallen on hard times since the show had ended.

"That's right—Fred and Judy, reunited!"

"Judy and Fred," Dolly corrected automatically.

"Only now Fred's a debonair man about town and Judy's a glamorous woman of the world!"

Dolly wasn't sure a drug habit made you debonair. "You don't think we'll look like a couple of has-beens?"

"What kind of talk is that?" Jerry scolded. Then he leaned forward and lowered his voice confidentially. "But Buddy's a little unreliable. I'd take Honey Bear."

"Let me sleep on it," said Dolly, helping herself to the creamed spinach. It was hard to concentrate on her career when the table was covered with food.

She thought over her options as she waited at the bus stop, barely noticing the flakes of snow that began to drift down.

Maybe Jerry was right and Honey Bear was the best choice. She felt for poor Buddy, but playing a glamorous woman of the world sounded like a diet and girdle job.

Boarding the bus, the unemployed actress wondered what Jackie would think of her choices. Last night the avid student actress had declared that acting was a craft you had to practice constantly. *Maybe I should take a few lessons from Sidney Meier,* the unemployed actress thought idly. *Play Hamlet's mother in summer stock at Loon Lake. Mrs. DeWitt was always encouraging me to try Shakespeare—*

Mrs. DeWitt! She'd promised her housemother she'd substitute for her at the Magdalena Arms trustees' meeting!

The unemployed actress looked at her watch in a panic. It was four fifteen. She pulled the cord and hurried off the bus at the next stop. She was still downtown—not far from the plush old mansions on Linden Lane. If she ran, she wouldn't be late—not very.

Dolly was out of breath when she rang the bell of 37 Linden Lane half an hour later. She tilted her head back to gaze up at the unadorned facade of grayish brown stone. Phyllis had told her that some of the mansions on Linden Lane were worth a quarter of a million dollars, but Mrs. Putney-Potter's plain row house didn't look like much to Dolly.

Inside, it was a different story. A maid in a lace-trimmed apron left the actress waiting in the high-ceilinged entryway, under the eyes of a marble mermaid who was seated in a burbling fountain. "Tell her Mrs. DeWitt sent me," Dolly called after the servant as she retreated down a wide hall. The maid was back before Dolly had more than a minute or two to wipe the perspiration off her face and crane her head at the frescoed ceiling, where some Roman gods were having a party.

"Mrs. Putney-Potter will see you in the library." She led Dolly down the hall, opened a door on the right, and then stood aside.

When Dolly stepped into the library, her feet sank into deep pile carpet that spread like golden sand on a beach from one wall to the other. The room was paneled halfway up the wall in dark wood, and hung with red and gold wallpaper above. Dolly had only seen such opulent comfort in the movies.

At the far end of the room, a fire crackled in the big fireplace, and a group of women were gathered around it on overstuffed chairs upholstered in red and pink chintz with gold braid. One of them rose to her feet at Dolly's entrance. "Where is Mrs. DeWitt?"

She was a shrewd-faced woman in her forties who reminded Dolly ever so slightly of Mad Morganstern; another polished, powerful woman of affairs. A talented hairdresser had almost succeeded in softening her sharp features, surrounding them with smooth waves of her dark hair. Her brows were drawn together as she looked at Dolly suspiciously.

"Mrs. DeWitt is in the hospital. She fell and broke her hip."

There was a flurry of concern from the group by the fire. "She asked me to come to the meeting for her," Dolly added. "I'm Dolly Dingle—I'm kind of senior tenant at the Magdalena Arms."

"How did the accident happen? Was she—" The standing woman stopped.

Dolly wondered if the woman had been about to ask, "Was she drinking?" The actress ignored the unfinished question. "She slipped on some spilled water in the kitchen yesterday morning."

"Dora, ask Miss Dingle to sit down," interposed a white-haired woman. "There's no need to keep the poor child on her feet while we interrogate her."

Dora Putney-Potter—for it must be she, she matched the enormous portrait over the mantel—came out of her brown study. "Yes, do sit down. Have a cup of tea."

Dolly sat and took the dainty white and gold cup and saucer, wondering where the eats were. The table in front of the fireplace was set with a fancy lace cloth and tea service, including a stack of china plates and some silverware. While the trustees twittered about a bouquet for Mrs. DeWitt, the maid returned, pushing a heavily laden tea cart. Dolly's eyes brightened. Sandwiches, muffins, little cakes—even after her meal with Jerry, she still had an appetite. There was a lot of bouillon and celery to make up for.

As the unemployed actress filled her plate, she sorted out the trustees. The nice white-haired one was Mrs. Pryce; next to her was Miss Craybill, a bright-eyed little bird of a woman. There was an ancient, sleepy-eyed dowager in the corner, as interested in the muffins as Dolly, who was introduced as Miss Barnes. Dolly was taking her third crustless ham and cream-cheese sandwich when a man with a briefcase came in, remarking, "The snow has turned to sleet." He was introduced as Mr. Hagney, "our lawyer."

"How do you do?" said Dolly, her mouth full. She was basking in the warmth of the fire and the crass comfort of the wealthy woman's room, with its shirred silk shades shutting out November's bad weather. Mr. Hagney shook her hand perfunctorily and sat down.

"Now that we're all here, why don't we begin?" said Mrs. Putney-Potter peremptorily. She looked at Dolly and hesitated a fraction of a second. Mrs. Pryce said:

"Oh, I think Dolly should stay. We may have questions she can answer."

That reminded Dolly of her duties. "I forgot." She put down her sandwich and picked up her purse. "I have more bad news, I'm afraid." She pulled out the plumber's bill. "The hot water heater in the sub-basement gave out, and we had to have the plumber put in a new one—"

Mrs. Putney-Potter snatched the bill from Dolly's hand and studied it. To the actress's surprise, there was a triumphant gleam in her eye.

"Well! I certainly think this is an adequate reason to reopen the debate from last quarter!"

"Dora, we agreed to table that discussion," Mrs. Pryce protested.

"Unless circumstances changed," put in Mr. Hagney. "I agree with Dora. This question needs to be discussed."

"Of course you two agree," said Mrs. Pryce pettishly. "You're cousins."

Dolly studied Mr. Hagney, searching for a family likeness to Mrs. Putney-Potter while wondering idly what the question was that had them all worked up. Would they finally decide to revamp the Arms' antiquated plumbing? Or fix the elevator? Dolly helped herself to a slice of seed cake and made up her mind that before she left this luxurious mansion, she would put in a word for additional phones—say, one per floor.

"I think I agree too, Chaddy," Miss Craybill put in regretfully. "After all, Mrs. DeWitt may not be able to manage the Arms after the accident, and so her promises at the last meeting are moot."

"She's devoted her life to the Arms—"

"And now deserves to be pensioned off in fine style," Mrs. Putney-Potter interrupted the flushed Chaddy Pryce. "But as I've said before and will say again until you finally pay attention, the Arms has outlived its purpose. Girls don't need boardinghouses and chaperones these days. There's no sense pouring money into a deteriorating physical plant"—she waved the plumber's bill— "which is half empty! The Magdalena Arms should be shut down."

Dolly dropped her teaspoon, wondering if she'd heard correctly. Her mouth opened and closed like a fish's as she looked at the woman sitting calmly behind the laden tea table, the plumbing bill held authoritatively aloft. Why, Mrs. Putney-Potter was planning to destroy the only real home the footloose actress had ever known!

Mrs. Pryce said hotly, "You are forgetting the terms of my late aunt's bequest! 'To provide a shelter for young girls who find themselves alone in Bay City, with naught but their own resources to rely upon.'"

"But surely," wheedled Mr. Hagney, "the manner in which the trust is executed is open to interpretation. There's nothing in your aunt's bequest that specifically says we need to run a boardinghouse. We might explore other options that respond to the vital needs of *today's* generation."

"What is more vital than a place to live?" Dolly demanded in a voice that rattled the china. She clenched her fists, crushing the piece of poppy seed cake in her hand.

Mrs. Putney-Potter darted a venomous glance at Dolly. "Of course we'll find replacement housing for the current tenants," she told the irate actress. "We're not going to put you out into the street! After all, I'm an old Magdalena Arms girl myself."

"You think your replacement housing could even hope to match the Magdalena Arms?" Dolly scoffed, eyes blazing. "Don't you know that those particular four walls and roof are more than just a building? How are you going to replace the sense of sisterhood, and belonging? How do you relocate the history? Where are all the ghosts of the girls who have gone before going to go, when you evict them? Anyone who touches a brick of yon red brick building, should die like a dog!"

The trustees stared, stunned by Dolly's unexpected eloquence. Dolly herself didn't quite know where it had come from, although a line from Whittier's "Barbara Frietchie" seemed to have crept in, along with bits of dialogue from the "Clubhouse" episode on *Meet the Jarvises*, when Judy and her brother save their tree house from being torn down.

She wheeled on Mr. Hagney. "And if you don't think the modern generation needs the Arms, you're just plain nuts! Why, over the weekend we took in a girl who'd been put out into the street, through no fault of her own." Dolly decided not to go too deeply into the whys and wherefores of Jackie's housing crisis. "Who knows what might have happened to her if the Magdalena Arms hadn't taken her in! Why, she might have been strangled or put in a coma, or—or worse!" She glanced at Chaddy Pryce, whose eyes shone with encouragement. "Maybe girls today don't need chaperones anymore, but they sure need a room of their own!"

"As I said, I was a Magdalena Arms girl myself," Dora Putney-Potter tried again.

"And another thing," Dolly burst out. "Why does everybody blather on about today's generation as if they're so special? Lots of us from the last generation are still around, and I didn't stop needing a place to live when I turned thirty-five!"

In fact, she needed it more than ever, Dolly realized. There would be no moving out to the Riverside apartment she'd dreamed of last Friday.

"Hear, hear," said a voice. The irate actress had woken the dozing Miss Barnes. Dolly turned to Miss Craybill.

"About Mrs. DeWitt—sure, you'll need to get someone to run the Arms while she recovers, but do you really want to put her out to pasture? Remember the words of the poet." Dolly recited,

> " 'Do you think, O something something
> Because you have scaled the wall,
> Such an old something as I am
> Is not a match for you all?' "

Before the trustees could recover from the poetic grenade she'd lobbed, the actress added, "All Mrs. DeWitt thought about as the ambulance drove away was 'her girls.' Why, right before they turned the siren on, I heard her faint cry, 'Who will take care of my girls?' I think taking her away from her home for the past forty years would be just like sending a faithful workhorse to the glue factory and replacing its old barn with a parking lot!"

Dolly put a little quaver into the glue factory line. She noted, with some satisfaction, that Miss Craybill was wiping away a tear. Mrs. Putney-Potter's lips were pressed tightly together.

"Well, I've said my piece. I'll be going." Dolly rose and waited expectantly.

The trustees all burst into speech at once.

"Hear, hear!"

"Of course she's right—*I* certainly didn't want to retire when *I* turned sixty-five!"

"We've gotten quite off track—"

"I'm all for sentimental bilge on greeting cards, but—"

"Dolly." Mrs. Pryce turned to her. "Don't go just yet. Wait in the back parlor."

Dolly was pacing up and down in the reproduction Dutch farmhouse parlor wondering if her impassioned plea had done the trick when Chaddy Pryce and Miss Craybill found her half an hour later. She put down the pewter candlesnuffer she'd been fidgeting with. "Well?" she asked anxiously, but their beaming faces told her the news.

"The Magdalena Arms lives!" Chaddy was practically weeping with joy.

"And we all agreed that *you* should be Mrs. DeWitt's substitute, until she can return to her duties," added Miss Craybill, as if conferring an honor. "You'll collect a salary of course."

"Me!" Dolly was taken aback. "But I'm an actress—I have no experience running a boardinghouse!"

"Oh dear." Miss Craybill frowned. "I'd hate to have to go back to Mrs. Putney-Potter and reopen the question."

"Dolly, the Magdalena Arms needs you," Mrs. Pryce begged. "You've watched Mrs. DeWitt all these years—you just need to keep the place running for a few weeks, and mother the girls a bit."

Mother—the word reminded Dolly of her lunch with Jerry. What better way to get new experience for all the mothers she planned to play than by substituting for Mrs. DeWitt? Dolly smacked her fist into her palm.

"Okay, I'll do it!"

Chapter 7
New Renters

It was a perfect fall day—cold and clear, with impossibly blue skies and a snap in the air. Dolly was on her knees outside the Magdalena Arms' front door, busily polishing the brass grille. She was wearing an old blue coverall she'd found in the storeroom—no need for a girdle under this garment! And she'd covered her bleached waves with an orange bandana.

The best defense for the Arms, she'd decided, was to put the place in apple-pie order as quickly as possible. The next time the trustees met, they'd find the rent rolls full, a waiting list for rooms, and a spruced-up "physical plant."

"Tell your acting friends," she'd instructed Jackie, then turned to Kay: "And your musician friends."

The temporary landlady hadn't told anyone the reason for this new-tenant drive. In fact, Dolly had confided to only one person the threat hanging over the Arms. Meeting Phyllis in the fifth-floor hallway after her return from the trustees' meeting, she'd poured out the whole story in a jumbled rush.

Mid-sentence, Phyllis had pushed Dolly into her room and closed the door. "Don't let anyone else know about this," the social scientist had cautioned. "If the girls hear that the Arms is in danger, they'll start looking for someplace else to live, and pretty soon you'll have a panic, like a run on the bank in the depression. I've seen this happen to whole blocks in some neighborhoods," she assured the doubting Dolly. "A rumor gets started that a water treatment plant is being built next door, or that a Negro family is moving in, and boom! Everyone's in a tizzy and the real estate agents swoop in like vultures and buy up properties for less than their worth!"

The social scientist's insistence had scared the usually gossipy Dolly into silence. She certainly didn't want to panic her tenants!

My girls, she reminded herself, as she dipped her rag in the jar of brass polish and rubbed it on the next tarnished curlicue.

Dolly had started her sprucing-up campaign with the Magdalena Arms' front door, reasoning that a welcoming entrance would help her new-tenant drive. But there were enough items on her to-do list to keep her busy for weeks.

She took her list out of the breast pocket of her blue coveralls and unfolded the creased paper.

polish brass
wash door glass—also front windows?
patch cracks in marble—how?
tuck-pointing—get estimate
remove front desk, install fountain like PP's (next month)
mosaic tiles—clean, replace missing
lounge tv reception—fix
paint lobby—also lounge, hallways?
stair carpet—re-lay
woodwork—refinish

flush radiators (see p. 332)
3rd floor toilet—leaky seal?
dishwasher! Investigate.
phones??

Dolly frowned. Her list had gotten awfully long, even if some of it was wishful thinking. She wasn't sure how she'd fit in an acting class in the Meier Method around all this home improvement.

Taking a pencil stub from behind her ear, she wrote, *sub-basement storeroom—organize* at the bottom.

As she tucked the pencil behind her ear, she saw a girl coming down the street, carrying a suitcase. She was hatless, and her dark red hair flamed in the sunlight like an autumn leaf. She wore a belted brown suede trench coat, and she slowed as she approached the Arms, gazing up at the building.

Dolly brightened. Could the word-of-mouth advertising be working already?

It could. The girl turned down the walk, a questioning smile on her face, as she began, "Hello..." Then she stopped in her tracks. "Why, it's Dolly! Well, hello, Dolly!"

"Ramona?" An incredulous smile spread over Dolly's face. "Ramona!"

The former tenant dropped her suitcase and laughingly embraced the astonished ex-actress. "Careful, my brass polish!" Dolly warned breathlessly. "I can't believe it's you! When did you become a redhead?"

"I didn't recognize *you* in that getup!" retorted Dolly's long-lost friend. "I just thought, gee, the Magdalena Arms has hired an awfully good-looking janitress!"

"Where have you been all these years? Are you visiting or back for good? You know, your old trunk's still in the storeroom—"

"I'm not sure how long I'll be in town." Ramona retrieved her suitcase. "I'm hoping Mrs. DeWitt can find a corner for me, for a little while, at least. I need to catch my breath and look around."

"Mrs. DeWitt's out of commission. You're talking to the Magdalena Arms' acting landlady." Dolly struck a haughty pose. "And your old room's ready and waiting!"

"Marvelous!" The two girls linked arms and went inside, chattering away as fast as they could. There was so much to ask: about where Ramona had been and what she'd been doing. And so much to tell: about Mrs. DeWitt, about Dolly's acting career, about the old gang, and who was with whom and where now.

"Netta said you were working in a boarding school," Dolly said as they crossed the lobby. "I sent you a postcard, but by then I guess you'd moved on."

"Yes, things there didn't work out quite as I'd planned," Ramona said carelessly.

The former tenant skimmed breezily over the past seven years, touching on an assortment of jobs and locations in an offhanded fashion. She'd been a bus driver, a cafeteria cook ("that was in Nevada"), a librarian-guard in a juvenile detention center ("Not so different from the boarding school," Ramona remarked with a laugh), and even a guidance counselor. "It was a tiny town, and they never figured out I had no qualifications." She'd ended up in California.

"Doing what?" Dolly asked.

"Oh, different things." Ramona was vague. "I worked in a curio shop, and then I was a cocktail waitress, and then—" They'd reached the first landing, and she broke off, looking around in wonder. "It's like coming home! Nothing's really changed here."

"Well, the elevator's still broken," Dolly joked. "I hope you don't have too much luggage."

"This is it." Ramona swung her suitcase. "I left San

Francisco on the spur of the moment. I'll send for the rest of my things once I'm settled."

Dolly wondered, not for the first time, what Ramona was leaving out of her account. Her old friend had presented her peripatetic wandering and frequent job changes as one long lark, but the adventurous girl looked tired. Her cheekbones seemed sharper, her chin more pointed, and there were dark shadows under her eyes.

The softhearted landlady decided not to press her. "Not everything's the same." She reverted to more neutral topics. "Pam moved out. She lives with Lois—you don't know Lois. She came after you left. Janet's moved out too. Did you know she's a lawyer now?"

"Good for her," said Ramona. "And handy for her friends."

"That's truer than you know," Dolly told her long-lost friend. "Janet helped Maxie set up both her businesses. She runs a publishing company and owns a bar in Dockside."

"Maxie, a businesswoman! I can't wait to see her."

"You'll have to wait until she gets back from Paris." Dolly explained again about Maxie's manuscript-buying trip. "But Phyllis is still in her same room," she added. "And so is Netta."

She looked sideways at the other girl as she mentioned Netta, wondering how the returnee would react. Ramona and Netta had been a couple, back before Ramona's abrupt departure.

How is it, the actress couldn't help wondering, *that no-fun Netta finds herself surrounded by ex-steadies, while I've had nothing but one-night stands?*

"Good old Netta," said Ramona absently. "You know, that's too bad about Maxie being out of town."

They had reached the fifth floor. "Oh, and now there's Beverly, in Janet's old room. She's studying to be a nurse—

just as handy as a lawyer, I think. And there's a new girl, Jackie, who's subletting from Maxie. With you back in 503, the fifth floor will have a full house again!" She was unlocking Ramona's old room as she spoke. "Maxie will be back by New Year's."

"New Year's, eh?" Ramona frowned. "That complicates things."

"Complicates things how?" Dolly stood in the doorway as Ramona crossed the room. The traveler set down her suitcase and sank down on the bed with a little sigh.

"I was hoping she could spot me some cash," Ramona confessed. "The bus ticket took practically my last dollar and I'm stone-broke."

"Oh!" Dolly's heart sank, and she wondered again about Ramona's sudden departure from San Francisco. Then she rallied. "You don't need to worry about a little thing like money!" the substitute landlady told her old friend heartily. "The Arms can keep you fed and housed."

"Really, Dolly?" Ramona lay back on the bare mattress wearily. "Just till I have a chance to get the lay of the land. You know I'm good for it . . ."

Ramona's eyes fluttered shut. Now that the euphoria of return had worn off, it was clear that the Magdalena Arms' prodigal tenant was exhausted. The substitute landlady backed quietly out of the room and closed the door. She stood in the hall, thinking.

Sure, Ramona had skated south of the law more than once; she'd moonlighted as a marijuana pusher, and Netta insisted that she'd taken to blackmail before she left Bay City, although Dolly wasn't too clear on the details. And yes, probably Ramona had left out the more unsavory parts of her cross-country adventures during her brief account. Dolly supposed that most landladies wouldn't consider a girl with such a checkered history an ideal tenant.

But darn it! Dolly whacked her fist into her hand emphatically. She couldn't turn away a friend in need, any more than a mother cat could refuse milk to its kitten. The Arms was Ramona's home, for however long she needed it. Wasn't there a poem on this subject that Mrs. DeWitt used to recite?

Ramona is okay, the substitute landlady told herself staunchly as she started down the stairs. Whenever Netta talked about her delinquent students, she'd say, "There's no such thing as a bad girl," and Netta should know.

Just then she spotted her teacher-neighbor trudging up the stairs. "Netta! You'll never guess who's upstairs!"

"Santa Claus come early?"

Dolly ignored Netta's waspishness. The teacher was extra cranky lately, having been forced to direct her delinquent girls in a play about the pilgrims landing on Plymouth Rock. "No—Ramona! Ramona Rukeyser! She just walked up the street not half an hour ago, fresh from California and wanting her old room back. Isn't it terrif it was available?"

"Ramona!" Netta was as surprised as Dolly had been, but much less pleased. "What on earth is she doing here?" Immediately she answered her own question: "She's probably on the lam from the law. Watch out she doesn't steal your newly polished brass." She resumed her climb to the fifth floor. As she passed, Dolly heard her mutter again, "Ramona!"

Dolly stood, deflated. Netta's day with troubled teens had left her with no patience for anyone else's troubles, apparently, not even an old girlfriend's.

The Arms doesn't provide bedding, Dolly remembered, *and she only has the one suitcase.*

"Do you have any spare sheets or blankets?" she called after the disappearing teacher. "Ramona's things are being sent later—she just collapsed on the bare mattress, poor thing." She added the last bit, hoping to stir up some sympathy in the stiff-necked schoolteacher.

"There's bed linen in her trunk in the storeroom," said Netta briefly. "I know. I cleaned out her room and packed her belongings away when she cleared out the first time. But I'm not cleaning up whatever mess she's in now!"

Dolly headed to the storeroom, trying to quell the uneasiness Netta had awakened. "Darn that old sourpuss," she muttered, "putting suspicions in my head!"

Unfortunately, Netta did have a point. The Arms could ill afford a deadbeat tenant. If only Ramona had returned a few days ago! Then Dolly could have put her in Maxie's room, and Jackie could have taken 503. Ramona would have owed Maxie money, and Jackie would be paying the Arms instead of Maxie.

Dolly shook herself mentally. She shouldn't let Netta get to her. Ramona wouldn't stiff an old friend.

She puzzled over her neighbor's callousness as she opened the trunk and unearthed blue-sprigged sheets smelling faintly of cedar. Obviously, the high-minded teacher had once cared enough to protect Ramona's linen from moths. But lately Netta seemed impervious to basic human feelings. It was as if her radical ideals left her no patience for the imperfections of regular people.

Dolly tucked the sheets under her arm and turned to climb the stairs with a sigh. *If I was Netta, I'd be pleased as punch to find an old girlfriend as nice as Ramona had reappeared*, Dolly thought wistfully. *At the very least I'd be a little curious!*

The substitute landlady stopped when she came to the lobby. A well-dressed girl was looking the room over critically, like an inspector from the Bay City Building and Permits Department. She prodded a gap in the tiled floor with the toe of her shoe, and Dolly half expected her to pull out a white handkerchief and run it along the molding to check for dirt.

But when Dolly asked, "Can I help you?" The girl whipped around with a wide smile. "I hope so," she said. "I'm looking for a room."

Chapter 8

Arlene

"Well, sure!" said Dolly heartily. "We have room! Let's get you all set up. I'm Dolly, your temporary landlady."

"My name's Arlene Sutton." The girl followed Dolly as she took out her keys and opened the door to Mrs. De-Witt's suite of rooms on the first floor. This would be Dolly's first time filling out the paperwork required for a new Magdalena Arms girl. Mrs. Pryce had told her that record keeping was one of her duties as Mrs. DeWitt's stand-in. "Don't forget to cross your *t*'s and dot every *i*!" the friendly trustee had instructed. "I don't want Dora to have any excuse for . . . well, just be careful."

"Have a seat," Dolly said, leading the way into Mrs. DeWitt's sitting room. Arlene raised an eyebrow as she looked around the dim room, crowded with heavy Victorian furniture and cluttered with knickknacks. Dolly put down the sprigged sheets and moved a pile of fat photograph albums off the love seat, plopping them on the floor where they raised a puff of dust. Arlene sat down gracefully, smoothing her skirt beneath her.

She was an attractive girl, Dolly thought, sitting at

Mrs. DeWitt's desk and eyeing the prospective tenant covertly as she wondered where the application forms might be. It wasn't her coloring that made you notice her—she was a medium-sized brunette—but a certain flair that was hard to pinpoint. It was in the sleekness of her geometric haircut, and her erect posture, and the way her amber eyes took in everything—which unfortunately included the drawer full of empty gin bottles Dolly had pulled out in her search for the tenant applications.

"This is Mrs. DeWitt's desk," Dolly said as she shut the drawer hastily. "She's the Magdalena Arms' regular housemoth—that is, landlady. The gin is medicinal."

"I see," said Arlene.

"Here we are!" The second drawer held a folder that said *Magdalena Arms Residence Applications,* and Dolly pulled it out triumphantly. But the yellowing forms it contained were from 1947. She put the folder back, with the sneaking suspicion that Mrs. DeWitt had *not* been crossing her *t*'s and dotting her *i*'s, paperwork-wise.

Dolly finally found a blank form on top of some old issues of the *Bay City Sentinel,* weighted down by a china figurine of a bulldog. "Now," she said, uncapping a pen with a flourish. "Reason for application?"

"I wanted something more affordable than my current address," Arlene said.

Dolly wrote *affordable place to live,* even as she wondered why a girl who dressed in the latest fashion, an imported wool tattersall coat in cream and chocolate with a matching tattersall skirt and a cashmere ribbed sweater the exact same shade as the mulberry silk lining of her coat, needed to scrimp on the rent.

"You see, I work in the theater," Arlene said, as if she'd read Dolly's mind. "And while my income is quite good, it can be a little—unsteady." She flashed her appealing smile.

"Are you an actress?" Dolly was delighted.

"A scenic designer," Arlene corrected. "I often go out of town, and it just didn't make sense, paying for a big expensive apartment I hardly use."

"You'll be right at home at the Arms," Dolly assured the new girl. "We have a strong theatrical tradition here."

"Wonderful," said Arlene. As Dolly looked down at the form to fill in the next question, Arlene added, "You're an actress, aren't you? Dorian Dingle—you were Judy Jarvis and now you're on that daytime drama. What's it called?" She snapped her fingers.

"*A Single Candle*," Dolly felt flattered. This was twice in one week a girl had recited her credits. "But I'm no longer on the show—"

"You haven't given up your acting career to run a boardinghouse?" Arlene raised her eyebrows until they touched her bangs.

"No, no, this is just temporary," Dolly assured her. "I'm just resting between parts—working on a new image—boning up on motherly motivation. I'll be back in the saddle soon enough."

"I'm happy to hear that," Arlene said gravely. "The theater can be a hard taskmistress, but she's worth it, I've found." After a brief hesitation she added, "I have a few contacts . . ."

"Well, thanks, I may take you up on that," Dolly told her. It was awfully nice of the newcomer to take an interest in her career. "Next question: Who referred you?"

Arlene hesitated. "I heard a young actress talking—"

"Was it Jackie?" Dolly guessed. "Short girl, dark hair, big eyes?"

"She was telling another girl that there were rooms for rent and that the breakfasts were out of this world."

It was nice to know her fresh baked buns were appreciated. "Mother's maiden name?"

The eyebrows went up again. "Eberle." Arlene spelled it out.

Carefully Dolly filled out the old-fashioned form. Place of birth, occupation, employer—"Put 'freelance,'" said Arlene. Education, previous residence—Arlene supplied an address in the swank Lakeside neighborhood. The scenic designer would certainly save a bundle moving to the Arms! Dolly wondered if Arlene had had trouble finding work lately. She didn't need another tenant with employment problems.

"This is quite a thorough form," Arlene commented as Dolly asked her for "current place of worship."

"The Magdalena Arms is kind of like a club," Dolly explained. "It was founded by Mrs. Payne-Putney after World War I. She wanted young working women—especially theatrical types—to have a respectable, affordable place to live."

"I see."

"So that's why I have to ask things like, 'Have you been thrown solely on your own resources?' We'll just put 'yes.'"

"True enough," said Arlene thoughtfully.

"And I'm supposed to get two letters of recommendation, one of which is from your hometown clergyman, a judge, or a past or current tenant of the Magdalena Arms. Gee, we really should update this form!"

"Do you need those right away?" Arlene was nonplussed.

"No, no, don't worry about that." Dolly didn't want to lose a prospective tenant over these antiquated requirements. "I tell you what. We'll get Jackie to write one letter—she qualifies as a reference, seeing as you heard about it through her—and I'll write the other."

"Well—"

"We're almost done, and then I'll give you your key and show you the room. I just need a list of male visitors—you get five." Dolly explained, embarrassed, "The Magdalena Arms doesn't allow its girls to receive male callers, except in the visitors' parlor, between the hours of two and nine on weekdays, and ten and eleven on weekends. I know it sounds a little odd." She added, "But none of our girls mind."

And Jackie ignores it completely, Dolly thought ruefully. Several times she'd brought her acting classmate Angelo, a cherubic Puerto Rican boy who lived up to his name, right into the lounge to practice their scenes.

Arlene smiled faintly. "I don't mind either. In fact"— she looked at Dolly through lowered lashes—"I can't think of even one name for your list."

Dolly's spirits rose. This was indeed the ideal tenant! "Then if you've got the first month's rent and deposit, I'll give you your key."

Any reservations she had dissolved as Arlene pulled a thick wad of bills from her purse. Dolly wrote her a receipt and opened the key cabinet. "There's a lovely room on the second floor—"

Arlene interrupted. "Anything higher up? I like a room that gets the sun."

Dolly half-wished there was an open room on the fifth floor. She wouldn't mind having Arlene for a neighbor. "How about 402? That faces the street and gets lots of light. But I should warn you, the elevator doesn't always work—"

"That's all right." Arlene held out her hand for the key. She seemed anxious to finish the transaction.

"I'll give you a quick tour." Dolly got up as she handed the scenic designer her key. In the lobby the twice monthly cleaning lady was swabbing the marble floor. To Dolly's newly critical eye, it looked like she was doing little more than moving the dirt from one side of the room to the other.

"That's where the mail comes." She pointed at the wall of hotel-style pigeonholes behind the deserted front desk. "And that's the phone. We all share it, so if it rings, grab it and take a message."

Arlene looked at the lone black phone in amazement. "One phone—for how many girls?"

"Twenty-four," Dolly told her reluctantly. "That is, when all the rooms are filled. It isn't quite that now. Anyway, we'll be getting more phones soon." Mentally she moved "phones" to the top of her to-do list.

She opened the double doors to the visitors' room, barely giving Arlene the time to glance inside at the dusty whatnot, the horsehair sofa, and an old oil painting darkened by time, before leading the new girl to the lounge, the big room that ran the width of the back of the building.

"This is where the girls spend most of their leisure time," she said, proudly displaying the cheerful room with its comfortable couches and armchairs, the old upright piano against the back wall, the Ping-Pong table in the other corner, the bookshelves with paperback novels, chess and checker sets, decks of cards and poker chips, and even a game of Parcheesi. And in pride of place: "This is our new color TV!"

"How do you decide what to watch?" Arlene asked, looking at the gleaming appliance. "I imagine there are some arguments!"

"Oh no," Dolly told her firmly. "The girls here are as compatible a bunch as you could hope to find." She decided not to mention that the television only got three stations clearly. That would change as soon as she built and installed that antenna she'd read about in *Popular Mechanics*.

Downstairs she showed Arlene the dining room and took the opportunity to punch down the pan of cinnamon rolls rising on the kitchen stove.

"Oh, and the elevator." She remembered to point it out when they were back in the lobby. The "Out of Order" sign propped against it had a layer of dust on it. "Even when it's working, we don't use it after ten p.m.," she instructed the new tenant. "It's too noisy."

The front door opened, and a gust of cold air made them both look up.

"Jackie!" called Dolly. "Meet our newest tenant, thanks to you."

But Jackie paid no attention to Arlene. "Where were you? You were supposed to meet me for the Meier Method drop-in class! We did animal exercises, and it was absolutely inspiring!"

Dolly had forgotten about their date completely. "It was just one thing after another, all day," she apologized.

"Sprucing up the Arms is all well and good," scolded Jackie, "but you *must* make time to work on your craft!"

"Jackie's right," said Arlene, who'd followed the interchange with interest. "Talent is too precious a commodity to waste."

As she waved good-bye to the new tenant a little later, Dolly wondered if Arlene was interested in the career welfare of every girl she met or if perhaps the substitute landlady had perked her interest. Arlene had certainly interested her!

Chapter 9

Miss Watkins's Study

Dolly was doing the dishes after breakfast and Jackie and Ramona were keeping her company, lounging on chairs they'd dragged from the dining room into the kitchen.

"You should really price out a dishwasher," said Ramona, lighting a cigarette to keep her second cup of coffee company. "We had an old Hobart at Metamora. Of course, we were producing three squares a day for more than three hundred."

Metamora was the boarding school where Ramona had worked, and now Jackie asked, "Was Metamora a hotbed of passion, like the school in *Boarding School Hussies*?"

Jackie had taken to Ramona. "She's hip," she'd told Dolly. Miffed, the landlady wondered if that meant she wasn't.

"Well, we didn't ski naked," Ramona admitted. "But there was the winter—"

Her story was interrupted by a distant "Hellooooo? Anybody home?" The next minute, a smiling woman stood in the doorway.

"Miss Watkins!" Dolly greeted the older woman. "Pull up a chair. How about a cup of coffee?"

The competent career counselor was a frequent visitor to the Magdalena Arms, where more than one girl had benefited from her wise advice on what position would best suit her. Despite her years of counseling experience, Doris Watkins looked little older than Dolly. As usual, her chestnut curls were smoothly coiffed and she was smartly dressed in a moss-green mohair fleece coat.

"Sounds wonderful," Miss Watkins said. She unbuttoned the coat to reveal a matching moss-green dress. Dolly wondered wistfully what dizzying heights her career might have reached if she'd been as petite and polished as Miss Watkins. *But if I was that short, I'd need a stepstool to reach the top shelf in the pantry,* she cheered herself.

Jackie fetched another chair from the dining room and urged their guest to try a cinnamon bun. "Dolly baked them this morning, and they're simply out of this world!"

"Jackie, Ramona, this is Doris Watkins. These are two of our newest tenants, Miss Watkins, although strictly speaking Ramona isn't new—she's one of the Magdalena Arms' old guard."

"Ramona Rukeyser?" Dolly could see Miss Watkins's razor-sharp mind had matched Ramona to some of the stories she'd heard. "I've been wanting to meet you for some time." The counselor bit into her cinnamon bun and her eyes closed in involuntary pleasure. "Dolly, this is delicious! I had no idea you were so talented in the kitchen."

"Ramona helped," said Dolly modestly.

"All I did was multiply the recipe and give you some efficiency tips," Ramona protested. To Miss Watkins, she added, "I used to housekeep for a couple hundred girls, so cooking for the masses is old hat for me."

"What are you doing now?" Miss Watkins asked with interest as she licked sugar glaze off her fingers.

"That's the big question, isn't it?" Ramona parried.

"Maybe I can help you answer it," the career counselor suggested. "In fact, that's the reason I'm here. I'm planning to present a study on "actual appropriateness"— that is, how often girls work at jobs that really suit them— at the next Career Counselor Conference. It occurred to me that the Magdalena Arms would provide me with the perfect data set—the ideal cross section of girls!"

"You want to move in and study us?" Dolly wrung out the dishrag and turned the idea over in her mind. Another renter—that would be good. But maybe the tenants wouldn't like living under the personnel professional's magnifying glass.

Miss Watkins laughed merrily. "Nothing so thorough, I'm afraid. I merely want to administer a career questionnaire to all the girls, along with the PPA, for those who haven't yet taken it."

"What's the PPA?" Jackie's eyes were wide beneath her fringe of bangs. "It sounds like a welfare program."

"It's short for the Spindle-Janska Personality Penchant Assessment," explained Miss Watkins. "It's a test that was devised to help young people determine the correct career path."

"Gosh, what if I took it and it told me I wasn't cut out to be an actress?" Jackie tormented herself with this horrible possibility. "I'd have to be a waitress the rest of my life!"

"We focus on positive indications," Miss Watkins told her. "Your proclivities and talents, especially those you may be unaware of."

"I wonder what it would say about me?" Ramona looked intrigued. "But I guess my age lets me out—I'm hardly young."

"You're not so old!" Dolly looked sharply at Jackie as she uttered the protest. She wasn't sure she liked the way the young girl was gazing at Ramona.

"While it's primarily used on young people, we've come to the conclusion over the years that the Personality Penchant Assessment is valid for all ages," Miss Watkins told Ramona. "Can I count on you both?"

Ramona and Jackie assented. "I guess it would be better to find out now, rather than later," Jackie mused.

"What about you, Dolly? Can I count on you as well?"

Dolly was taking off her rubber gloves. She looked up at Miss Watkins in surprise. "Me!" she hooted. "You don't need me to take that test! Just put in your data set 'Dolly Dingle, Miss Showbiz.' Why, I've been doing this for thirty-one years, ever since my mother pushed me onstage to sing 'The Good Ship Lollipop' in the Shirley Temple look-alike contest."

And thirty-one years later, all that awaited her was the role of Honey Bear. Involuntarily, she sighed. It wasn't an auspicious career, but it was all she had.

Unbidden, a couplet from one of Mrs. DeWitt's poems echoed in her head:

> *What is that which I should turn to,*
> *Lighting upon days like these?*
> *Every door is barred with gold,*
> *And opens but to golden keys.*

"Yet you may have other abilities you've never explored," Miss Watkins was saying. "Like your evident flair for cooking."

"I just like to eat." Dolly waved the idea away. "Doesn't everyone?"

"And she patched the plaster over the sideboard," Ramona told Miss Watkins.

"I hate to be idle," Dolly explained, sweeping the kitchen.

"You intrigue me, Dolly," Miss Watkins eyed her. "Are you sure you won't take the PPA?"

"Well, not today anyway." Dolly didn't want to tell the career counselor she thought her test was a little like consulting a carnival fortune-teller. "I'm just leaving to visit Mrs. DeWitt in the hospital."

"Mrs. DeWitt is in the hospital!" the career counselor exclaimed. "What happened?"

Jackie and Dolly told the story of the landlady's accident. "She came through the surgery just fine," Dolly reported. "She should be home early December."

Miss Watkins clicked her tongue. "The poor woman! Has she any family?"

Dolly doubted it. "I think they cut her off years ago."

"I'm going to go too," Ramona said suddenly. "I'd like to say hello to the old girl." She promised Miss Watkins to take the PPA and questionnaire another day, and they left the career counselor preparing to administer her test to the trepidatious but willing Jackie.

They were winding scarves around their throats in the lobby when Kay came down the stairs. Hearing of their errand, she said she'd join them. "I have a little time before rehearsal."

"Has any of your old gang been to see Mrs. DeWitt?" Kay asked as they walked to the bus stop.

"I don't know," Dolly admitted. "I don't even know if they know!" She'd been so busy with the new tenants and the improvements at the Arms, she hadn't thought of the old gang all week. Maybe she should put together a dinner at Luigi's, a sort of "welcome back, Ramona" affair.

She glanced at Ramona, who was stamping her feet to keep them warm as they waited at the bus stop. Or maybe not, she reconsidered reluctantly. Netta was avoiding the returned tenant, Pam would disapprove, and Lois, who'd only heard Netta's one-sided stories about Ramona's misdeeds, wouldn't be kindly disposed either. Even idealistic Phyllis had hesitantly suggested that Dolly make sure Ramona wasn't wanted by the Bay City Police.

"The Magdalena Arms is Ramona's home," she'd told Phyllis firmly. "Isn't home the place that when you show up on the doorstep, they have to invite you inside?"

Her old friend certainly didn't *look* like a girl with a guilty conscience. Red-cheeked with cold, she was chatting gaily to Kay about various Bay City jazz musicians. "Is Buzz Bixby still around? Maxie and I used to sit in on his jam sessions, above Club Lucky. In fact," she added, climbing aboard the bus that wheezed to their stop, "I'm tempted to stop by the club and see if they remember me. Maybe I can pick up a few cocktail shifts while I wait to find out my penchants from your Miss Watkins."

See? Dolly told the invisible critics triumphantly. *There is no reason to be so suspicious of good old Ramona.* She asked as they sat down, "I always wondered why you didn't stick with being a librarian, after all that schooling."

With a disarming smile, Ramona answered, "I guess the slow and steady way just isn't for me." She gazed out the window thoughtfully, and Dolly knew her mind was busy with her next scheme and that she wasn't even seeing the wintry gray sky, or the dirty red brick buildings of Swensonville, or the blaring advertisements in shop windows for Thanksgiving turkeys.

"If only I could put my hands on some capital," Ramona murmured to herself. But her next words surprised Dolly. "I'm kind of curious about this personality test. You should take it too. Who knows what you'll find out!"

"Don't tell me you take that stuff seriously?" Dolly

pulled the cord for their stop. "I'm too busy to take tests. Anyway, I already know my proclivities and what I'm going to do with them." They dropped the subject, and the three girls disembarked, hurrying through the bitter cold to Bay City General's big, forbidding entrance. "It looks like a jail," Ramona murmured, pulling open the heavy door. Once inside, wide hallways led off in all directions, and signs pointed the way to radiology, urology, psychiatry, geriatrics, and the morgue. The steamy warmth was tinged with antiseptics.

"Hospitals, ugh," said Kay.

They had to ask for directions twice, and Dolly wandered into obstetrics before they found Mrs. DeWitt's room on the orthopedics floor. Their old housemother was dozing, her eyelids twitching slightly. She looked gaunt and pale. As they tiptoed in, she opened her sunken eyes. For a moment, she stared at them as if they were strangers. Then her eyes settled on Dolly and she lifted her head.

"Dolly." She beckoned her favorite tenant forward urgently.

"How are you feeling, Mrs. DeWitt?" Dolly approached, covering her shock at her landlady's appearance with a hearty lie: "You're looking about ready to hop out of bed!"

Mrs. DeWitt grasped Dolly's arm and pulled her closer still. "Gin," she said hoarsely. "I need my gin!"

Dolly asked helplessly, "Are you sure it would be good for you? We brought you some cinnamon buns." She extricated herself from Mrs. DeWitt's alarmingly strong grip and put the buns on the patient's bedside table. Mrs. DeWitt plucked at the bedclothes as if she couldn't keep her hands still. Except for her nervous hands and constantly turning head, she was unnaturally still, her lower half immobilized.

Ramona tried to distract her. "Hi, Mrs. DeWitt! It's Ramona—Ramona Rukeyser—remember me?"

Mrs. DeWitt coughed, and then winced in pain. "I thought you were in jail," she murmured, before turning to Dolly again. "Dolly," she began pleadingly.

Dolly tried to avert another request. "I also brought a tenant application to show you—you can tell me if I've filled it out okay—"

Mrs. DeWitt barely glanced at the papers Dolly held out. "Those forms are a bunch of foolishness," she muttered, confirming Dolly's fears about misfiled forms. "Not worth the time it takes to fill them out." She pushed them away. "I can't think, for the pounding in my head—*la migraine*—it's been nothing but *la migraine* since I've been here!"

Mrs. DeWitt was growing more and more agitated, and the girls looked at each other anxiously, unsure what to do. To Dolly's relief, a nurse bustled in. "Hello, Harriet," she caroled. "I see you have some visitors!" The sight of her seemed to subdue Mrs. DeWitt. "I still have that headache," said the old housemother meekly. "Can't you give me something for it?"

"Still feeling ouchy? Hmmm." The nurse frowned as the Magdalena Arms' fallen landlady sneezed and winced. She took Mrs. DeWitt's pulse and wrote something on the chart. "It's not quite time, and I'm a little worried about that cold." She turned to the girls who were standing uncertainly at the foot of Mrs. DeWitt's bed. "Why don't you wait outside a minute or two, while I try to make Grandma more comfortable?"

They filed out, not bothering to correct the nurse, and stood for a second in depressed silence.

"She's worse than I expected," Kay said finally.

Ramona agreed. "She looks terrible! What have they done to her?"

Dolly was too disheartened to reply. Was it just the hospital? Or had Mrs. DeWitt's years finally caught up with her? She wished she could launch herself on a to-do list of improvements for the old landlady, the way she had for the Magdalena Arms. "She'll be better once she gets home," she said with a confidence she didn't feel.

Kay looked at her watch. "I have to leave or I'll be late for rehearsal. Tell me what you find out from the nurse."

After she was gone, Ramona turned to Dolly. "Are you going to get her the gin? She seemed pretty desperate."

"I don't know," said Dolly doubtfully. "Do you think it would be okay for her, while she's recuperating?"

"She always said it was the only thing that cured *la migraine*," Ramona replied. "I just wish there was *something* we could do!"

The nurse joined them. "She's sleeping now. Why don't you let her rest and come back another time?"

Dolly asked, "Is this normal? I mean, is she recovering?"

The nurse wasn't forthcoming. "She's doing as well as can be expected. She's an old woman, with an old woman's problems. Of course this cold she caught isn't helping. The doctor can tell you more."

She hurried away. Dolly wished Beverly were the one taking care of Mrs. DeWitt. Beverly wouldn't call her Harriet or ask if she was ouchy.

Mrs. DeWitt hadn't even recited any poetry, Dolly realized. Not one line of verse.

The substitute landlady murmured some for her:

> " 'God in his mercy lend her something,
> The Lady of Shalott.' "

A fter the visit to the hospital, Dolly threw herself into the Magdalena Arms improvements with renewed vigor. These were problems she could solve with elbow grease and energy, and she had an irrational feeling that the more items she checked off her list, the faster Mrs. DeWitt would recover.

The front door and the windows sparkled. She spent one long day untacking the carpet from the stairs and then retacking it so that the unworn parts were now on the edges of the treads and the worn parts tucked back in the inside corner where the tread met the riser. Kay helped her on the last two floors and was dismayed when they were short one step's worth of carpet at the very top. But Dolly was prepared for this dilemma and triumphantly produced the square she had measured and cut from a remnant in the storeroom.

"The old carpet was so faded the colors don't match anymore," she said, "but no one on the fifth floor will make a fuss."

Kay also helped her bleed the radiators, although Dolly alone oiled the pump, installed an adjustable valve on the radiator in the dining room, and rewired the lobby's chandelier. The substitute landlady spent her days hunting down odd items, like tile squares the right shade of blue to replace the missing ones in the lobby floor.

But underneath it all, her worry about Mrs. DeWitt persisted. She had buttonholed Beverly one morning, to consult her on the gin question. The student nurse was adamantly opposed to Dolly's idea of taking the Magdalena Arms housemother a gift-wrapped bottle of her favorite brand.

"But she always said it was the only thing that cured *la migraine*," Dolly pleaded. "And she looked so miserable!"

"Likely all that gin she drank is what was *giving* her headaches," Beverly retorted, her Southern accent more evident than usual. "Didn't you ever wonder why she always had a bottle handy?" The nurse hid her own concern under a professional cloak of scientific detachment. "She presents several symptoms consistent with a dependence on alcohol."

"You mean she's a *drunk*?" Dolly was shocked at the idea. Drunks were the old men you saw on lower Pingst, slumped in doorways with shabby clothes and stubble on their chins. Not Mrs. DeWitt, who had played Emilia, Iago's wife, at the Orpheum! "If Mrs. DeWitt has a drinking problem, then so do half the girls in the Arms!" Dolly sputtered.

"I think so too," Beverly agreed at once. "If they could see the state of their livers, they wouldn't be barhopping every night. And they wouldn't need these heavy breakfasts you serve the next morning. Now, I know you thought my idea about serving just fruit and nuts was too extreme, but I have a recipe for a muffin I want you to try. It's called a *bran* muffin—"

As a conscientious housemother, Dolly was glad that Beverly had come out of her shell. However, she had to admit she was disconcerted by the health nut who'd emerged. Beverly's concern for the digestive systems of fellow tenants was relentless, and she had proposed a series of drastic changes to the Magdalena Arms diet.

"All right, I'll try it," promised the harried housemother, just to hush the health professional.

"And don't you go giving Mrs. DeWitt any gin, you hear?" Beverly pulled her tasseled stocking cap down over her ears and headed into the cold.

Dolly carefully fit the last tile into the *M* in the center of the lobby floor, wondering what she could substitute for gin on her next visit to the ancient landlady.

"What was that all about?" Arlene was descending the stairs, pulling on a pair of two-toned gloves that matched her tattersall coat. She'd landed a stint at a production company that made educational films on historical subjects and had told Dolly that her work constructing a miniature colonial village would keep her busy through the end of the year.

"Oh, just Beverly, lecturing me about health," said Dolly. "She thinks drinking is bad for us." The temporary landlady sat back on her heels and surveyed the lobby floor, pleased with her handiwork. All the lobby floor needed now was a good scrub. She made a mental note to look up marble in her *One Thousand and One Ways* and find out if it needed special soap.

Arlene dismissed Beverly impatiently. "Those medical types always have some bee in their bonnet about diet." And then she asked, "Have you talked to Kay about those lengthy showers?"

"Gosh, I'm sorry." Dolly climbed to her feet feeling guilty. "I haven't had a chance yet."

It was unfortunate that Arlene's schedule coincided with Kay's. Dolly had discovered that whipping the Arms' physical plant into shape was child's play next to the task of managing twenty-two girls with their various fixations and foibles.

And Arlene seemed to be having a hard time adjusting to life at the Magdalena Arms. Her jaw had dropped to her knees when she understood that the bathroom on the fourth floor was shared by four girls, and that the number might increase to six.

"Are you sure this conforms to the current housing code?" she'd demanded.

Dolly had assured her the Arms had always operated this way. "That's why rooming here is so cheap—I mean, economical." She felt sorry for the scenic designer, who was clearly used to ritzier accommodations.

"Of course," Arlene had muttered, a miserable look in her eyes.

Dolly was more convinced than ever that Arlene had suffered some kind of financial setback. She'd brought only one large suitcase when she'd moved in—an expensive one, naturally, of cured cowhide with brass buckles.

The novice housemother wished she had the time to do a little tactful probing and extract the sad story that she was sure lurked behind Arlene's appearance at the Arms. But so many other things clamored for her attention—the repairs, the unfortunate animosity between Ramona and Netta, and the foolish crush Jackie had developed on Ramona, which only added fuel to the fire. Then there were the antiquated bylaws of the Magdalena Arms, which Dolly had been studying harder than any script, discovering that they were booby-trapped with awkward demands on the new housemother.

Take the knotty issue of food in the rooms, a rule Dolly had always been the first to flout. The softhearted substitute landlady had solved the problem by shortening Mrs. DeWitt's well-known dictum, "No food in your room. It attracts vermin" to the more succinct, "No vermin in your room." *It comes to the same thing*, she reasoned, even though Ramona said that it sounded like Dolly was forbidding the tenants to keep pet cockroaches.

Now, the harried housemother promised Arlene, "I'll talk to Kay tonight. Why don't you join us in the lounge? We're going to watch that space show."

Beverly was keen to see the new television program, which featured a Negro actress, and Ramona had promised to make cocoa. It was the perfect scenario for "fostering new friendships," as the bylaws recommended.

"I have an engagement," the scenic designer responded briefly. "A cocktail party where I hope to make some business contacts."

"Oh, too bad." Dolly was stymied again in her efforts to integrate standoffish Arlene into the Arms.

"By the way," the attractive girl hesitated, her hand on the doorknob. "A casting agent friend is on the lookout for a matronly type—I told him all about you."

Dolly was flattered that Arlene remembered the conversation they'd had about Dolly's new acting strategy.

"Awfully swell of you to think of me!" she told the attractive girl.

"Not at all." Arlene smiled slightly. "I just hate to see talent go to waste."

Dolly watched her swing down the walk, wondering again if there was more behind her interest in Dolly's career than simple showbiz sisterhood. Arlene's unrelenting efforts to further her own design ambitions made Dolly feel a little lazy. She really should do *something* about her neglected career—get a new head shot, at least.

I might as well wait until Stella comes back in January, she excused herself, as she put away the tiling tools. Her photographer friend would take the photo for free.

The fact was, in spite of her worry about Mrs. DeWitt, and the trustees' threats, Dolly was enjoying her vacation from the showbiz grind, the open calls, the uninterested agents, the depressed feeling she used to have, returning from a day of making the rounds with the empty promise "we'll call you" echoing in her ears. It was a relief to have the immediate satisfactions of a pan of brioche bread, a clean kitchen, or a polished lobby floor—not to mention a steady salary.

In addition, she was enjoying the companionship of the new gang that had coalesced with the addition of Jackie and Ramona. Sitting on the couch in front of the television that night, with Beverly curled up under an old afghan (the Southern girl was always cold) and Kay and Jackie teasing the young nurse that she needed more fat in her diet, Dolly had a deep feeling of contentment. What did it matter that the TV's picture wavered or that Ramona still hadn't paid any rent? So what if the tuck-pointing estimate she'd gotten earlier that day was astronomical? Here she was, the center of an attractive bunch of girls again, and there was Ramona, pushing open the door to the lounge with the glad words, "Cocoa's ready! Who wants a cup?"

If only Netta would forget her resentment and join in the friendly warmth. "Come on, Netta!" Dolly pleaded, when the schoolteacher declined her invitation to join an old-fashioned bull session in Jackie's room. "We're going to toast the repaired elevator!"

Fixing the out-of-order elevator had turned out to be a simple matter of realigning the contacts that had prevented the mesh gate from closing properly and allowing the elevator to operate. However, every girl at the Arms marveled at the newly repaired elevator, as if Dolly had built the Taj Mahal.

"I appreciate that too, of course," Netta conceded. "And all the work you've been doing for the Arms." The stiff-necked girl was nothing if not fair. "All right, I'll stop by after my meeting," she agreed reluctantly. "But I'm not sitting next to Ramona!"

When Netta slipped in, Ramona was sharing the bed with Jackie, which Dolly knew would scarcely soften the stern schoolteacher. Dolly disapproved too. *Ramona shouldn't encourage Jackie's crush!*

Jackie was looking particularly young, sitting up on Maxie's pink satin-covered bed, her eyes wide and excited as she announced, "According to Miss Watkins, I'm just bursting with penchants!"

Tonight, after toasting elevators, the topic had turned to careers. All the Arms was in a ferment over "career appropriateness" as Miss Watkins worked her way through the building, administering the questionnaire and PPA to her precious "data set."

"She said I had a penchant for promotion!" Jackie bragged. "She said my unbridled enthusiasm and extroverted personality were compatible with acting, but would be a greater asset in the sales field."

"Which will you pursue?" inquired Phyllis. The social scientist was sitting cross-legged on the floor.

"I can do both!" Jackie overflowed with the enthusiasm Miss Watkins had noted. "Maybe I'll form a theater company with Angelo and a couple of the other kids from class. I can act in our productions and handle the promotion on the side!"

Dolly couldn't help smiling. Jackie reminded her of herself as a little girl, wanting to be a ranch hand and a movie star both. She poured the dregs of the cocktail shaker into Jackie's glass and toasted her. "May you realize both your ambitions!"

"What about you, Phyllis?" Jackie asked in turn. The young statistician had fallen into one of her brown studies. Lately the idealistic bureaucrat seemed preoccupied with something more than Bay City building policy.

Phyllis blinked and came back to the present. "Me? Well, I first took the PPA ages ago, in high school." She sighed. "All the indications were that I should become a social scientist. My guidance counselor even said that government work was indicated rather than an academic career, and that bureaucratic negotiation was my strong suit."

"And that's exactly where you ended up!" Netta looked down at Phyllis affectionately from her perch on the dressing table chair.

"Yes," said Phyllis dolefully. "I got eighty-five out of one hundred on Miss Watkins's career experience questionnaire."

The girls exchanged glances. That meant Phyllis had scored in the top percentile for career appropriateness. Yet she seemed oddly cast down by her results.

"Criminy," murmured Ramona. "I only got a forty-two."

"But what difference does it make?" Phyllis burst out. "Does career appropriateness bring you happiness?"

"Miss Watkins never promised any of us a rose garden," Netta defended the career counselor.

"Oh, I'm not blaming Miss Watkins." Phyllis's shoulders drooped.

"I know what Phyllis means," Ramona said suddenly. "Miss Watkins's tests and questionnaires kind of stir you up—make you look at your life with a new perspective. You go along for years, doing what you have to to get by, and when you look back and see what it all adds up to, it kind of frightens you!"

"Why should you be frightened?" Jackie looked at Ramona admiringly. "You've had so many wonderful experiences!"

Netta snorted, and Dolly said hastily, "Has it got you stirred up, Phyllis?"

Phyllis burst out: "Suddenly it seems my graphs and

charts proving that simple zoning changes will improve people's lives are unimportant! I mean, even if I succeed in convincing the higher-ups in Bay City government to approve my amendments to the zoning code, I'll still be alone—I mean, not alone exactly, but—"

Dolly helped the stumbling statistician: "What you mean is, statistical success means nothing without someone special like Miss Ware, is that it?"

Phyllis nodded gratefully.

Then Ramona voiced the question they'd all wanted to put to the torch-carrying statistician at one point or another: "Phyllis, why don't you forget about Miss Ware, and find someone who's a little more *available?*"

The social scientist replied stubbornly, "There's no one like Miss Ware."

Netta added, with a disdainful look at the pair on the bed, "Love isn't just about finding someone handy!"

"A girl in the hand is more fun than one in the bush!"

Ramona was being deliberately provocative, Dolly could tell. The temporary housemother hastened to smooth over the argument. "I guess to Phyllis we're like the merry comrades in that poem of Mrs. DeWitt's— you know, 'They to whom my foolish passion were a target for their scorn.'"

Ramona teased, "Goodness, Dolly, you're determined to substitute for Mrs. DeWitt in every way, even to supplying us with appropriate poetic quotations!"

"Oh, don't be silly, I can't remember half as much poetry as Mrs. DeWitt." Dolly was secretly delighted by Ramona's remark. She picked up the empty cocktail shaker, her trustiest tool for making peace between enemy factions. "Why don't I make up another batch?"

"How about you, Dolly?" Jackie asked the substitute landlady, who was peering at the level of gin left in the bottle. "What did the PPA say about you?"

"Me? I haven't taken it." Dolly emptied the bottle into the shaker.

"You haven't? Why not?" Jackie was round-eyed with astonishment. Before Dolly could answer, Ramona said, "Dolly's old-fashioned. She thinks the PPA is a bunch of hooey."

"I'm not old-fashioned," Dolly protested, offended. She was starting to sympathize with Netta. Ramona could needle a girl to distraction when she chose.

On cue, the schoolteacher snapped, "Oh, stop trying to pressure Dolly into doing something she doesn't want to!"

"It's not that I don't want to," Dolly said, trying to keep the peace. "I just haven't found the time—"

To her relief there was a tap at the door and Beverly peered in. "Did you all hear those noises coming from downstairs?" As always when worked up, Beverly's Southern accent was stronger. Her "you all" sounded like "yawl."

"You think someone's down there? I mean, someone who shouldn't be?" Dolly started to get to her feet, but Jackie beat her to it, scrambling off the bed. "You've been on your feet all day, Dolly, I'll go check."

"Better two of us." Ramona followed her out the door.

"What are you all doing up so late?" Beverly lingered in the doorway loathe to leave until her nervousness was allayed.

"Career talk," Netta told her. "What did your PPA say? Was it helpful?"

"Well," Beverly said dubiously, "Miss Watkins didn't advise me to get a job as a maid, which is better than the career advice at home. She just spouted some nonsense about how I'm a crusader type, with a penchant for educating, persuading, and browbeating people. Honestly, all I want to do is finish nursing school and get a job so I can help my folks."

Miss Watkins's assessment of the young nurse made Dolly wonder if there *was* something to this PPA. Then Jackie and Ramona returned, reporting everything was all clear downstairs, and Beverly spotted the gin bottle and began to lecture them about their livers, and the bull session broke up.

Brushing her teeth a little later, Netta told Dolly, "Include me out of any future get-togethers! The sight of Ramona cozying up to Jackie makes me gag!"

"Don't be jealous." Dolly tweezed a stray hair from her chin.

Netta flushed. "This has nothing to do with jealousy," she declared. "I simply can't stand watching Ramona exert her evil influence over an innocent young girl!"

It was hopeless to argue. And once again, Netta had succeeded in infecting the optimistic landlady with worry. *Was* Ramona using Jackie for one of her shady schemes?

Watching the two girls at breakfast the next morning did nothing to relieve Dolly's suspicions. The way Jackie hung on Ramona's every word was simply irritating, but their secretive whispering was worse. And why did Ramona look around cautiously before beckoning Jackie up the stairs? It was unfortunate that the girls were together so much, what with Ramona's unemployment and Jackie being on the night shift at the dinette.

As if I don't have worries enough, Dolly fretted, as she descended to the sub-basement storeroom after breakfast. Arlene had complained about the chill in her room, and Dolly needed to retrieve the roll of weather stripping on top of one of the stacks of stuff.

Distractedly, she dragged out the rickety ladder, pushing aside an old baby carriage. Teetering at the top, she put a hand on the wooden beam to brace herself. The wood felt soft and moist to the touch. Dolly frowned.

That wasn't right. She nicked the soft wood with a fingernail. A feeling of alarm began to grow as the amateur repair woman pulled out the switchblade knife she'd taken from the thug. She flicked out the blade and pushed it against the beam.

The knife sank in as easily as a butter knife slicing a quivering custard.

Wood rot! Dolly had read about this dread disease of older structures in her *One Thousand and One Ways to Save Money on Home Repair*. This was worse than a busted water heater! How was she going fix this without Mrs. Putney-Potter finding out?

Suddenly, the substitute landlady realized someone was calling her name, an urgent cry that was coming closer. She climbed down from the ladder and was halfway up the stairs when the door above her opened and Ramona panted, "Dolly! Didn't you hear me shouting? The trustees are here! They're waiting for you in the visitors' parlor!"

Chapter 11

The Trustees' Visit

The trustees! Here! For a panic-stricken moment Dolly wondered if Mrs. Putney-Potter had somehow discovered the rot and come armed with condemned signs to shut the building down. Then her common sense took hold and she hurried up the rest of the stairs. They *couldn't* know—and they mustn't find out. She had to keep the trustees out of the sub-basement storeroom and the rot it contained!

There were only two trustees when Dolly burst into the visitors' parlor, out of breath. Mrs. Putney-Potter and Mrs. Pryce sat at opposite ends of the slippery horsehair sofa. Even in her flustered state, Dolly noticed, with relief, that for once the cleaning woman had done a thorough job on the seldom-used room. She'd even placed a vase of fresh flowers on the spindly-legged side table.

These amenities left Mrs. Putney-Potter unimpressed. She sat with a tight-lipped expression, determined to disapprove everything. Mrs. Pryce greeted Dolly with an anxious smile.

"So sorry to drop in on you like this with no notice, but we did want to see how you were getting along."

"Sure, why not?" panted Dolly. "We have nothing to hide! How about a cup of coffee, or tea, or—" She almost added gin to the list of beverages, she was so flurried.

Mrs. Putney-Potter spoke up. "This isn't a social call. We're here solely to determine the state of the Magdalena Arms and assess your guardianship of its girls." As she said "guardianship," her eyes raked Dolly from head to toe, taking in everything from the oil-smudged orange kerchief on her head to the scuffed toes of her work boots peeping out from the hem of her worn blue coveralls.

Darn it! She should have taken the time to change. "Pardon my dust"—she tried to lighten the mood—"while I make improvements! I was in the sub—the kitchen, doing the dishes."

Mrs. Putney-Potter merely sniffed. "Wouldn't rubber gloves be sufficient?"

"What can I show you?" Dolly's brain drew a blank, all the projects she'd been working on fleeing her mind like rabbits before an oncoming storm. "How about the radiators? We bled them a week ago, to keep them working at peak efficiency. Save on heating costs!"

They all looked at the parlor's radiator, which looked the same as usual. "Splendid," said Mrs. Pryce gamely.

"I'm very saddened to see this painting in such an appalling state." Mrs. Putney-Potter pointed at the darkened oil painting that hung over the horsehair sofa. "It's an original copy of a very famous original, painted by a former Magdalena Arms girl who went on to an illustrious career as an artist. It has been shamefully neglected!"

"Really, Dora," snapped Mrs. Pryce. "Mabel Burnside taught art at the Waukesset Art Center for forty years. Her career was hardly that illustrious."

"We'll clean it up," Dolly promised, wondering if her *One Thousand and One Ways* covered oil painting restoration. "Did you notice the mosaic tiles in the lobby are all fixed?"

She ushered them into the lobby, and Mrs. Pryce took the opportunity to whisper in the temporary landlady's ear, "I tried to call and warn you as soon as Dora sprung this, but the phone was off the hook!"

Dolly glanced at the phone. The receiver was in its cradle now, just where it was supposed to be.

Mrs. Putney-Potter was frowning up at the lobby ceiling. Dolly had scraped off the old paint and patched the plaster, and she planned to paint that afternoon. "Quite a mess!" snapped the critical trustee.

"Well, you have to break eggs to make an omelet, don't you?" Dolly was getting tired of the wealthy woman's attitude. "Look at this swatch of Ashes of Rose, and picture how nice it'll look when it's done!"

Mrs. Putney-Potter disregarded the swatch Dolly proffered and said to Mrs. Pryce, "I wonder if it's a good idea to let Miss Dingle do all the work instead of a licensed contractor. Are we creating insurance issues?"

"Don't be such a grump, Dora," Mrs. Pryce defended the beleaguered handywoman. "It's part of the Magdalena Arms tradition to help where help is needed. Surely you remember the line in the bylaws, 'Neither servant nor mistress but all girls together!' "

Despite Mrs. Pryce's cheerleading, the trustees' inspection continued to travel around the same repetitive track—Mrs. Putney-Potter finding fault while Dolly pointed out that the scratched woodwork, or the stained grout, or the closet door that stuck was cosmetic, fixable, and in the end hardly hindered the boardinghouse's function.

"The Arms is in solid shape!" she declared, slapping the sideboard and praying Mrs. Putney-Potter wouldn't ask to inspect the sub-basement storeroom. "Why, I was up on the roof yesterday, installing a new television antenna, and I can tell you, that roof will weather winter storms for a good many years to come."

"New television antenna? It seems to me that there are several other items more worthy of your attention!"

Would this tedious trustee never weary of her picayune criticisms? "The new antenna will make a big difference to the girls who live here," Dolly retorted, trying to keep her temper. "We're at almost eighty percent occupancy and I'm doing everything I can to bring it up to one hundred percent!"

Mrs. Putney-Potter pounced. "Ah, the new tenants. I wonder if we might glance over the tenant paperwork while we're here."

From the way Mrs. Putney-Potter's eyes gleamed, Dolly realized at once that *this* was the real reason for the unexpected visit. How had the devious trustee sniffed out the disorder in Mrs. DeWitt's desk? Dolly was suddenly extra thankful that she'd called on her fifth-floor friends to help straighten out the mess. Phyllis, with her analytical mind, had been a whiz at putting Mrs. DeWitt's records into order, while Ramona and Jackie filled in the missing pieces. Ramona had shown particular skill in imitating Mrs. DeWitt's handwriting, and it had been her idea to "age" some of the supposedly older documents by baking them briefly in a slow oven.

Ramona herself made an appearance as Dolly returned from Mrs. DeWitt's desk, carrying the paperwork to the visitors' parlor with her heart pounding. Dolly gave a double take as she deposited the stack of tenant applications by Mrs. Putney-Potter. This was a Ramona transformed; gone was the beatnik girl who lounged in the kitchen in her blue jeans, smoking cigarettes. Now she wore a full-skirted pine-green wool jumper with a fitted bodice and carried a silver tray with a matching tea service.

Where on earth did she get that? Dolly wondered, as her friend set down the tray. She'd put out a plate of Dolly's fresh-baked pecan rolls.

"Hello!" she caroled. "I thought you ladies could use a little refreshment!"

Mrs. Pryce beamed. "Just like the old days, isn't it, Dora?" She nudged her fellow trustee. "I always thought it was too bad they let the daily tea lapse after the war."

"I was once a housekeeper at Me—a girls' boarding school," Ramona told Mrs. Pryce after Dolly made the introductions. "So I try to give Dolly a hand. Not that she needs one," Ramona prattled on gaily. "She made these pecan rolls. Marvelous, aren't they?"

"Delicious!" said Mrs. Pryce.

"She cooks, she cleans, she fixes, she mothers us all—I hope you realize how lucky you are that she sacrificed her acting career to help out like this!" Ramona fixed the two trustees with a stern look.

"Of course we appreciate her!" Mrs. Pryce replied warmly. Mrs. Putney-Potter gave up flipping through the stacks of neatly labeled folders with tenant applications and records dating back to 1924.

"This seems to be in order," she said vexedly.

Dolly bent to pick up a recommendation letter that had floated to the floor. Where had Ramona found the state senator's stationery? She'd written a very nice recommendation letter for Jackie on it, before signing the senator's name.

Mrs. Putney-Potter stood up. "I have an appointment

downtown. I'll say good-bye now." And without any thanks, she stalked out.

The three left behind relaxed. Mrs. Pryce heaved a frank sigh of relief. "What an ordeal! I've often wor—er, wondered about Mrs. DeWitt's record keeping, but I see now I was wrong."

Dolly didn't bother to enlighten the good-natured trustee. Already the relief that she'd felt at Mrs. Putney-Potter's frustrated departure was seeping away, and wood rot worries filled her head once more. "Mrs. Pryce," she began.

"Call me Chaddy, dear," said the trustee chummily. "We're colleagues after all—coconspirators, even!" She trilled a little laugh and took another pecan roll. "These really are quite good," she murmured.

"Chaddy," Dolly tried again, "say—hypothetically speaking, of course—that something big *was* wrong at the Arms, something I couldn't fix, like the roof blew off, or"—she gulped—"the stairs collapsed because of wood rot. How would I go about getting repairs paid for?"

Chaddy shuddered. "You wouldn't. That would be all the excuse Dora needed."

This confirmed Dolly's worst suspicions. "What about paying for it on the q.t., maybe funded by a wealthy trustee—"

Chaddy smiled. "I hope you're not thinking of *me*, Dolly, my dear." Dolly's hopes, which had already sunk to her knees, now descended to the toes of her work boots. "I'm comfortably off, but no more. You see, Aunt Cornelia left her own fortune to the trust, and the rest of the estate—"

Ramona interrupted. "What I don't understand is why Mrs. Payne-Putney is *your* aunt, but your name is Pryce, and how Mrs. Putney-Potter fits in."

"My mother was Cornelia Payne-Putney's cousin, so we're actually cousins once removed. I married a man named Harold Pryce, and Dora Potter married Horace Putney, from the Putney side of the Payne-Putneys," Mrs. Pryce explained. "It's only since her husband's death that she started calling herself Putney-Potter, like the arriviste she is!" Chaddy showed a little spleen toward her fellow trustee. "Unfortunately, the Putney part of the Payne-Putney fortune went to Horace, including the house. Now Dora calls Aunt Cornelia's house, where I was practically raised, the Putney-Potter mansion even though *everyone* knows it as the Payne-Putney house!" Mrs. Pryce gave a disdainful sniff. "It's part and parcel with the rest of her pretentions!"

Dolly was thoroughly befuddled after being pelted with all these Putneys, Paynes, and Potters. "So the upshot is, Mrs. Putney-Potter got your cousin's money, not you?"

"The Putney part," Mrs. Pryce corrected patiently. "And she had to marry Horace Putney to get it, poor girl!"

Ramona had been following this with perfect comprehension. "So Dora Putney-Potter really was a poor Magdalena Arms girl at one point—when Dolly told me, I wondered why someone like her would have lived here."

"Oh, yes." Mrs. Pryce nodded wisely. "She was working as an assistant sales agent in a real estate office when she met Horace Putney and saw an easier way to butter her bread. The Putneys have a finger in every important development pie in Bay City, you know! But still, she never lets a board meeting pass without reminding everyone that she lived here and knows more than everyone else about what should be done."

"I wonder what room she had," Ramona mused.

"So you see"—Chaddy Pryce turned to Dolly—"I'm in

no position to make a private donation, in the hypotheti-
cal situation you mentioned. It's fortunate that, as you
said, the repairs are all cosmetic—aren't they?" she
added a little anxiously.

"Oh yes," said Dolly in a hollow voice. "All cosmetic."

Chapter 12

A Transatlantic Phone Call

After Mrs. Pryce departed, Dolly picked up the tenant applications Mrs. Putney-Potter had scattered about. "Thanks for pitching in," Dolly told Ramona distractedly. "My coveralls didn't go over so well. Where'd you get the fancy tea service?"

"I found it in the storeroom when I was poking around one day." Ramona was stacking the tea things tidily on the tray.

Dolly couldn't help wondering if Ramona had been looking for valuables to sell. The next instant she reproached herself for the disloyal suspicion, as Ramona added, "Did you like the way I talked up your hard work? You really should ask for a raise—you do so much more work for the Arms than Mrs. DeWitt ever did." She held the door for Dolly.

"I don't mind, but thanks for the thought," Dolly said. "That *and* playing respectable."

"Keeps me in practice." Ramona smiled as she headed upstairs.

Dolly carried the pile of paperwork across the lobby to Mrs. DeWitt's suite to put away, but all she could think about was wood rot. It was only a matter of time before someone besides Ramona went poking into the sub-basement storeroom and exposed the shocking structural weakness hidden there. And how, in good conscience, could the novice housemother continue to let girls keep her company in the kitchen, when the floor might collapse under them at any moment?

Abandoning the painstakingly prepared paperwork on Mrs. DeWitt's desk, Dolly went to the phone and dialed the contractor who'd estimated the tuck-pointing. As the line rang, Dolly wedged herself into the little closet-office hidden behind the pigeonholed wall, a necessary precaution for a private conversation.

A few minutes later she staggered out, white-faced. "Replacing a rotted joist?" the contractor had said. "Could cost you as much as a thousand." At Dolly's audible gasp, he added kindly, "Could be less. I'd have to take a look."

When he came by after lunch and looked, he halved his estimate. "Easy to get to, and no ceiling to replace. Looks like it's just this length here—must have been a leak from the sink overhead."

"Yes," said Dolly miserably. If only she'd discovered that leak and patched it sooner!

Five hundred dollars—Dolly had to come up with five hundred dollars. After the contractor left, she flipped through the accounts book, halfheartedly hoping she might discover an overlooked balance or some sort of cash surplus in an obscure column. But it didn't take a statistical whiz like Phyllis to see there was just no cash to cover this unexpected expense. The only extra money in the bank was earmarked for taxes in January, and even if Dolly fired the cleaning lady and scrubbed the floors herself, or went back to serving stale pastries, she'd never save enough to pay back the tax account in time.

Dolly closed the book with its rows of tidy figures, furious at the injustice of it all. Mrs. Putney-Potter acquired her water-spouting statuary and silk-tasseled draperies just by marrying some real estate mogul, while Dolly, who was slaving away without even a dishwasher, didn't dare ask her for the price of repairing a measly spot of wood rot!

Suddenly, Dolly snapped her fingers and her eyes lit up. She knew a mogul too, someone she wouldn't have to marry to get the money for the repair: Maxie Mainwaring, publishing mogul!

Dolly went to the phone again. "I'd like to make a person to person call," Dolly told the operator tersely. "Maxie Mainwaring, Hotel Belloc, Paris, France. Yes, ring me back as soon as you have the call."

Dolly paced impatiently up and down in front of the abandoned front desk. The phone rang, and Dolly snatched it up. "Hello, Maxie?" she said, taking the phone once again into the little closet. The cord stretched tight, and she could barely close the door.

"Hello, Dolly!" The line crackled, but Maxie's voice was clear, except for a faint echo, as if Dolly was on the line with two Maxies. "You're lucky you caught me! We were just leaving to go to a discotheque in Montmartre— Stella, Lon, it's Dolly!"

As Dolly strained to hear the distant double hellos of her faraway friends, she was invaded by jealousy. They sounded so gay, so carefree! Why was it her lot to drudge at home like Cinderella?

"How are things at the Arms? Mrs. DeWitt isn't worse, is she?" Maxie's echoey voice turned anxious.

"No, Mrs. DeWitt is fine. We're all fine—I was—well, the fact of the matter is—" Dolly wasn't sure how to begin. She tried a lighthearted approach: "I'm calling about a real estate investment opportunity. You haven't spent all your money on manuscripts, have you?"

"What, Dolly? I can't hear you very well—you sound like you're underwater—no, not you, Lon, Dolly. Have I spent my money on what?"

"On manuscripts!" Dolly shouted into the phone.

"Not a dime—the trip to Tangier was a complete washout. I think the writers were on a hashish binge and the tripe they churned out didn't make any sense. But it all turned out for the best because I needed every penny for my new restaurant!"

"New restaurant!" Dolly repeated, stupefied. "But you're a publisher—you're supposed to put out books."

"Oh, publishing," Maxie discounted her business. "I've gotten a little bored with books." As Dolly listened, the undependable dilettante launched into an enthusiastic account of how she'd been seduced by the culinary pleasures of Paris and decided to take the plunge into the restaurant business. "After all, I have some experience in the hospitality field," she defended her decision. It took Dolly a second to realize that the ex-publishing mogul was referring to her ownership of the Knock Knock Lounge, a seedy dive in Bay City's Dockside district. "I think there's money to be made here in Paris. All they think about is food!"

"But what do you know about French food?" Dolly demanded angrily as she saw her solution slipping away.

"Nothing!" Maxie rejoined cheerfully. "That's why we're going to open an American-style, Western-themed restaurant. We'll serve hot dogs and hamburgers, and maybe some cassoulets and steak frites as well. We're thinking of calling it 'Buffalo Gals'—did you know the French are crazy about American cowboys?"

Dolly hadn't known.

"You ought to join us, Dolly. Take a little vacation from your soap opera and teach the chef I've hired how

to make that delectable strawberry shortcake of yours—
or do you think a cherry pie would have more of that all-
American je ne sais quoi?"

"I can't come to Paris, Maxie," Dolly said with a
heavy heart.

"All it would cost you is a plane ticket," Maxie urged.
"You could bunk here at the Belloc with us. We'd have a
ball!"

"Until Mrs. DeWitt is better, I have responsibilities at
the Arms," Dolly told her.

"Oh, of course. Well, as soon as she's back on her feet,
you get on that plane. I'll expect you for New Year's!"

"You better get to your discotheque." Dolly hung up
the phone and emerged from the closet, dazed and depressed. She looked around at the scabby walls, scraped
and patched and ready for paint. What was the point in
painting? Would the Arms still be standing, come New
Year's Eve?

The overburdened landlady had to confide in someone. The secret she'd been carrying since the trustees'
meeting was suddenly too much for her. She climbed the
stairs to the fifth floor, forgetting, in her misery, that the
elevator was fixed. She pondered the six closed doors
that confronted her. Phyllis was still at work, and Netta
was probably at a meeting. And really, wasn't Ramona the
best confidante, after all? Maybe the queen of schemers,
the girl with plenty of experience squeezing out of tight
spots, would be able to contribute some new ideas—because Dolly was fresh out!

"Ramona, I need your help." Dolly pushed open the
door to Ramona's room after a perfunctory knock.

Ramona had evidently taken a shower. Her head was
wrapped in a towel, turban style, and she was reclining
on her bed, cigarette in one hand.

Jackie was lying next to her, legs entwined with Ramona's, as they looked up from what had evidently been an ardent kiss!

Dolly started to back out in red-faced embarrassment, with a muttered, "Sorry!"

Then she stopped, sniffing the air suspiciously. "Ramona!" She said accusingly, "What's that you're smoking?"

Chapter 13

The Late Show

Ramona stubbed out her cigarette hastily. "Nothing!" At Dolly's stern expression, she wilted. "I swear, Dolly, it's just a souvenir of San Francisco. Scout's honor!"

Jackie was carefully collecting the marijuana cigarette stub from the ashtray. "Look how much is left!" she mourned.

"Give me that!" Dolly swooped down on her young protégée and confiscated the contraband. "Jackie, I'm surprised at you!"

So this was what the two girls had been whispering about at breakfast! Dolly was torn between anger and jealousy. If she hadn't been subbing for Mrs. DeWitt, maybe she would have been invited to join this pot party—and maybe Jackie would think *she* was hip enough to kiss!

The would-be bohemian stuck out her lower lip and sulked, "Killjoy!"

That tore it. "I'm a killjoy, am I?" Dolly stormed. "If it wasn't for me playing propriety in Mrs. DeWitt's place, you wouldn't have a roof over your head right now!"

Ramona tried to soothe the irate landlady. "Jackie didn't

mean that. She's grateful for you for rescuing her from the mugging, and I'm just as grateful for the way—"

"That's not what I'm talking about!" Dolly stampeded on. "When I went to the trustees' meeting, Mrs. Putney-Potter and her henchman Hagney were *this close* to shutting down the Magdalena Arms and kicking us all out!"

"Wha-a-at?" gasped Ramona. "They wanted to shut down the Arms?"

"I only took this housemother gig to prevent that from happening, but I could use a little help!"

Now that she had the two girls' attention, the hard-pressed housemother poured out the whole situation, from the tense trustees' meeting to the just-discovered wood rot and the bleak bank account.

"I'm sorry," said Jackie repentantly. "I won't smoke weed in the Arms anymore!"

"Forget the marijuana," said Dolly impatiently. "How are we going to come up with the five hundred dollars?"

Ramona too was remorseful. "You need every paying tenant you can get, and I show up, the unemployed dead-beat!"

"Oh, Ramona." Dolly couldn't stay angry at the guilt-ridden girl. "Your rent wouldn't pay for half a joist. If you want to help, stop kicking yourself and think!"

Her old friend pulled herself together and narrowed her eyes, muttering calculations. "Sell the stuff in the storeroom—no, mostly junk from what I've seen. Loan shark—too risky. Take the tax money to the track? Ditto." Suddenly her eyes lit up. "Maxie!" she exclaimed.

"I tried that, and she's spent all her dough on a new restaurant," Dolly reported glumly.

The three girls slumped back into hard-thinking silence. "Could we pass the hat?" Jackie ventured.

Dolly shook her head. "Any money-raising we do would

get back to Mrs. Putney-Potter before we'd collected more than a few bucks," the ex-actress informed her grimly. "Look at the way she came here today, checking up on the paperwork. We're just lucky the visitors' parlor was presentable. The cleaning lady even put out a vase of flowers."

"That wasn't the cleaning lady—" Jackie began.

"That was me," finished Ramona. "My old house-keeping instincts, I guess. But listen—here's what we do about Putney-Potter. We get something on her."

"You mean—blackmail?"

"Why not? Think about it—she was a poor but ambitious girl who married into money and is trying to make it in Bay City society. She's got to have a few skeletons in the closet she'd like to keep there. Most people do." Ramona spoke with the authority of experience.

Dolly supposed she should object on moral grounds, but the situation was desperate. She was more concerned with practicalities. "You want me to hire a private detective?" she asked skeptically.

"Start by asking Mrs. DeWitt about her," Ramona retorted. "Look through the stuff in the storeroom! Maybe she left, oh, I don't know, evidence that she worked as a B-girl, or had an illegitimate kid, or pulled the wings off flies."

It seemed like a long shot to Dolly, but it was the only scheme they had. "I guess I can ask," she said, getting up. "I'm seeing Mrs. DeWitt on Friday, after Thanksgiving." She lingered to add dolefully, "I s'pose I'll go drown my sorrows in a can of paint."

She thought maybe the two girls would feel sympathetic enough to offer to help, but Ramona only unwound her towel turban, distracting the depressed landlady. "You dyed your hair!" said Dolly.

"Chocolate chestnut." Ramona examined herself critically in the mirror. "It was time to change my look. What do you think?"

"I think it looks terrific," said Jackie adoringly.

On that nauseating note, Dolly made her exit. "Don't worry, Dolly, we'll come up with something," Ramona promised, almost as an afterthought.

It was evident to the despairing landlady that Ramona and Jackie were eager to get back to their interrupted activities and would soon be lost in each other's arms, passion driving away purely practical problems, like unpaid repairs, and how they were going to keep a roof over their heads, much less the floor under their feet!

I'm sure I'd be positive too, if someone was looking at me all agog, Dolly thought resentfully, as she opened a can of paint. *Someone who thinks I can do no wrong!* She stirred the paint so vigorously that a little of the Ashes of Rose slopped over the side of the can and onto the drop cloth. Why didn't anyone ever look at Dolly the way Jackie looked at Ramona?

Okay, I'm jealous, she admitted to herself. She guessed she'd had a little yen for Jackie all along. It wasn't that she was in love with the would-be bohemian, but after all, she *had* saved her life! Why was it Ramona the younger girl went all starry-eyed over?

Dolly brooded on, as she carefully cut in the wall along the molding just the way *One Thousand and One Ways to Save Money* said to. She moved the stepladder a few feet along the wall. It sure seemed like romance was doled out awfully unevenly among the fifth-floor inhabitants. Here was Dolly, stuck painting the lobby, while Ramona and Jackie got intimate upstairs and Maxie danced in a Paris discotheque with Stella and Lon!

She splashed paint impatiently on the wall, and it dribbled down and formed a droplet. Dolly pulled the paint rag out of her pocket to wipe it smooth. As she stuffed the rag away, her fingers encountered the cigarette stub she'd taken from Jackie. She pulled it out and looked at it.

She'd asked Maxie about these tea sticks once, and the madcap girl had claimed they weren't much different than a cocktail. And wasn't it just about "*l'heure de l'apéritif*" as Mrs. DeWitt used to say? There was that poem she'd recite:

> *Between the something and something*
> *When the night is beginning to fall*
> *There comes a pause in the something something*
> *That is known as the Children's Hour.*

Dolly looked around, warily, before defiantly striking a match and lighting the forbidden substance.

To her disappointment, it had absolutely no effect on her. *They probably smoked the potent part,* she realized. *This is like a watered-down drink.*

Oh well. More fun that had passed her by. The substitute landlady felt more philosophical than bitter as she climbed down the ladder to refill her paint tray and took another drag on the impotent cigarette. At least the painting was soothing her, putting her in a meditative mood. Maybe when they were all evicted she'd get work as a painting contractor, covering Bay City in Ashes of Rose. The do-it-yourselfer couldn't suppress a guffaw at the goofy picture.

Dolly painted steadily, her cares falling away as she concentrated on the relaxing sensation of smoothing the brushfuls of pale pink on the wall. She didn't notice how much time had passed until a voice said, "You're working kinda late."

It was Kay, carrying her clarinet case and looking up at Dolly quizzically. It was dark outside the lobby's glass doors.

"What time is it?"

"It's after ten." Kay sniffed the air. "Someone's been smoking something they shouldn't!" she diagnosed.

Dolly climbed down the ladder, surprised at how much time had passed, and at how small an area she'd covered with Ashes of Rose. Yet the corner of the ceiling she'd painted was perfect, she thought proudly, even layers of painstakingly smooth paint without dribble or drip.

"I'm starving!" Dolly staggered slightly as she reached the floor. She hadn't had dinner, she realized, and now she had a dull headache.

Kay steadied her, studying the loopy landlady. "Tell you what, Dolly," she suggested, "why don't you relax on the couch in the lounge, and I'll rustle up some sort of snack from the kitchen."

"Tenants are not permitted access to cooking facilities," Dolly started to say. But the word *snack* sounded so appealing she made an exception. "Just this once," she said sternly, and then added, "I think there are some home fried potatoes from this morning in the refrigerator!"

The temporary landlady was staring at the television set in a daze when Kay returned with a plate of scrambled eggs and reheated potatoes, along with a mug of hot tea. "Eat up!" Kay plunked the dish on one of the TV trays. Gently she tugged off the kerchief Dolly had forgotten was still on her head, tossing it on top of the coveralls Dolly had shed.

"Don't want you getting paint on the couch," she teased. "You'd have to sew up a new set of slipcovers, or reupholster it from scratch or something!"

As Dolly attacked the food with gusto, Kay commented, "I never figured you for the locoweed type. What gives?"

So the jazz musician had identified the pungent smoke that clung to Dolly's coverall. "I've been under a strain!" the embarrassed landlady defended herself. "So, yes, I tried the cigarette I confiscated from Ramona. A house-mother ought to understand just what her girls are up to. Anyway." Dolly wiped the plate with her forefinger and licked it. "The drug didn't have any effect on me—I must be immune or something."

"Maybe you ought to cool it on the fix-it side of things," Kay suggested. "You've been working too hard."

"It's not that," Dolly told her. "It's worrying about what'll happen to the Magdalena Arms that's driving me crazy!" For the second time that day, the gossipy land-lady forgot Phyllis's warning and poured out the prob-lems she'd kept secret to another tenant.

"I'm at the end of my rope," she finished. "I've got to find a way to repair the wood rot, but if I tell the trustees, it's curtains for us all!"

Kay patted the agitated ex-actress soothingly. "We'll find a way, Dolly, I'm sure of it. You've only been wrestling with the problem for one day. Relax and stop worrying. The solution will come to you."

"How do you come by your composure?" questioned Dolly. "Is that hair natural?" Kay's short hair was the color of a copper penny.

The clarinetist laughed. "I was just born this way. Miss Watkins said that if I ever gave up music I could have a future throwing pots. Apparently, it's an occupation that takes a steady hand and a cool head."

Dolly was thinking that maybe she should try Miss Watkins's crazy test when Kay exclaimed, "Look, Dolly, it's you!"

She pointed at the television, where a bunch of teenagers were having a beach party. Sure enough, there was a much younger Dolly, sitting on a towel in the corner of the screen. The substitute landlady recited the line in unison with her tiny television self: "Swellisimus! Simply simpatico!"

"You still remember?" Kay asked.

"I didn't have a lot of lines," said Dolly sadly. The teen movie had been made just after *The Jarvises'* demise. But like all her acting attempts since that show, it had gone nowhere.

"I'm just a has-been!" the ex-actress burst out bitterly. "I guess that's why Jackie picked Ramona over me!"

"Don't tell me you're sulking over *that* baby beatnik!" the clarinetist exclaimed unsympathetically. "Why, she's so wet behind the ears, you'd have to sop her off before you slept with her." As Dolly automatically protested, Kay added, "Anyway, you're too cute to be a has-been."

Kay's comforting arm was still around the substitute landlady, and she tightened it as she turned to Dolly and kissed her. Dolly felt almost as dazed as if Mrs. DeWitt had suddenly turned amorous. Kay had been a fixture on the fourth floor for so many years, Dolly had just never thought of her that way!

"Why, Kay!" said Dolly, but before she could go further, Kay kissed her again, and like a good actress picking up her cue, Dolly responded ardently. Kay broke away and began unbuttoning Dolly's shirt with businesslike efficiency. "You're just plain worn down and need to relax," she told the astonished ex-actress.

"I wasn't looking for pity!" Dolly bristled a little as she shrugged her perennial plaid Pendleton off her shoulders.

Kay ran her hands over the bared flesh, and then slipped them under Dolly's arms, reaching around her back to unclasp her brassiere. "Who said anything about pity?" the musician asked equably. "You're so hung up on this little beatnik, you've forgotten all the girls who've fallen in your lap over the years. I was one once, remember?" With one sinuous movement she pulled her own shirt off and pushed Dolly down on the couch. She fit herself on top of the conflicted girl with a satisfied "ahhhh."

"You were?" Dolly said. She tried and failed to conjure up a previous encounter with Kay. "I mean, sure, I'd forgotten, but now I remember," she ad-libbed, helping Kay kick off her pants. She kissed the shadowy girl, seeking a familiar taste or sensation. The television burst into canned applause, as if in appreciation of the two girls' sudden intimacy. For a moment, the whiff of Dial soap wafting from Kay's neck uncovered a long-buried picture of a younger Dolly doing something acrobatic with a shy, redheaded farm girl in the backseat of a car as it careened down a country road. Could that have been Kay? Dial was a pretty common brand.

In the midst of desire mounting like an ocean's slow surge, Dolly was caught in a backwash of embarrassment. Maybe she'd been Kay's rite of passage all those years ago, the way Sylvia had once been hers. Did that mean this interlude was a replay of Dolly's mistaken tryst with Sylvia a few weeks ago? Except now Kay was Dolly, Dolly was Sylvia, and this couch was the Prescott Hotel. Even as she lost track of who was who, Dolly knew she didn't want to take advantage of a younger girl's momentary lapse of judgment!

"Wait a second," the ex-actress muttered. She couldn't think straight with the warm, stimulating sensation of Kay's mouth and tongue on her breast. She stilled her hands, which of their own accord were urging Kay into a crouching position.

"Come on, Dolly," coaxed Kay, "I need distracting

too. I've got to go on this small town tour tomorrow and then back to the farm for Thanksgiving. The holidays always give me the blues, and this is the best cure I know." She paused a moment, the afghan draped over her naked back. The television screen had turned to white fuzz. "No one will come in—it's late and they've all gone to bed."

"That's not it," Dolly confessed. "I was just thinking, you've been down this road before, and isn't there some poem about how the road not taken is better—"

"Forget your poem. In jazz, no matter how many times you play a tune"—Kay moved against her and Dolly caught her breath—"there's always a new way to spin it."

Chapter 14
A Bottle of Gin

Dolly woke up the next morning full of her old optimism. The problem of paying for the joists no longer seemed so insoluble. She climbed out of bed and stretched luxuriously. Her back was sore and she had a crick in her neck, but last night's interlude with Kay on the narrow couch had distracted her from her problems, just as Kay had promised!

Of course the ex-actress wasn't kidding herself that her fling with her fourth-floor neighbor was anything more than two ships that had paused in the night purely to satisfy a mutual craving; but aside from the physical pleasure she'd experienced—Dolly stopped right in the middle of smoothing her sheets, shaken by the mere memory of some of last night's sensations.

Where was she? Oh yes, in addition to the panting, moaning excitement of this second encounter with Kay, there were other benefits. Not only was a little hanky-panky the perfect cure for the blues, but whereas yesterday she'd been too worried to think straight, today she had a sunny certainty that a solution would come to her.

She pulled on her clothes, went down to the kitchen,

and started frying bacon, humming "Buffalo Gals" all the while. She'd always enjoyed starting breakfast in the quiet kitchen, but today this peaceful moment with the weak sunlight making a warm patch on the floor by the stove seemed extra pleasant.

"And dance by the light of the moon," she sang as she set the coffee brewing. She wasn't even mad at Maxie anymore or resentful of this Buffalo Gals restaurant. She wished the dabbling dilettante every success in her quixotic quest to conquer the critical palates of Paris.

And indeed, now that Dolly was no longer caught in a repetitious round of worry, ideas were popping like the drops of bacon fat bouncing in the pan. Maybe she could take a leaf from Maxie and start a sideline selling baked goods. Or what if she offered her tenants more meals at an additional charge?

The substitute landlady was putting the platter of bacon on the sideboard as the girls began to drift in for breakfast. Jackie and Ramona appeared with twin expressions of sleepy satisfaction. Dolly could observe them without envy this morning.

Netta, however, looked peevishly at the two lovebirds. "Please, Dolly, don't invite Ramona to the Friday night dinner," she instructed the temporary landlady. "To you she's an old friend and all faults are forgiven, but that's not the case with some of us."

Dolly almost dropped the wooden spoon she was using to stir the oatmeal. "That's it!" she exclaimed.

"What's it?" Netta asked.

"Never mind." Dolly stirred jubilantly. The idea that had just popped into her head was the winner.

Jackie had given her the clue when she'd suggested passing the hat. The trick was to do it on the q.t., approaching only the most dependable parties. And who better to ask for help than the old fifth-floor gang? Who were more dependable and loyal to the Arms than Pamela, Lois, Janet, Phyllis, and Netta? None of them was as flush as Maxie, but if they all pooled their resources . . .

She'd make the appeal at their annual day-after-Thanksgiving dinner, Dolly planned. A few of them had made a date to visit Mrs. DeWitt at the hospital before joining the rest of the gang at Luigi's. If the sight of the bedridden housemother didn't soften the hearts of these former Magdalena Arms girls and incline them to open their wallets, Dolly didn't know what would!

"What's put you in a good mood?" Arlene asked curiously, handing Dolly her oatmeal bowl. "Did you hear yet from Eddie? He said he'd call."

It took the substitute landlady a second to remember what the scenic designer was talking about. "Not yet." She beamed at the attractive girl. "But I've got plenty else to keep me busy!"

All through the week, Dolly mentally practiced her appeal, whether she was painting the lobby ceiling, listening to Ramona's earnest assurance that she'd come up with her rent soon, or setting mousetraps in the visitors' parlor, where she'd heard some suspicious rustling noises that night on the couch with Kay.

Dolly wished she could tell Kay how well her distraction had worked, but the dedicated musician had departed at dawn following their unexpected tryst and wouldn't return until after the long weekend. She'd led the exodus that emptied much of the Arms by Thursday.

The holidays had never meant much to Dolly. Thanksgiving was merely the prelude to the Friday get-together with her friends, a tradition that had started when the old gang used to pool leftovers from their respective holiday dinners in Maxie's room.

However, humoring the girls who thought Thanksgiving was important, the temporary housemother fried up doughnuts Thursday morning as a treat for her remaining tenants. They munched them happily, watching the Thanksgiving Day parade on the lounge television. "I can actually see Santa," said Sue, impressed by the improved picture.

Arlene joined the group, to Dolly's surprise, and after the program was over, thanked Dolly for weather stripping her window. "It's made a real difference," she reported.

The attractive girl looked a little forlorn, and on an impulse Dolly invited her to join the left-behinds in the kitchen that night for takeout chop suey. "I'm starting a new Thanksgiving tradition," the novice housemother declared heartily. "Dish-free dinners!"

Arlene declined, and Dolly demanded, "You're not working, are you?"

"No." Arlene managed a smile. "There's just something I have to do—a kind of duty visit to—to a sort of relative."

Dolly offered silent thanks that she had no relatives making similar claims on her time. The scenic designer looked positively wistful at the idea of a dish of chop suey!

Finally it was Friday. "Netta, are you ready?" Dolly knocked impatiently on her neighbor's door. "If we're going to see Mrs. DeWitt before dinner, we ought to get going."

Netta came out, pulling on her shapeless winter coat, skipping, for once, her usual snappish comments. She locked the door behind her while Dolly waited impatiently. Most girls at the Magdalena Arms left their doors unlocked, but Netta was always security conscious, a result of her days spent surrounded by juvenile delinquents.

Dolly was silently rehearsing her speech as they rode over to the hospital. She had butterflies in her stomach. *It won't be a cakewalk*, she cautioned herself. All the girls had expenses, and Pamela in particular could be a real penny-pincher. But once she pointed out that the Arms was Mrs. DeWitt's home, and what it would mean if the laid-up landlady were to lose it—

She realized that she'd been ignoring Netta, who was unusually quiet. "I wonder why Phyllis dropped out," Dolly remarked, belatedly making conversation. At the last minute, Phyllis had bowed out of the hospital portion of the day and said she'd join them at the restaurant.

"Huh?" Netta was preoccupied as well. She shrugged. "Phyllis has been awfully busy lately," she offered. "Probably some zoning change up for approval."

Their arrival at the hospital put an end to the two girls' lackluster efforts at conversation. By now they knew the way to their old landlady's room and navigated the maze of corridors quickly. As they approached the orthopedics ward, the sound of their ancient housemother's agitated voice gradually became audible. Dolly and Netta exchanged anxious looks and quickened their pace.

"Slimy things!" Dolly could make out Mrs. DeWitt's words now. "Slimy things that crawl with legs upon the slimy sea!" The ancient landlady's voice brimmed with horror.

"There are no slimy things, Mrs. DeWitt! It's just an African violet we brought to brighten your room!"

It was Lois's voice, high with anxiety. The next moment a handsome redhead burst out of the patient's room, almost colliding with the two girls. "What's going on?" demanded Dolly.

Without stopping, Pamela Prendergast panted, "Mrs. DeWitt has lost her wits!" The sportswear buyer brushed past them. "I'm going to get help!"

The two girls hurried into the hospital room, where they were met by a painful sight. Mrs. DeWitt was pummeling the covers frantically, while Lois Lenz tried vainly to capture her hands.

Dolly pushed the petite brunette aside and succeeded in grabbing one of the flailing hands. "Stop it, Mrs. De-Witt, you'll hurt yourself!"

"Dolly!" Mrs. DeWitt looked at her old tenant, her rheumy blue eyes wide and staring. "Dolly, *I* shot the albatross!"

"She thinks she's the Ancient Mariner," realized Dolly as Mrs. DeWitt tried to wrench free. The elderly landlady was wheezing and coughing with her exertion, an alarming cough that came from the depths of her being and shook her frail frame. "What set her off?"

"I don't know!" The efficient office manager was uncharacteristically flummoxed by this unfamiliar situation. "She was raving when we came in!"

A Single Candle*'s research department was right,* Dolly decided as the two girls struggled to restrain Mrs. DeWitt. *Delirious patients* are *surprisingly strong!*

Mrs. DeWitt was reciting, "Her lips *are* red, her looks *are* free, her locks *are* yellow as gold, her skin *is* white as leprosy!" She stared with fearful fixity at a corner of the room as she spoke.

Pamela returned with Beverly in tow. "Mrs. DeWitt," the student nurse said sharply. "Mrs. DeWitt, you're in a hospital!" She snapped her fingers in front of Mrs. De-Witt's staring eyes.

The old woman jerked away convulsively. "Water, water, everywhere, and nary a drop to drink!" she wailed.

In her frenzy, she'd pulled loose the neatly tucked sheets and tidy hospital corners. Now an object that had been nesting under the bedclothes with her rolled out and landed on the floor with a heavy *thunk*!

It was an empty bottle of gin.

Chapter 15
The Dinner at Luigi's

The group of girls who straggled downheartedly into Luigi's for dinner was a demoralized bunch. Janet and Rhoda looked up from the big round table in the corner with festive smiles that faded when they saw the stricken expressions on their friends' faces.

"Is Mrs. DeWitt worse?" asked Janet Kahn at once. The attractive young lawyer's usually calm face wrinkled with worry, and her eyes behind her tortoiseshell glasses were anxious.

"She's suffering from incipient pneumonia," said Lois dolefully.

"And a bad case of delirium tremens," Pamela added flatly. "Someone sneaked her a bottle of gin."

While the orderlies fastened restraints on Mrs. DeWitt, Beverly had asked Dolly point-blank if she were behind the bottle's mysterious appearance. And even though Dolly's fervent protestations of innocence had convinced the suspicious nurse, a faint cloud of guilt clung to the hapless ex-actress.

Dolly didn't intend to share her own suspicion, that Ramona was the real culprit. She could imagine only too easily that the rule-breaking tenant had smuggled in the liquor as a well-meaning attempt to cheer up her former housemother, but it was unlikely the other girls would see it that way. They were all a little prejudiced against the gay and reckless girl. And in a way, Dolly blamed herself. *If only I'd told Ramona what Beverly told me!* she mourned.

Phyllis hurried in, out of breath, and slipped into the last chair. "Sorry I'm late," she said. Then asked as she took in the dour circle of faces, "What's happened?"

Netta filled in the shocked social scientist, ending, "Since she's not exactly an orthopedics case anymore, they're moving her to the Happy Valley Sanatorium, outside the city."

"Well, maybe it's for the best," Rhoda tried to brighten the mood. "I'm sure they'll take good care of her!"

The other girls said nothing. Rhoda didn't really know Mrs. DeWitt—she'd never lived at the Magdalena Arms. The plump, comfortable girl, clad as usual in a sober tweed suit, was the perfect partner for self-assured Janet. A supervisor at the Women's House of Detention, she'd met the young lawyer when Janet was visiting a client. All the girls liked Rhoda, but she couldn't feel as they did about Mrs. DeWitt.

Now, as the group of old friends glumly picked over their pasta and sipped the Chianti, Rhoda made a game attempt to keep conversation going. She asked after Pamela's promotion, and whether she and Lois had made progress finding a new place. She told a funny story about an incarcerated pickpocket and gossiped with Phyllis about the vast Bay City bureaucracy. "I hear your Miss Ware is due to climb up another rung at the department of human services."

"My Miss Ware!" Phyllis started. "What do you mean? I've hardly seen her since I was her assistant on the dock commission."

Rhoda gave up and turned to the temporary landlady. "How are things at the Arms, Dolly? Janet said you had some news."

Dolly decided she might as well take the plunge. "Yes, but it's not very good news, I'm afraid. The Magdalena Arms needs help."

Six faces looked up attentively, as Dolly drew a deep breath and for the third time, explained the situation: the trustees' meeting, the threat to the Arms, the discovery of the wood rot, and the need to conceal this structural weakness from Mrs. Putney-Potter.

"So, it's just a matter of coming up with some scheme to raise enough money to pay for the repair," she summed up. She looked around the table, hoping someone would draw the obvious conclusion.

God bless Pamela. "It's simple," the sportswear buyer said with her usual decisive energy. "We'll each pitch in a hundred dollars or so, and Dolly will pay us back when the Arms is full again and the rents are rolling in."

"Yes!" said Dolly eagerly. "I know I'll be able to repay you."

Janet, however, was hung up on a point of law. "But, Dolly, the trustees are responsible for the structural integrity of the Magdalena Arms. Once you tell them, they'll *have* to allot the necessary funds or face a suit for criminal negligence!"

"Mrs. Putney-Potter would simply persuade them to condemn the Arms!" Dolly argued. "You weren't at that trustees' meeting! The Magdalena Arms was literally one step away from the wrecking ball!"

Rhoda was thinking out loud: "Putney-Potter—is your trustee connected to Putney Real Estate Planning and Projects? I wonder if she has her eye on the Arms' property as a site for one of the new housing developments the city is planning. Do you know if Putney has put in a bid, Phyllis? That's your province, isn't it?"

Phyllis came out of a private reverie. "I don't know," she said as if it didn't matter. "I'm taking some time off from zoning policy to work with the Bay City Beautification Committee."

Everyone stared at the statistician in astonishment. "Bay City Beautification Committee?" Janet repeated. "But you never take time off and you've always said the Beautification Committee was beside the point!"

"I've changed my mind," said Phyllis defiantly. "Anyway, my vacation days have been piling up, and—I—I—well, surely I'm entitled to a personal life?"

Personal life! It was as if a bombshell had exploded from the tiramisu the beaming Luigi had just set on the table. This was unprecedented behavior from the young social scientist. Her personal life had been sacrificed to the public good for as long as they'd known the idealistic girl.

Lois and Pamela were whispering back and forth, trying to puzzle out what Phyllis could possibly mean by "personal life."

Dolly tried to steer the conversation back to the plight of the Magdalena Arms. "If Mrs. Putney-Potter is plotting to replace the old Arms with some shiny new housing project, we have to act fast—"

"But maybe the trustees are right," objected Lois. Dolly gaped at her. This was another bombshell. "I read a piece in the *Sentinel*," the ad agency executive went on, "pointing out that it's high time we replace Bay City's deteriorating tenements with new, modern, efficient housing which will better serve its poorer population."

Dolly recalled, with a sinking heart, that the organized office manager had always been a demon for cleanliness, efficiency, and modern methods.

"Lois, it's the *Arms*," Pamela said patiently. "Can you imagine what our lives would have been like if we hadn't had the Arms to take us in?"

"Times have changed," Lois insisted like a junior version of Mrs. Putney-Potter. "This article said the new projects are the right solution for today's housing needs. They'll have studios with efficiency kitchens and all the latest appliances!" Her eyes shone as she pictured this miracle of modern housing.

"I could contribute to the repairs too," Phyllis said belatedly. Dolly could tell she wasn't even following the conversation. "But I've spent a lot lately, what with the expense of joining the Beautifiers—"

Netta turned on her. "You haven't forgotten the Christmas donation you promised to the DTs?" the schoolteacher asked sharply. "The Democratic Teachers for a New Society," she explained at Rhoda's puzzled look.

Dolly said hopelessly, "But, girls, how are we going to come up with the money? The only other scheme we've got is Ramona's idea to get something on Mrs. Putney-Potter!"

Pamela recoiled. "Don't tell me Ramona is back to her blackmailing ways!" The sportswear buyer was all indignation.

Mentally, Dolly kicked herself. She'd forgotten that Pamela was a stickler for good behavior from her sapphic sisters. "We must never give society an excuse to brand us as criminals!" she would lecture.

"Did you know about this, Netta?" Pamela asked the upright teacher. "I'm surprised *you* put up with such behavior."

Then Netta dropped *her* bombshell. "I guess this is as good a time as any to tell you all I'm moving out," she announced. "A bunch of us Democratic Teachers are getting a house together—we're calling it 'Experiment in

Living,' and we plan to live communally, making conscious choices that express our ideals every minute of the day!"

The whole table was in an uproar now, with Netta expounding on her group's experiment and the superior way of life she was embarking on, while Pamela and Lois were arguing in an undertone about the money they'd set aside for the new apartment. "It's not that I begrudge the money," Dolly heard Lois say. "But I don't believe in fighting progress!" Janet was probing the evasive Phyllis about her personal plans, and as a disheartened Dolly drank the last of Luigi's coffee, Rhoda tried to comfort the substitute landlady by telling her she'd "look into Putney Projects" for her.

"Thanks," Dolly said briefly. By the time any of these distracted girls got around to doing anything, the Magdalena Arms would be dust!

"Dolly," Netta said diffidently as the three Magdalena Arms residents walked to the bus stop in the freezing cold, "please consider this my thirty-day notice. I'll need my deposit back before Christmas."

Dolly grunted an affirmative. *So much for the old gang!* she thought wrathfully.

Dolly stalked into the Magdalena Arms trailed by Netta and Phyllis. She was bitterly disappointed in her old gang. She'd counted on them. She'd believed that even though they no longer all lived at the Arms, they still felt the same way about the old place she did. How mistaken could a girl be! They'd left behind the boardinghouse and the shared past that was so precious to Dolly, like a toy they'd outgrown.

A fine one Pamela is, criticizing Ramona! Dolly thought hotly. *Ramona is the only one of the old gang with an ounce of loyalty left!*

Pointedly ignoring Netta and Phyllis, who lingered uneasily in the lobby, Dolly went to the wall of pigeonholes and took down her mail. She pretended to be absorbed by the circulars and bills. There was a phone message from Miss Watkins, pestering her again about taking the test and questionnaire, which Dolly crumpled up. She couldn't think about career appropriateness now!

"I can ask Miss Ware—" Phyllis began timidly. Dolly turned a freezing look on her.

"If the girls the Magdalena Arms has fed and sheltered like babies in a mother's bosom, if *they* won't lift a finger to help the old girl in her hour of need, why would Miss Ware?"

"It's just a building, Dolly," Netta said placatingly. "We DTs believe that it's people that make the difference, not bricks and mortar!"

"You're even worse than the rest!" Dolly lashed out. "You're using your ideals as an excuse to abandon the Arms when the real reason is you can't stand watching Ramona canoodle with Jackie!"

Netta stiffened. "I'm simply choosing my battles. I can make a difference with the DTs, but I think this attempt to save the Arms is romantic nostalgia." She went toward the elevator.

"Don't be angry, Dolly," Phyllis pleaded. "It's not that we don't care—"

"It's just that you care about so many other causes," Dolly interrupted, "including the most hopeless one of all, the wonderful Miss Ware, who doesn't even know you're alive!"

"She does know I'm alive!" Phyllis cried passionately. The elevator dinged in the distance, and she hurried to join Netta before the door closed.

I don't need them, Dolly told herself. But she put her mail down on the front desk, feeling very alone.

"Dolly?" The landlady looked up. Arlene was standing in the lounge doorway, outlined in an aureole of light. She closed the door behind her and crossed the polished marble floor. "I thought I heard your voice." Her friendly smile was a balm to the hurt housemother's bruised spirit. "Did you see my message?"

"What? No, I haven't." Dolly shuffled through her mail and messages again, this time really looking at them. "You mean this?" *Call Eddy—he has a part for you!* the scenic designer had written in her tidy print.

"Well, whaddya know?" murmured the unemployed actress. "Do you think it's too late to call?"

"Of course not," Arlene assured her. Her new friend stood at her elbow as Dolly made the call, listening as the unemployed actress explained who she was and apologized for calling after business hours.

"Not to worry, Miss Dingle." The casting agent's energetic voice crackled in Dolly's ear. "I've got a hot proposition for you and no sense in waiting till it turns stale." He spewed out the details in machine gun bursts. "World Teleplay Pictures. They want you. New show. Plum role. Is it a yes?"

"It sounds too good to be true," stammered Dolly. "What's the part?"

"You're a secretary—"

"Not a mother?"

"You've heard about the office wife? You're the office mother. Get it? All these young execs getting into wacky situations, and you're Mom. A new concept. Very now. So here's what I want you to do. Get yourself on a plane and be in Los Angeles tomorrow morning—"

"But—"

"We'll reimburse. Let's not waste time—"

"It's not that," Dolly explained. "But I can't leave Bay City right now!"

Arlene was shaking her head vigorously at Dolly as Eddy said, "What's the holdup? Whatever it is, solve it, but quick. This one's rush-rush."

"Let me think about it, and I'll call you tomorrow," Dolly promised.

Scarcely had she hung up the phone than Arlene was saying, "Oh, Dolly! Why not? You can't keep burying your talent in the basement of this old boardinghouse!"

"I don't trust the big hurry," Dolly told her thoughtfully. "I need to think."

Maybe she just couldn't trust such luck, arriving on the heels of her disastrous dinner. An advance on her salary would solve all the Arms' problems!

"Come and have a drink with me," Arlene proposed. "We'll go to that bar you told me about. I'm a good listener, and maybe it will help you to do your thinking out loud."

"I really shouldn't," Dolly demurred, thinking of the Chianti she'd drunk at dinner.

"My treat," Arlene insisted. "I'll just run up and get my coat. Don't go anywhere."

Arlene was back almost instantly, still buttoning the chocolate and cream tattersall coat as if she were afraid Dolly wouldn't wait. *A beer won't hurt*, Dolly reasoned, succumbing to the scenic designer's flattering attention. Ten minutes later, the landlady and tenant were descending the steps to Francine's, which Dolly had avoided ever since that embarrassing incident with Sylvia.

The familiar beery, smoky atmosphere of her old haunt swaddled Dolly like a favorite blanket as soon as she pushed open the swinging door. Friday night meant the dim bar was crowded. Dolly took a quick look around. No Sylvia. *Of course not*, she remembered. *It's Thanksgiving weekend.* Relieved, she waved to Jessie behind the bar and a few of the regulars. Arlene spotted two girls getting up and pushed through the crowd to secure the tiny table. "Lucky!" she shouted to Dolly over the din.

Her old gang was for the birds, Dolly decided, eyeing the attractive Arlene. *The new generation is where it's at!*

"Howdy, stranger," Jill, the waitress, greeted Dolly. "Long time no see! What'll it be? The usual?"

"For two of us," Arlene put in quickly with her captivating smile.

One martini wouldn't hurt, Dolly supposed. She'd never been fond of beer.

"I like this place," said Arlene, looking around.

"It's kind of like a clubhouse," Dolly agreed. "And it's good to get some new blood in the old hangout. We should have invited Jackie, and maybe Beverly." She added the nurse's name as an afterthought, remembering her teetotaling tendencies.

"I'd just as soon have you to myself." Arlene quickly looked down at the table. "I mean, you're always so surrounded at the Arms."

Was that how it looked to Arlene? The drinks arrived, and both girls picked up their purses. "No, no, I invited you," Arlene insisted until Dolly gave in.

"I'll get the next round," she promised. She still worried about the young scenic designer's finances.

"Now, let's talk seriously about your career." Arlene took a dainty sip from her drink. "Maybe it's none of my business, but I just hate to see someone with your years of experience throwing it all away."

"Is that just another way of saying I'm an old hack?" Dolly laughed.

"There you go again, putting yourself down!" Arlene exclaimed. "You've got to get out of that habit—positive thinking is essential in getting ahead." Earnestly she outlined all the reasons why Dolly owed it to herself to return to her acting career, ending with: "Maybe I'm talking out of turn, but we girls need to boost each other up the ladder any way we can!"

Dolly remembered her long-ago daydream about a girlfriend in showbiz. Arlene seemed made to order for the role. And even if no ladder was involved, the young scenic designer's polished appeal and flattering attention were enough to awaken Dolly's lascivious side.

Maybe it was the interlude on the couch with Kay, maybe it was a Pavlovian reaction to the scents and sounds of Francine's, but lustful thoughts began bubbling up in Dolly's brain as she watched Arlene's soft, red mouth forming words Dolly barely heard. A girl leaving the dance floor tripped over Dolly's chair, giving her an excuse to hitch it closer to Arlene's.

"But I can't leave Mrs. DeWitt in the lurch," said the substitute landlady, casually resting her arm along the back of the other girl's chair.

"She has nurses and doctors looking after her," Arlene argued.

"But someone has to manage the Arms in her absence—if only I could do both!"

For an instant Dolly felt like Jackie, imagining a life evenly divided between two competing callings.

"You have to choose," Arlene told her. "And it makes no sense to sacrifice your acting for Mrs. DeWitt. Being a stand-in landlady is no kind of career!"

"I know," said Dolly a little wistfully. What had started as research into the maternal instinct had ended with Dolly feeling a motherly attachment to her whole houseful of girls.

But Arlene was right, she thought ruefully. It would be foolish to throw away thirty years as a practicing thespian to be nothing more than a glorified janitress.

Besides, she reminded herself grimly, how would she get a girl without her showbiz glamour? Would Arlene have invited her for this drink to discuss wood rot?

There was a line Mrs. DeWitt used to recite, "A something to fortune and to fame unknown." That fate was not for Dorian "Dolly" Dingle!

Jill paused by their table. "Another round?"

"Sure," said Dolly, even though Arlene had barely touched hers. "Maybe you're right," the actress told Arlene. "Maybe I *should* fly to Los Angeles."

"Of course I'm right." Arlene put her hand on Dolly's.

"You're right and you're awfully cute." Dolly leaned forward to kiss the scenic designer. Arlene froze for a moment, long enough for Dolly to wonder, *Did I get my signals crossed?* But the next instant the scenic designer cupped Dolly's face in both hands and kissed her thoroughly. Dolly's pulse leaped at the touch of those soft, red lips. She wanted to undress Arlene right there in the bar and explore what lay beneath the snug sweater and pleated wool skirt, but she contented herself with caressing Arlene through her clothes. *She's wearing one of those cone-shaped brassieres,* Dolly concluded, fingering the circular seaming through the soft wool sweater.

The two girls broke apart as Jill set down their drinks. "For a minute there, I wasn't sure you liked me," Dolly told her.

Arlene slid her arms around Dolly's neck. "I guess I'm having a little trouble getting back on the horse that threw me."

"Bad breakup?"

"And how. But let's not talk about that now."

They kissed again, more passionately. Dolly desperately palpitated the padded bra, in an effort to reach the actual flesh underneath. "I think you're doing the right thing, going to Los Angeles." Arlene sighed against Dolly's shoulder.

"I hope you'll miss me," Dolly told her.

"Maybe I'll follow you and find a job out there," the younger girl murmured. "We'd get a little bungalow— something modern, with clean lines—"

The date was moving faster than Dolly had dreamed, and the substitute landlady put her hand out for her drink to steady herself. She was surprised to find the glass was filled to the brim again. She couldn't remember ordering another round.

"Of course, I still have my responsibilities at the Arms," she said out loud, taking a gulp. "I don't want whoever takes my place falling through the floor!"

"Of course not," Arlene purred, snuggling against her.

"I could use the tax money, and then repay it with my salary," Dolly continued thinking aloud.

"Sure." Arlene was looking around the bar. She'd clearly given up trying to follow Dolly's nonsensical nattering.

"And I could fly home on weekends, finish the plastering and painting," Dolly planned. Who said a girl couldn't have a dual career?

Arlene stood up. "Come on, Dolly, let's dance!"

To make up for boring the scenic designer with her domestic preoccupations, Dolly threw herself into the Freddie with such verve that she lost her balance as she stuck out her left hand and leg.

That last martini was a big mistake, Dolly thought, climbing unsteadily to her feet. She'd miscalculated her alcoholic intake, counting only the Chianti and forgetting the sweet liqueur Luigi had served with the coffee. The spinning girls around her blurred together as Dolly attempted to apologize to Arlene, who was holding her up. She was chagrined to hear herself slurring her words. "I think I have had a liddle too much," she enunciated carefully, as Arlene propelled her up the stairs into the street.

The cold made her head hurt, and Arlene was saying something about how Dolly had to fly to Hollywood. Dolly didn't want to fly anywhere. She clutched the scenic designer to steady herself for the block and a half back to the Arms, thinking the fifth floor was a more reasonable goal.

Then she was lying in bed and Arlene was pulling off

her shoes. Dimly, Dolly regretted that she was too far gone to take advantage of the intimate situation.

One good thing about leaving glamour behind for the life of a landlady, Dolly realized dizzily as her bedroom door clicked closed, there was no danger of passing out in your girdle.

Chapter 17

Dolly Gets an Idea

"No, I never heard of World Teleplay Pictures," Jerry said. "Oh wait, maybe I have. Strictly bottom-feeders." Dolly heard her agent suppress a yawn. "You know the kind—trying to hustle the networks with nothing but an idea that has a bunch of hopefuls and has-beens attached. Tell this casting agent to give me a call."

"Gotcha—thanks, Jerry. Sorry again for waking you up."

Dolly hung up the phone not sure whether she was relieved or disappointed. She descended to the kitchen to finish the breakfast dishes. In the weak wintry light that filtered through the high window, the rosy daydreams of last night seemed just that, daydreams. She was glad she didn't have to fly to Hollywood—the very thought fatigued her. But neither was she going to pay for the wood rot removal from her television star salary. She was back to square one.

Except for her new romance. Arlene had seemed really interested in her, even if they weren't quite ready to move into a bungalow in the Hollywood Hills. Unless, of course, the housemother had spoiled it, swallowing all that hooch last night. *No more three martini evenings*, Dolly vowed, taking down the bottle of aspirin over the sink.

She was anxious to see how Arlene would act after last night, but the attractive scenic designer hadn't appeared for breakfast that morning. *Sleeping in, after their wild night,* Dolly supposed. She bent to light herself a cigarette from the gas burner and pulled on her rubber gloves. Would it be forward to knock on Arlene's door with a cup of coffee? *If I hadn't had so much to drink, maybe I'd be curled up with her!* the substitute landlady reproached herself.

Netta and Phyllis edged into the kitchen. "Would you like me to give you a hand?" Phyllis asked with polite solicitousness. Dolly wondered at her old friends' formality until she remembered she was mad at them both. So much had happened since that demoralizing dinner party.

"Guess what," she began, on the verge of telling them about her date with Arlene and the ersatz job offer. Then she stopped. *They're not my friends anymore,* she reminded herself. She'd have to break herself of her old habit of sharing the latest gossip and news with them.

When Phyllis asked, "What?" Dolly muttered, "Never mind," and turned back to the sink. "I don't need any help, thank you." She felt rather than saw the two girls fade away and suppressed the impulse to call after them. *I'll bring Arlene some breakfast,* Dolly decided instead. *A sort of "sorry for getting sloppy drunk."*

She found a tray and fussed around making it look nice, with a linen napkin, little glass salt and pepper shakers, and a tiny pitcher for syrup. She even took the time to snatch a carnation from the bouquet in the visitors' parlor and put it in a little vase. Then before the fried eggs and pancakes could get cold, she boarded the wheezing elevator for the fourth floor.

As it rose she tried out different lines in her head. "Hi, Arlene, I thought you could use some breakfast" or "Sorry about boozing it up last night—care for some grub?" or "Arlene, I've got a breakfast here fit for a princess—any takers?" Dolly frowned. None of them was quite right.

"Arlene," she called softly, tapping on 402. "Are you up?" There was no response.

Dolly looked around. The fourth-floor corridor was deserted. She put the tray on her floor and unlocked Arlene's door with her master key. She'd just take a peek inside. After all, the Magdalena Arms bylaws recommended monthly room inspections.

The bed was empty and tidily made. Arlene must have left the house at the crack of dawn.

The substitute landlady opened the door a little wider and stepped inside. The room had only the bare necessities. There were no pictures on the walls or bureau, no figurines or mementos, no furniture except for what the Arms provided. Arlene didn't even have a rug on the floor, which most girls found a necessity—just a pair of blue slippers at the foot of the bed.

Dolly knew she shouldn't snoop, but she took a quick step to the closet and swung open the door. A few good dresses and separates hung forlornly on the clothes rod.

Dolly backed out to the corridor and locked the door. Poor Arlene! Dolly was certain now she'd fallen on hard times. She'd hinted at a bad breakup the other night— was that the cause of her current impoverished state? The softhearted substitute landlady picked up the tray, thinking hard.

"Dolly, you darling!" It was Ramona, looking over the bannister from the floor above. In a flash she'd descended the stairs and seized the tray. "Let me help you— wait, why only coffee for one? Where's Jackie's?"

"This wasn't for you, Ramona. I made it for—oh never mind, you can have it."

"You made it for whom?" Ramona eyed her speculatively. "Kay's out of town, so it must be that Arlene you've been eyeing."

"Never mind my love life." Dolly blushed in spite of herself, wondering how Ramona had sniffed out her strictly carnal interlude with Kay along with her interest in Arlene.

"Well, since Arlene's not available, grab two more cups and come on up to Jackie's room. I've got a surprise for you—two, in fact."

When Dolly returned with the coffee, she found Ramona sitting on one of Maxie's slipper chairs, polishing off the plate of pancakes, while Jackie reclined in bed, heavy-eyed, sipping the coffee. Dolly handed Ramona her cup and sat down in the other chair. "What's the big surprise?"

Ramona pulled a roll of bills from her pocket. "Ta-da! My rent, this past month and next."

"You got a job! Terrif," enthused Dolly, smoothing and counting the bills. It was a relief to know she hadn't misjudged her old friend. "Doing what?"

"I'm kind of all-around factotum at Club Lucky," Ramona told her. "I run errands, do a little bookkeeping, and hostess at night."

"Would Miss Watkins approve?" Dolly teased. "Is this job truly suited to your strengths?"

Ramona shrugged. "I'm not going to make a career out of it." A shadow dimmed her expression, but her animation returned as she continued. "Now for my other surprise." She took a sip of her coffee. "I went to see Mrs. DeWitt yesterday, to ask her about old Putney-Potter—"

"Yesterday!" Dolly sat up straight. "When yesterday?"

"Before lunch. I didn't want to run into any of the old crowd and have them purse their lips at me, the way Netta does."

"Old meanies!" Jackie yawned.

That clinched it; Ramona *must* have given Mrs. De-Witt that fateful bottle of gin. Dolly was on the point of accusing her, then stopped herself. She didn't want to quarrel with her oldest remaining friend, her only real ally. What was done, was done. Dolly knew Ramona had meant well.

"How did she seem?" Dolly asked instead.

"She wasn't too coherent. I thought maybe she had a fever—"

"She has pneumonia," Dolly told her. "They're moving her to a sanatorium."

"Like my great-aunt," Jackie said sepulchrally.

Ramona looked stricken. "Poor Mrs. DeWitt! I'm extra glad I got to talk to her. She seemed to remember Mrs. Putney-Potter—at any rate, she got riled up at the name. Called her 'Dora the pill,' and said she was a sneak and a tattletale. 'A borrower and never a lender,' she said. She went into a long spiel about how the rest of the girls all shared their duds, but this Putney-Potter wouldn't lend a girl so much as a glove, when she had a whole drawer full."

"I don't think we can get her kicked off the board of trustees for hoarding gloves," Dolly said dubiously.

Ramona put down her coffee. "Wait, I haven't gotten to the good stuff. When I finally got through to Mrs. De-Witt that we needed real dirt on Dora, she started babbling about 'buying babies'!"

"Buying babies!" Dolly stubbed out her cigarette. "Mrs. DeWitt must have been delirious." She tried to picture the shrewd president of the board of trustees running a black market baby ring. "Did she say anything more? Where's the incriminating infant?"

"She said"—Ramona jabbed her cigarette in the air for emphasis—"*we should look in the storeroom.*"

"The mystery of the storeroom," said Jackie sleepily.

"It sounds like one of those books your friend Maxie puts out."

Ramona looked at the young girl indulgently. "Are you ever going to get up or should I bring you lunch in bed?"

"No vermin in the room," Dolly reminded them automatically.

"What time is it?" Jackie stretched and yawned.

"Eleven thirty."

Jackie sat up and threw back the covers. "Oh lord, Angelo's coming to rehearse in half an hour!"

As Dolly stacked the coffee cups on the tray, Ramona told her, "Maybe there's a tiny skeleton buried in the cellar, and we just have to figure out where to dig!"

Dolly doubted it. The sub-basement storeroom floor was covered with concrete. She suspected Mrs. DeWitt's story of Dora Potter purchasing children was nothing more than the delusional ravings of a drunkard.

Nonetheless, she descended to the sub-basement storeroom and poked around halfheartedly, trying not to look up at the wood rot overhead. She'd have to shift all this stuff anyway, to make room for the eventual repairs.

Dolly grunted as she moved a heavy Victrola and a broken chair. There was that old-fashioned black baby carriage again, just behind them.

It was an odd thing to find in the Magdalena Arms sub-basement storeroom. Perhaps some overzealous babysitter had acquired it? She jiggled the dusty vehicle experimentally and peered under its hood. There was a folded plaid blanket, draped over an irregularly shaped object. Cold fingers of fear walked their way up Dolly's spine, as she remembered Ramona's gruesome suggestion. Nerving herself, she snatched up the blanket and let out a sigh of relief. No tiny skeleton was cradled in the old carriage, just a haphazard pile of *National Geographic* magazines from 1950.

Dolly abandoned the storeroom and climbed the stairs to the kitchen to try the healthy muffin recipe Beverly had pressed on her. As she mixed the batter, she cocked an ear to the odd wailings in the lounge—Angelo and Jackie doing their vocal warm-ups. All at once, they burst into some pop song, probably a Meier Method exercise.

They sound pretty good, the ex-actress thought, adding two cups of bran to her mixture. *Good enough to win a radio talent contest.*

Her sudden brainstorm was like a blinding flash of light in the dim kitchen. Talent! The Arms was overflowing with talent! They'd do what Mrs. DeWitt and her acting pals had done in the days of the Depression—they'd pay for the repairs by putting on a benefit, this time raising money for the Arms instead of the Spanish Loyalists!

Dolly raced up the stairs and burst into the lounge, startling both the aspiring thespians and a group of girls engaged in a hand of pinochle.

"Hey, kids," she beamed. "How about we put on a show?"

Chapter 18
The Telephone Benefit

It was heartening, how enthusiastically the budding actress responded to Dolly's idea. "Of course!" she exclaimed. "A benefit to raise money for—"

"For more telephones," Dolly finished quickly, with a broad wink at Jackie. It was essential that the real purpose of the Magdalena Arms Benefit be concealed.

"More phones?" Second-floor Sue looked up from her pinochle hand. "I'm in!"

Word of the proposed benefit winged as swiftly as swallows through the Arms, and soon an impromptu organizing committee filled the lounge's couch and all available chairs, before spilling over onto the floor.

"Let's have a holiday theme," Ramona suggested. "We'll schedule it for Christmas Eve, a matinee show!"

Round-faced Angelo shyly suggested a slogan: "Ring in Christmas at the Magdalena Arms." The assembled crowd applauded in approval. Thus encouraged, he improvised an accompanying jingle: "Telephone bells, telephone bells," he sang in his high, sweet tenor, to the tune of "Jingle Bells," and volunteered, "I can compose a whole medley!"

With the date set and the advertising campaign settled, it was time to figure out what the show would look like.

"How about a hootenanny?" one girl burst out excitedly. "I play the banjo!" There was a stirring of enthusiasm from the group.

Before the folk music faction could get too carried away, Dolly said firmly, "I was picturing a kind of variety show, something to showcase *all* the Magdalena Arms talents."

Jackie backed her up: "We can mix music with dramatic monologues!"

Ramona wrote it down on the pad of paper. "Variety show—the Magdalena Arms Christmas Capers. Suggested acts: banjo picking, dramatic monologues." She looked up. "What else?"

All sorts of hidden talents emerged, and several days' worth of acts were suggested. One girl had a comedy routine that "killed them in the Catskills." Another was an amateur contortionist. "No baton twirling," Jackie vetoed, immoveable in the face of Sue's disappointment. Ramona softened the rejection, adding, "For the Fourth of July, sure, but not Christmas."

However, Ramona overruled Jackie when it came to Ilsa's clog dance. "People love that sort of stuff," she assured the mutinous thespian. "At the boarding school, I helped out with plenty of living picture pageants, talent shows, choral concerts, and musical extravaganzas." She raised her voice to address the whole group. "The trick is to keep each number short, keep 'em varied, and keep 'em moving." In an undertone to Dolly, she added, "And involve as many girls as possible. The more people onstage, the more in the audience!"

By the end of the afternoon, the show had taken shape. There would be banjo playing, an operatic solo, a jug band, and a string quartet; there would be tap dancing, clog dancing, impersonations, and monologues—Jackie urged Dolly to do something Shakespearian, while "I'll balance it with a more modern piece, Brecht, or Pinter maybe." The Sisterhood of Swing would play, assuming Kay was agreeable. Angelo would lead a chorus line of girls in a medley of songs with the words *bell* or *ring* in the lyrics.

"And we'll end with a big ensemble number," Dolly planned. "Maybe some kind of kick line, with girls dressed in telephone costumes. Yes, that's it!" Her eyes brightened as she pictured the number: Magdalena Arms girls in mod, striped shifts, each partnered with a color-coordinated dancing telephone.

"I know what you mean," a mousy girl said eagerly. "Like the opening number in *Bye Bye Birdie*!"

"Only bigger phones," Dolly agreed.

"Wait a sec—" Jackie tried to interrupt.

"I can work on the choreography," the mousy girl offered. "I'm a dance instructor at the Castle School of Dance."

Dolly beamed at the mousy girl—was her name Margie? The nice thing about the benefit was the way it was bringing the whole house together. "That sounds wonderful!"

"Shouldn't we end with carol singing?" Ramona objected. "People will expect something Christmasy in a holiday show. Let's at least give 'em carols."

"We'll segue from the telephone bells medley into Christmas carols," Angelo suggested. He began singing "I calllled up-ah-ahn a midnight clear," by way of illustration.

"No, no, no!" Jackie broke in, horrified. "Carols and kick lines—that Rockettes kind of corn is so—so yesterday! I think we should write a kind of morality play, maybe a folk opera—"

"Remember, keep it short," warned Ramona.

"That will show everyone how important the Arms is. Like, maybe a girl is walking down the street, seeking shelter, and she keeps getting turned away, and then a gang springs from the shadows and knifes her. And then"—Jackie was warming up—"then the fellows who knife her turn toward the audience and walk among them, kind of menacing them with switchblades—"

"That sounds awfully depressing," Dolly said. "We want to send our audience home humming and tapping their feet. Dancing telephones aren't corny—they're cute!"

"Audiences today don't care about cute—they want to be intrigued, provoked—"

"Frightened, mugged?" Dolly asked pointedly.

"Enough!" Ramona held up her hand. Her years of experience in quelling teenage quarrels was evident. "I say we stick to the musical theme. And since it was Dolly's idea and she has the showbiz background, let's make her our director and give her final say on the details. *This* time," she added, as the avant-garde girl continued to pout. "We're going to need your energy and enthusiasm for promotion, Jackie."

"All right," Jackie gave in. "But I call dibs on directing the next benefit!"

Angelo consoled her. "I thought your morality play was very Christmasy, very baby Jesus."

Phyllis had been sitting cross-legged and quiet on the floor. Now she said, "I'm not much of a performer and my showbiz know-how is nil, but I *do* want to help." She shot a glance at Dolly. "What can I do?"

"Plenty," Ramona assured her. "Costumes, props, stage management—"

"You should be stage manager," Jackie told her girlfriend.

"Look how you're managing us already," piped up mousy Margie. Everyone laughed.

"Is there a party?" said a new voice. Dolly twisted around. Arlene stood in the doorway, a quizzical expression on her wind-reddened face. The benefit director's pulse beat faster.

"Just what we need!" cried Ramona. "A scenic designer!"

Arlene strolled over and perched on the arm of the couch next to Dolly, listening as the girls eagerly explained the benefit in a jumble of folk-singing Lady Macbeths and clog-dancing telephones.

Arlene seemed taken aback by the idea. "Isn't it kind of—well, *tacky*, asking strangers to pay for our phones?"

Jackie started to say, "But really, it's for—" then hushed, when Dolly nudged her hard. A half dozen other girls were indignantly explaining why raising money for phones wasn't the least bit tacky.

"I take it back!" Arlene gave in with good grace. "I'll design your dancing phones and decorative backdrops."

Dolly analyzed Arlene's attitude after dinner, as she descended again to the sub-basement storeroom. This time she wasn't looking for skeletons, but supplies. "That storeroom has lots of stuff we can use onstage," Ramona had reminded the substitute landlady. "I have to be at Club Lucky tonight, but you could start looking for sign-making materials—paints, poster board, and what have you." The ex-housekeeper was going full-steam ahead with the advertising campaign. "It's more important than rehearsals!" she told Dolly seriously.

Arlene is the independent type, Dolly mused now as she looked at the storeroom, wondering where to start. She wanted to help the proud girl somehow, but Arlene made it difficult.

"Dolly? Are you down here?"

It was Arlene herself, tripping down the stairs in her stylish shoes. "Ramona suggested I give you a hand."

Was Ramona playing matchmaker? Dolly tried to keep her pulse under control. Sure, she was attracted to the young scenic designer, but she was also supposed to be a source of guidance for the troubled tenant. It was her job to convince the closemouthed girl that there was no percentage in pretending everything was hunky-dory and to encourage her to share any unhappy secrets with her understanding landlady. *I'm her housemother first, and have the hots for her second,* Dolly told herself sternly.

She had to clear the air about the other night. "Sorry I got so blitzed at Francine's," she told the scenic designer. "I don't make it a habit, honestly."

Arlene dismissed the apology with a flip of her hand. "It happens to the best of us. Where do we start?"

The two girls gazed around at the haphazardly piled goods, some now water-stained. In addition to the broken chair and old Victrola Dolly had moved earlier, there was a velvet upholstered love seat, a cinderblock substituting for its missing foot, a bunch of canvases leaned against the wall, behind an ancient typewriter with a diving mask on top, and of course the ancient trunks and piles of boxes.

"This could take all night," Arlene murmured. She turned in a circle, gazing up at the boxes stacked almost to the beams.

"Let's start here." Dolly dragged the ladder next to the stack beneath the wood-rotted beam. She'd have to clear this space for the carpenters anyway. Climbing to the top, Dolly sneezed as she opened the topmost box and discovered a red crinoline. "Here." She handed it to Arlene.

"Put it over there." Dolly indicated the opposite wall. She remembered to add, "And if you see anything that

says Dora Potter on it, set it aside." She might as well in-
dulge Ramona in her wild-goose chase.

"Dora Potter," echoed Arlene obediently.

"It was awfully nice of you to take care of me, pull my
shoes off and all that," Dolly said, struck by an idea. She
opened the next box, which contained a pair of ice skates.
"But that's the way girls are here at the Arms—everybody's always helping everybody else."

"Right," Arlene agreed absentmindedly. She was looking at the canvases while she waited for the next box.
"These are pretty awful," she said critically.

Dolly wondered if she was being too subtle. She tried
again.

"And look at the way you helped me out, fixing me up
with your agent friend. Of course the part didn't work
out, but still—"

Arlene looked at her blankly. "What part? Oh, you
mean Eddy and the secretary show. Sorry it fell through."

Dolly could see that Arlene was too distracted by her
own worries to summon the interest she'd shown last
night. She decided to be more direct. "So there's no need
to hide the fact that you're broke," she told the younger
girl kindly, handing down the next box. "No one's going
to think less of you. In fact, they'll want to help!"

"Broke? What do you mean, broke?" Arlene was instantly on the defensive.

"Get wise to yourself, Arlene," Dolly advised. "This
foolish pride is hindering you, not helping!"

Arlene stacked a box carefully in its new spot, keeping
her back to her concerned housemother. "Money *is* tight,"
she said finally, turning around to face Dolly. "I had some
unexpected expenses this fall—"

"Something to do with your ex?" Dolly guessed shrewdly.

Arlene's lips twitched in a wry smile. "I don't even
need to tell you, do I?" Then she turned serious. "Oh,

Dolly"—she put her head in her hands and half sobbed—
"you don't want to have anything to do with me. I'm a
mess!"

"You don't look like a mess to me." Hot blood raced
through Dolly's veins, as fast as greyhounds after a me-
chanical rabbit, and she hurried down the ladder to continue the conversation. She contemplated the sad-faced
girl, and her gaze dropped to the swell of Arlene's breasts
beneath her stylish sweater. *Was she still wearing that
padded bra?* Dolly forced her eyes upward.

"Sit down." She pulled the girl toward the love seat
that sagged in the middle. "Tell your housemother all
about it." *I'll sort through the storeroom another day,*
she told herself. *Arlene needs counsel now.*

"I already have a mother," Arlene murmured brokenly.
"What I need is—I need—"

Dolly couldn't have resisted the impulse to slide her
hands under Arlene's sweater, even if the rotted beam had
broken in half then and there. "I can be whatever you
want me to be," she promised, accepting the new role.

Her warm hands caressed Arlene's torso, and in an instant, she'd undone the clasp of the scenic designer's
brassiere and freed her firm, young breasts. "No, don't,"
Arlene said in a voice that carried no conviction as she
pressed herself into Dolly. "You don't know about
Muriel!"

"Do I need to?" Dolly asked, forgetting her original
plan to elicit a confession from her troubled tenant, and
instead continuing to mold and shape the succulent flesh
like it was wood putty she was preparing for a patch. The
landlady's breath came faster, as the attractive girl leaned
back and closed her eyes with a little sigh. Dolly pushed
up Arlene's sweater and bent her head to the breasts
she'd uncovered.

Arlene was trembling now, giving voice to low moans,

and Dolly's hands roved over the girl's palpitating body like a gang of bandits over the Sicilian countryside. Arlene hooked her knee around Dolly's waist with wordless urgency, and Dolly took the hint, redoubling her efforts to empty Arlene's mind the way Kay had emptied hers. Arlene was shaking all over now, her hands tangled deep in Dolly's bleached blond hair, clutching at its brown roots. The heated excitement made Dolly feel like the teenager she'd once played, only now this kind of heavy petting would never have made it into the script, much less onto the television set—certainly not on a family show!

The decrepit love seat suddenly tilted, sliding off the cinderblock that stood in for its missing foot, just as Arlene uttered an ecstatic cry of release.

"Oh, Dolly," she said almost the next instant, "I'm taking advantage of you!"

"I didn't do anything I didn't want to," Dolly declared.

"I'm not really free," Arlene confessed even as she caught her breath. "Not while Muriel's still in the sanatorium. I can't dump her while she's insane and depending on me!"

The story came out in pieces, with Dolly's astute guesses pulling the narrative from the guarded girl. Arlene and Muriel had shared that swank previous address Dolly had seen on the tenant's application, until the sensitive Muriel had fallen into a depression, lost her job, and had a nervous breakdown.

"Why? It's hard to say." Arlene pondered a minute. "Maybe the strain of leading the gay life."

"Perhaps her parents were putting some sort of pressure on her—"

"They were," said Arlene. "They were always urging her to move out and get married. I guess it just became too much for her."

Something about the story was familiar to Dolly. She wondered if she'd heard about Muriel from someone else, or maybe even met her—after all, Bay City's sapphic pool wasn't that big, and Dolly had been swimming in it for some time!

She turned her attention back to Arlene. The scenic designer told her landlady how the sanatorium fees ate up her income. "The doctors say she's—what's the word? Catatonic. I'm not sure I love her anymore, but I can't let her be shipped to the state mental hospital! Yet some days I just wish she'd wake up and act normal long enough for me to break up with her—am I a cad?"

"I think you're acting like a hero!" the landlady told her admiringly.

"But do you see my bind?" Arlene's amber eyes begged Dolly to understand. "I'm not really available. The way things are, I can't even ask you to wait! I'm just suspended, between the past and the present. . . ." She finished her sentence by putting her hand in Dolly's, pleadingly.

"You're in a tight spot," the substitute landlady comforted her. "But I have a feeling it'll all work out. And don't worry about me." Dolly put her arm around Arlene and gave her a reassuring squeeze. "I'm the type who can wait without being asked!" She pulled Arlene up from the dilapidated love seat. "I know the wait will be worth it."

Arlene smiled up at the landlady, tears glinting on her eyelashes, and Dolly had the glow of good feeling that comes from helping someone in trouble.

They were crossing the lobby when a small crash came from the visitors' parlor. Arlene clutched Dolly. "Who on earth is in the visitors' parlor now?"

Dolly wondered the same thing. "Maybe that vase of flowers fell on its own," she muttered, shaking loose of Arlene and going to the parlor door.

On opening it, however, she discovered a human occupant picking up the broken pieces of china and bedraggled flowers from the floor—Angelo, who had inexplicably changed into a handsome pair of striped flannel pajamas. Dolly's eyes traveled over the horsehair sofa, neatly made up with sheets and a blanket, and the spindly side table that now held a battered alarm clock and a toothbrush glass.

"Angelo," Dolly asked in astonishment, "are you living here?"

Arlene crowded next to Dolly and took in the scene. "Isn't this against the rules?" she asked.

Dolly put her hands on her hips, remembering her responsibilities. "Arlene is dead right. Visiting hours end at ten p.m.!"

"Is it so late?" Angelo peered at the clock, as if he'd simply lost track of time and wasn't bedding down in the visitors' parlor for the night.

The girls who'd been watching the late show began to trickle out of the lounge, attracted by the brouhaha. Jackie pushed her way to the front. "It's my fault!"

Just behind her, Ramona contradicted, "No, it was my idea. No one ever uses the visitors' parlor anyway!"

It had been Angelo whom Beverly heard that night, Dolly realized, and his rustling she had mistaken for mice. If it hadn't been for the shattered vase, the young boy might have gotten away with camping out at the Magdalena Arms for who knows how long!

"You must have departed at dawn," Dolly realized. "But where did you stow your stuff during the day?"

Angelo demonstrated for his interested audience how cleverly his belongings could be whisked away into the cupboards on either side of the white marble fireplace. "I swept and dusted every morning," he said eagerly. "And I kept the vase filled with flowers!"

"Hmmph!" Dolly eyed Ramona reprovingly, remembering how she'd taken credit for the flowers.

"Please, can't he stay?" Jackie begged as if Angelo were a stray puppy she wanted to keep. "He has nowhere else to go, really!" She poured out a long list of justifications, designed to soften even the hardest hearted housemother: cruel parents—"They tell him working in a beauty parlor to pay for acting classes is no job for a man"; dishonest roommates—"*They* spent the rent playing pool, but he got evicted too"; and outlined Angelo's many fine qualities—"He's very neat, he's musical, he speaks two languages, and he can help with hairstyling!"

Dolly might have weakened, but the substitute housemother couldn't condone such an egregious breach of the Magdalena Arms' rules and regulations—not with a whole crowd of girls as witnesses! Somebody would blab, and it would inevitably get back to the ever-vigilant Mrs. Putney-Potter. Keeping this private would be like carrying water in a sieve. The housemother shook her head firmly.

"No. I'm sorry, Angelo, but it just won't do. The Magdalena Arms is girls only, and that means no men, not even one!"

"But he's helping with the Christmas benefit!" Jackie protested desperately.

"I'd pay regular rent," Angelo chimed in. "And I could style all your hair for nothing!"

There was an intrigued murmur from the group of girls. Beauty parlor bills were the bane of every career girl's existence.

Dolly stuck to her guns. She had to be the responsible one. "It can't be done." She shook her head emphatically.

"You're surely not going to put him out on the street this instant?" Ramona asked reproachfully.

Dolly hesitated. Angelo *was* already in his pajamas, and the sheets on the horsehair sofa looked awfully inviting.

"He can stay tonight," she allowed. "But that's it!"

Angelo dolefully turned down the covers for the last time as the disappointed girls drifted away.

"I never thought *you'd* be such a stickler for rules!" Ramona accused Dolly.

Dolly seized the aggrieved girl's arm with sudden strength. "Listen, Ramona!" she hissed. "You know I'm just trying to save the Arms for future generations—stop hindering and start helping!"

"I take it back—I'm sorry," her old friend muttered, and retreated to the elevator.

Surely Ramona could guess how temptation had tugged at the seemingly stern landlady when Angelo offered to pay rent! *If only I could find a loophole in the bylaws*, Dolly thought longingly.

The sound of a key in the front door made her turn. It was Kay, flushed and windblown, carrying her overnight bag and clarinet case.

"Kay! I thought you weren't coming home until Sunday!" The landlady's mood lifted.

"I'd had enough of my family by last night," confessed Kay. She smiled at Dolly, eyes alight and dancing. "It's good to be back!"

The warmth of her glance made Dolly a little uneasy. She was relieved when Kay turned her attention to Angelo. "Hello!" The clarinet player was unfazed by the pajamaed boy on the sofa. "I see we have a visitor!"

"Sort of," Dolly began.

Arlene broke in, "Oh, you've missed all kinds of excitement." She linked arms with Dolly and began to tell Kay about "our benefit."

The expectant look in Kay's eyes faded as she took in the twosome. Dolly detached herself from Arlene. As landlady, it was her duty to be discreet.

Not that Kay would care, of course, the substitute landlady thought, eyeing Kay as Arlene chattered on. After all, Kay had said she was just feeling blue, that night on the couch. But as Dolly knew from experience, you didn't need to be in love to feel left out! And Dolly hated to hurt anyone's feelings.

"I'm sure the Sisterhood of Swing will be happy to play the benefit," Kay was telling Arlene politely. "I guess I'd better get to bed now."

"And I have some research to do, into the Arms' rules and regulations," Dolly said hastily, before Arlene displayed their newfound intimacy. "Tooraloora, you two. 'Night, Angelo."

It wasn't just an excuse. Dolly let herself into Mrs. De-Witt's suite and switched on the desk lamp. Kay's remark about having a visitor had given her an idea.

She pulled out the bylaws and skimmed through the pages, searching for a half-remembered section. "Items stored may be considered abandoned property after . . . listen to confidences and supply sound and sage advice . . . establish a list of economical eating places . . ."

"In the case of out-of-town visitors . . ." Aha! This was it. Dolly read the section carefully. Yes—it would work. A few hoops to jump through, but that should be no difficulty. Dolly triumphantly put the brittle sheets back in their yellowed folder. Angelo could stay!

She climbed to the fifth floor and almost knocked on Jackie's door to give her the good news, but the sighs and moans coming from room 505 dissuaded her. Breakfast would be time enough.

The noises from next door were still audible after the weary landlady had strapped on her chin guard and climbed under the covers. Dolly's mind wandered to Arlene and their earlier encounter on the love seat in the sub-basement storeroom. Now that the earlier excitement had faded, she wondered what, exactly, she had agreed to when she said she was willing to wait.

After a restless sleep filled with frustrated dreams, it was a relief to get up in the morning and fall into the now-familiar routine of serving breakfast, chatting with her girls, and cleaning up afterward. "Ixnay on the muffins," Sue said, thrusting the offending baked good at the cook. "I'm no rabbit to eat all this kind of chow!"

Dolly was about to apologize for the fourth time that morning when a sharp-toned voice echoed down the stairs.

"Dolly Dingle! Dolly Dingle, where are you?" It was Mrs. Putney-Potter, clattering down the stairs, dragging Angelo triumphantly behind her.

"I drop in for a casual visit, and *this* is what I find!" She flourished the frightened boy like a hunter with a brace of pheasants he'd bagged. "I'm shutting the Magdalena Arms down at once on grounds of immorality!"

Dolly put down the muffin and lit a cigarette. "Angelo is an approved guest of the Arms, per section IIIc," she said calmly. "The girls voted him in."

It had been unanimous, which was enough to give Angelo a majority and thus official Arms approval, even without the girls who were gone for the holiday and Arlene, who'd departed before breakfast. *Spending the day at the sanatorium*, she'd written on a note she'd put on the percolator. She'd signed it with an imprint of her lipsticked mouth, which made Dolly feel warm all over until Kay spied it, and then she felt terrible.

"When? How?" sputtered Mrs. Putney-Potter. Dolly showed her the ballots she'd collected that morning at breakfast.

"Have some coffee, Angelo," she added, pouring the relieved boy a cup. "And a muffin—or maybe you'd rather have a cinnamon bun."

"But these are dated yesterday." Mrs. Putney-Potter stabbed the slips of paper accusingly.

"Yes?" Dolly eyed the trustee narrowly. She was glad she'd followed Ramona's suggestion to backdate the ballots. The devious girl's instincts were, as usual, on the money. Mrs. Putney-Potter was furious and frustrated. This was no casual drop by—she'd been looking for Angelo!

"Never mind." Mrs. Putney-Potter put down the ballots abruptly. The defeated trustee clicked angrily out of the dining room and up the stairs.

Angelo heaved a sigh of relief. "I'm glad she doesn't live here!"

She knew the vote wasn't really taken last night, realized the substitute landlady. How had news of Angelo's presence at the Arms traveled to Linden Lane so fast? Who had spilled the beans?

Chapter 20

The Discovery in the Storeroom

It bothered Dolly, wondering who had blabbed about Angelo. She pondered the question on and off the next couple of weeks. Was it an isolated incident, or had someone at the Arms told Mrs. Putney-Potter on purpose?

It had to be an accident, she reasoned. But some girl *had* been loose-lipped. Dolly wished she knew where the leak was located, so she could patch this particular hole!

Secrecy was more essential than ever, now that she'd taken the final step. The contractors had come and gone, replacing the wood-rotted beam and collecting a fee that had taken all the tax money and then some. While it was a relief to cross the kitchen floor without worrying about falling through, the misappropriated funds weighed heavily on the substitute landlady's mind. If the Christmas Capers didn't make money, how would Dolly explain the shortfall at the end-of-the-year accounting?

Ramona dismissed Dolly's fears. "If our cast and crew each sell six tickets at three dollars a ticket, we'll be in the clear, and that's not even counting additional donations!"

Phyllis wasn't much better. Dolly had forgotten her

anger at the well-meaning social scientist, but when she tried to talk to her about her worries, Phyllis displayed that same strange distraction she'd been afflicted with since Thanksgiving. "We'll be fine," she reassured Dolly absentmindedly. "Mamie McArdle is going to give the show a plug in her column. Win—a friend of mine says it'll be sure to send sales skyrocketing!"

This news at least was encouraging. "Lois arranged it," Phyllis informed her neighbor. "Are you still holding your grudge against the old gang?"

"I don't really think about them," Dolly lied. "I've got a lot on my mind—rehearsals, the mess in the storeroom, and wondering how Mrs. Putney-Potter's getting her information. Any ideas?" she ended hopefully. Maybe the statistician could narrow down the pool of possibilities.

"I'll look at the data later, Dolly." Phyllis was primping in front of her mirror. "Right now I'm late for a Beautification meeting." Pushing her frizzy hair impatiently, she declared, "And I think I'm due for some beautification myself!"

Dolly watched her go. What had gotten into the formerly staid social scientist? And who was this "Win"?

For that matter, what had gotten into Kay? Ever since she'd come back from the Thanksgiving holiday, the clarinetist had been acting awfully odd around Dolly. It was as if a valve had been turned, shutting off the comfortable give-and-take between the substitute landlady and her fourth-floor neighbor.

They saw plenty of each other—they were both working hard on the Christmas Capers. But the frenzied backstage atmosphere that had enveloped the lounge was hardly conducive to a confidential conversation. One evening the Sisterhood of Swing would be rehearsing on one side of the lounge while Margie coached the dancing telephones on the other. Meanwhile, Phyllis would be bent over the ancient sewing machine they'd dragged up from the storeroom, piecing together the simple striped shifts. The clatter of the old Singer only added to the cacophony.

On another night it would be the string quartet, or the chorus, or the folk girls with their banjos. Jackie might be declaiming her Pinter monologue under her breath and simultaneously addressing invitations to former Magdalena Arms tenants, while Ramona checked them off the list she'd culled from Mrs. DeWitt's file of forwarding addresses or shook her metal money box (also unearthed from the inexhaustible storeroom) and called, "Where's that ticket money, girls? Only twelve days till Christmas!"

And it seemed like whenever Dolly *did* sidle over to Kay to chat, Arlene would have a question for the director about one of her designs or ask the hapless housemother's advice about some construction detail—"my favorite handywoman," she'd say with a wink.

The only time the two old friends exchanged more than a few words was the day they helped set up the enormous Christmas tree in the curve of the lobby's grand staircase. As the tallest and strongest girls, they were deputized to hold the tree upright and get it straight, before little Jackie tightened the screws on the base.

And so they stood, deep in the prickly pine boughs, as Ramona called, "A little left—no, too far—back half an inch!"

Kay remarked in a carefully casual undertone, "You and Arlene seem to be getting along."

"Well—" Dolly wasn't sure what to say. Arlene could be awfully affectionate. But she was away so much, visiting the mad Muriel. And when she returned, she was inevitably too overwrought to respond to Dolly's overtures. "Can we just cuddle?" she'd ask plaintively. If Dolly was even slightly slow to follow this suggestion, Arlene would reproach herself, urging the substitute landlady to give her the heave-ho. "You deserve someone better," she'd declare.

Dolly hated to see Arlene unhappy. She wanted to do what she could to help the snarled-up scenic designer, even if it meant damping down the fires of desire that threatened to burn up her insides.

As she held the Christmas tree up, Dolly tried to express some of this to Kay without being disloyal to her new, sort-of girlfriend. "We get along pretty well, and she *is* the kind of girl I always thought I wanted—which isn't to say—"

Kay interrupted earnestly. "I'm glad. I've been wanting to kind of, clear the air. You know—make sure you weren't feeling bad on my account."

To Dolly the air seemed murkier than ever, roiling with charged emotions and motives she didn't know how to interpret.

"Perfect!" cried Ramona. "Screw the base in quick, Jackie."

The two girls emerged from the pine branches to admire the results. Ramona said, "Now for the mistletoe!"

"You don't need me for that," Kay excused herself. And again Dolly was left with an unhappy feeling, like there was some misunderstanding between herself and the clarinetist, some unfinished business she needed to take care of.

Dolly replayed the conversation for the ninth time one gray afternoon as she gazed at the now decorated tree.

"Isn't it beautiful?" The voice made her jump. It was Angelo, who had quietly come up behind her. He was holding a bottle of peroxide and looking up at the tree, eyes alight with admiration.

"Oh, hello, Angelo! You startled me."

Angelo had proved to be an ideal addition to the Arms. Dolly had moved the semipermanent visitor into Mrs. DeWitt's empty suite, figuring the ancient landlady's bed would be more comfortable than the horsehair sofa. The boy had turned the visitors' parlor into a rudimentary beauty salon, and almost every afternoon one girl or another would be getting a trim or touch-up. It couldn't have worked out better if Dolly had planned it. The Arms girls bragged to all their friends about Magdalena Arms' in-house stylist, and rental applications had picked up. Dolly thought they might have a full house by Christmas—maybe even a waiting list!

"You're working too hard," Angelo said now. "And your hair needs an update!"

Dolly laughed. "I'll be coming to you for a new look one of these days," she promised. "But right now I have to get back to my chores."

She turned toward the basement, wondering who Angelo was touching up today. It would be nice to relax in his swivel chair for a beauty treatment, but her to-do list was as long as ever. Today's agenda included putting the sub-basement storeroom back in order, and double-checking a list of items for the benefit. If that chore didn't take too long, Dolly thought she might do some Christmas shopping. She'd picked Beverly in the secret Santa drawing the other night and planned to price a juicer for the young nurse.

Dolly surveyed the storeroom. They'd gotten rid of the worst of the junk before the construction crew arrived. Jackie, Ramona, and Arlene had helped Dolly carry the broken furniture, the baby buggy, and three ancient typewriters to the trash. Ramona had rescued the canvases and some gaudy **SOLD!** signs Arlene had piled on top. "We can paint over these for backdrops and benefit posters," she'd planned.

Now, Dolly began methodically stacking the boxes by size, checking each for benefit props and materials. "Any black fabric or old telephones," Ramona had instructed.

"Or striped fabric," Phyllis had added.

"Scrap wood too," Arlene had chimed in.

Most of the boxes contained old books, outdated clothes, or odd knickknacks. *Criminy, another crinoline.* Dolly held up the limp blue net, wondering if it would be any use.

She took the lid off another shoe box and started, with a stifled exclamation. Instead of the pair of pumps she'd expected, she'd uncovered a face with wide, staring eyes. She pushed aside the white tissue paper, her heart still pounding, and lifted the creature out.

It was a doll—a lifelike baby doll with a plastic head and limbs and a soft, stuffed torso. There was a white crocheted blanket underneath.

Stranger still, it was a Negro doll. Dolly held it up to the light. "Whose little doll are you?" she asked it.

Ramona's half-forgotten efforts to dig up dirt on Mrs. Putney-Potter came rushing back. Could Mrs. DeWitt's cryptic comments about babies have anything to do with this odd toy?

Dolly put the doll back in its box and carried it upstairs to show to Ramona. *I'm probably making too much of it*, she told herself. Maybe Beverly wasn't the first girl to integrate the Arms, and this was someone's childhood toy. Still—

In the lobby she remembered that Ramona and Jackie were putting up posters for the Christmas Capers in the neighborhood today. Darn it! Dolly wanted to share her odd discovery with someone.

As if in answer to her wishes, the visitors' parlor door opened and a girl came out, touching her buttercup blond hair gingerly.

"Why, Phyllis!" Dolly's jaw dropped. "That's quite a makeover!"

It wasn't just that the dishwater-blond locks had been skillfully brightened. The frizzy hair, which the social scientist generally wore pulled back in a barrette, had been cut, straightened, and styled. She wore makeup, blue eye shadow, and dark pink lipstick. Her whole head blossomed like a hothouse bouquet out of her sensible brown wool shirtwaist.

Phyllis smiled self-consciously. "Do you like it?" She put on her gold-rimmed glasses and peered at her reflection in the glass of the front door. "Angelo suggested new glasses too."

"You need a whole new outfit, honey! Who are you vamping?"

Phyllis turned bright red. "I've bought a dress. I'm going to the Bay City Beautification Committee Christmas Party next week, and I want to look my best."

Dolly eyed the blushing statistician narrowly. She'd bet that Miss Ware—or maybe the mysterious "Win" whose name Phyllis had let slip the other day—was behind her old friend's odd behavior. But why the hush-hush? Was Phyllis planning some kind of surprise announcement?

"Well, while you're waiting to hobnob with society, take a gander at this." Dolly took the lid off the shoe box and showed Phyllis the doll she'd found. "What do you think?"

Phyllis pushed her glasses up her nose. "It's remarkably lifelike. Is it for the toy drive?"

Dolly shook her head impatiently. "I found it in the subbasement storeroom. Remember Ramona's theory that Mrs. Putney-Potter was doing something fishy with kids while she lived at the Arms? Maybe this is hers—maybe she integrated the baby buying racket!"

"You're jumping to conclusions," Phyllis pointed out.

"Hundreds of girls have passed through the Arms. Statistically speaking, the odds that this particular doll belonged to Mrs. Putney-Potter are negligible. It's just as likely it was a teaching tool for one of the dozens of teachers who have lived here. Have you shown it to Netta?"

"No, I haven't and I'm not going to!"

It was easy to forgive Phyllis, who was at least working on the benefit, but Dolly still bore a grudge against her crusading tenant whose time at the Arms was ticking down.

"Don't be so stubborn," Phyllis pleaded for the twentieth time. "I can't believe you're really still mad at Netta and the old gang! They're all coming to the Christmas Capers. Janet and Pam both bought blocks of tickets when Ramona told them"—Phyllis lowered her voice—"what it was really for."

"I'm sure it's awfully nice of them to find the time in their busy schedules," Dolly said, attempting an air of indifference. "As for Netta, I could hardly ask her advice when she's spending all her spare time at her 'Experiment in Living' headquarters!"

Phyllis opened her mouth to argue, but Dolly forestalled her objections, saying, "Let's see the rest of your outfit."

That was enough to distract the appearance-obsessed social scientist. Up in Dolly's room, Phyllis modeled a new red maxi dress with a deeply scooped neck. "Nix the nylons," Dolly decreed. "Buy a pair of those ribbed tights in the same shade of red. That'll catch anyone's eye." Dolly thought Phyllis looked ready to pop with excited anticipation.

Phyllis corrected quickly, "I joined the Bay City Beautification Committee not for the personalities, but purely to further our common goal of civic improvement. It's not so different from my zoning projects, really."

Dolly stifled the impulse to reply, "Whatever you say," and left Phyllis carefully cold-creaming off her new look.

Restless, her mind teeming with her tenants' romantic entanglements and the perennial worry about whether the Christmas Capers would get the Arms out of hock, Dolly drifted down to the fourth floor and found herself standing in front of Kay's door. The mournful wail of the clarinet told her Kay was at home.

I'll just ask her what she thinks of the doll, Dolly decided. *The more minds, the merrier!*

"Oh—hi, Dolly," Kay said, in that not-quite-normal way, when she opened the door to Dolly's knock. "Come on in."

The musician's room was comfortably messy, with sheet music scattered about, and a stand between the bed and the window. Dolly took the chair Kay pulled out for her and unwrapped the doll, explaining Ramona's scheme to dig up dirt on Mrs. Putney-Potter and their ancient landlady's delirious hints. It *did* sound pretty thin, she realized, saying it all for the second time.

Kay turned the doll over in her strong, sensitive hands. "Of course I never played with dolls much as a kid," she admitted. "But I don't remember Negro dolls being very common. Maybe you could trace it to the manufacturer?"

Dolly was barely listening. It was the first time she and Kay had been alone together since the night on the lounge couch, and she was unexpectedly affected by Kay's physical closeness. She realized she was staring at Kay's hands, and she forced herself to look away, her breath coming fast all of a sudden.

Gosh darn it, she scolded herself. *Don't go getting all hot and bothered over Kay!*

The anemic diet of kisses and caresses that Arlene had fed her these past weeks was insufficient nourishment for the hunger that had built up in Dolly. That must be why Kay suddenly held such an irresistible attraction for her, from the coppery red hair to the freckled cheeks, even to the hollows of fatigue under her eyes—the hot wave of lust that swamped the helpless ex-actress took her by surprise.

Kay looked up from the doll, and her gaze locked with Dolly's. "You didn't really come to talk about this toy, did you, Dolly?" The clarinetist laid the doll on her desk.

It was almost a relief, being caught looking so lustfully. "I thought I did," she confessed. "But I guess I just wanted to see you! I've kinda missed you, Kay."

Kay looked down and laced her fingers carefully together. "You've been pretty busy with Arlene," she observed.

"Not really." Dolly seized the chance to *really* clear the air. "I mean, sure, sort of. The thing is, she's got another girlfriend. Or sort of girlfriend. So she's kind of distracted, and—" She was only making things murkier, Dolly realized miserably.

Kay's mouth twisted in a wry grin. "You're looking for distraction too? To even things out?"

Dolly started to protest, but Kay continued, "I don't mind." She unclasped her hands and slid one up the sleeve of Dolly's old sweatshirt. The touch of her hand on Dolly's forearm was more stimulating than such an innocent gesture had any right to be.

"I'd never come between two girls playing a duet." Kay slid her hand farther up Dolly's arm. "But you two sound like you still haven't chosen a tune."

Dolly sighed, as Kay's strong hands kneaded her upper arms. Somehow, she'd explained enough to get what she needed. "I'm surprised you don't have a regular girl, Kay," she said, sliding out of the chair and joining Kay on the bed. She supposed it was an odd remark to make right before you kissed a girl, but Dolly meant it as a compliment. Kay was a catch, no mistake. Her touch was soothing and stimulating all at once. The hardworking landlady felt lazy and languorous, as if she might slip into a sort of sensual snooze.

Kay had other ideas. "Don't fall asleep on me, Dolly." She nipped the landlady's neck lightly. "I've only got half an hour before rehearsal."

The news that their time was limited stimulated the substitute landlady. She stripped off her sweatshirt and tugged up Kay's wool pullover. "I'm awake," she protested, as Kay, done tuning up, stripped off the rest of their clothes with record speed. Then the two neighbors plunged into a delicious tangle of bare limbs, torsos, and tongues, beyond conversation and thought. The tempo increased, from andante to vivace in the space of a few heartbeats, and all at once Dolly experienced a sensation of pleasure so profound she felt she was levitating two feet above Kay's rumpled bed. If anything, the feeling was more earth-shattering than that first time on the lounge couch. *I must need distracting more than I realized*, Dolly thought as she found herself earthbound again, back on the bed with her arms around Kay, looking into the clarinetist's flushed face and half-closed eyes.

"Did we make our deadline?" Dolly looked at her wristwatch. "It's four twenty."

"With time to spare," Kay said.

They lay there, listening to their pounding hearts, and the faint creak of the elevator as it climbed up the building. It stopped on the fourth floor, and they could hear the rattle of the mesh opening, and then the bang of the outer door closing. Footsteps came down the hall.

Arlene is in a good mood, Dolly noted. The scenic designer was humming a little tune. Perhaps Muriel was finally on the road to recovery.

The door across the way opened and closed.

Whereas a second ago their two hearts had beat as one, now Dolly felt a gulf like the Grand Canyon grow between her and the girl in her arms. Kay extricated herself and began pulling on her clothes. "What do you say we stop meeting like this," she proposed curtly.

Dolly sat up too and pulled on her sweatshirt. "Well, sure, Kay, whatever you say." She felt apologetic and chagrined, without being able to sort out why. "I hope I didn't do anything to make you mad."

Kay nodded at the door. "I think you're more interested in the girl across the hall than you let on, and I'm not the kind who can play second chair."

"Gee, Kay." Dolly felt worse and worse. She borrowed a line from Arlene: "You deserve better than me!"

"Cool it." Kay zipped her pants and ran a comb through her tousled hair. "It's not like I'm looking for a picket fence and all that. It's just—better not to head down this road." She picked up her clarinet case and walked out.

Dolly dressed and left, wondering if what Kay said was true. She didn't want a picket fence either—it didn't go with the Arms' architectural style. But what was the matter with the road they'd been strolling on? Why did Kay want to turn back?

When she left, Dolly completely forgot the storeroom doll, which lay facedown on Kay's desk, next to the empty shoe box.

Chapter 21
A Visit to the Sanatorium

Dolly felt nervous as the Bay City Transit bus stopped at Happy Valley. She followed the other passengers up the curving driveway to Bay City's most famous sanatorium, not sure what to expect.

Would Mrs. DeWitt be strapped in bed, catatonic like Arlene's Muriel? Or would she be raving like last time, maybe in a straitjacket? Dolly was a bundle of nerves as she approached the front desk.

"Your friend is in the sunroom," the receptionist told her. "I'll have an aide show you the way."

The sunroom was a glassed-in porch that looked out over the snow-covered lawn. The afternoon sun, streaming in the windows and bouncing off the white expanse outside, lit the cheerful room as brightly as for a Broadway musical. There were a dozen or so women, one or two alarmingly still, but most of them looking quite normal—chatting, reading the paper, or playing bridge, just like Magdalena Arms girls relaxing in the lounge.

When Dolly spotted Mrs. DeWitt, halfway down the room, she gave a sigh of relief. The ancient landlady looked quite animated as she sat in her wheelchair, conversing with another woman, whose pen was poised over her clipboard.

Dolly approached gingerly. "Mrs. DeWitt?"

Her old landlady turned. "Dolly, my dear!" she exclaimed with unfeigned delight.

The Magdalena Arms housemother was thin and worn, but the spark of intelligence had returned to her eyes and the color to her cheeks. "This is the Dolly Dingle I was telling you about," she introduced her young tenant to her companion. The middle-aged woman, her gray-streaked hair coiled in a tidy chignon, put away her pen and rose. "I'll let you visit, then," she said briskly. "We can finish this another time."

Dolly sat down. "Was that your doctor?" she asked.

"Ivy Gill?" Mrs. DeWitt laughed indulgently. "She's one of the oldest patients—she's been here since 1959, and the nurses tell me she tries to recruit every newcomer to her revolutionary cell. I told her I wasn't a joiner. But I want to hear about the Arms." The old landlady's voice was eager. "How are you getting on? How are all the girls? Is Beverly still on night duty? Have you had any difficulty with Ramona? And what about dear Phyllis? Netta tells me she's been behaving quite oddly!"

Dolly was astounded to hear Mrs. DeWitt reel off her tenants' right names with such ease. It was as if the fog that had surrounded her for so many years had suddenly lifted. Now her old white head positively glowed with acumen, like the snow-covered peak of a venerable mountaintop touched by the sun.

The ancient landlady prattled on, referring to Pamela's recent promotion and accurately naming Lois's advertising agency. She showed Dolly the series of postcards Maxie had sent from Paris and offered her candy from a box Janet had brought her. "My girls have been wonderful all through this distressing time!" She wiped unabashed tears away, and recited, " 'Plotting and planning together to take me by surprise!' "

If only I'd known! Dolly felt a little dewy-eyed herself, in her relief. All these wasted weeks worrying! "I wish I'd visited sooner," she told her old housemother. "I guess you looked so low the last time I saw you, that it scared me off coming back!"

Mrs. DeWitt patted her hand understandingly. "I was frightened myself. What visions I had, what strange and horrible hallucinations! It wasn't until dear Beverly brought me some helpful pamphlets that I understood the gin I'd used medicinally for so many years was pure poison!" She leaned confidentially toward Dolly. "She advised me never to touch a drop again. At first it seemed a daunting idea, but day by day, I've gotten more used to it. I'm a little like dear Tennyson's mariners, addicted to their lotos blossoms." Her voice rang out:

" 'The lotos blooms below the barren peak
the lotos blows by every winding creek.' "

"Fortunately, gin is easier to avoid," she chortled gaily.

Dolly marveled, "I hadn't realized how much the alcohol affected your memory!"

"Oh yes," Mrs. DeWitt said proudly. "I'm sharp as the proverbial tack these days. Try me!"

Eagerly Dolly took up the challenge. "We found a doll in the sub-basement storeroom," she started. "I was hoping you could tell me whose it was." She described the doll, adding, "I wish I could show it to you, but it's gone missing."

When Dolly had awkwardly asked the clarinet player for the mysterious doll, Kay claimed she'd returned it to Dolly's room the day after their final tryst. The landlady had ransacked the Arms from top to bottom—no doll.

"I don't remember such a doll." Mrs. DeWitt wrinkled her forehead. "We housed another Negro girl briefly in 1934, an actress with a rather daring touring production of Othello, but she brought no toys with her, to my knowledge."

Dolly was disappointed. "I thought maybe it had something to do with Mrs. Putney-Potter, and the thing you told Ramona about her buying babies."

"Buying babies? Did I say that? I meant borrowing babies." The ancient landlady clicked her tongue impatiently. "I'm sorry for any confusion my confusion has caused. Shortly before she left the Arms, Dora Potter was pestering everyone, asking if they knew any mothers with small children. Then she bought that baby carriage, and that seemed to satisfy her."

Dolly was more bewildered than ever. "She bought a baby carriage? Why?"

"I'm afraid I don't know. I never inquired into her affairs. Such an unpleasant girl! She left under a cloud, suspected of card sharping. Several girls said Dora had marked the decks in the lounge and was winning money by dishonest means."

Dolly wondered if there was any way to use this old scandal to put pressure on the troublesome trustee. But Mrs. DeWitt said there had been no real evidence.

"Oh well," Dolly dismissed the idea. "We don't really need to dig up any dirt on Mrs. Putney-Potter. Ramona says the box office for the benefit is booming."

Mrs. DeWitt beamed. "I haven't had the opportunity to tell you how proud I am of the way you've taken hold at the Arms and solved the difficulties that seemed so dire!"

"I got the benefit idea from you, Mrs. DeWitt!" Dolly was both embarrassed and pleased.

"Call me Harriet," said the older actress. "These recent events have made me realize that the day-to-day care of the Magdalena Arms is beyond my strength. I'd happily retire, if I could be sure you would continue as my successor!"

Even though Dolly had discovered the flaws in Mrs. DeWitt's stewardship, she was taken aback. "But—you are the Arms!" she protested.

"We are all the Arms," Mrs. DeWitt corrected. "It occurred to me that I might occupy my old quarters as a sort of landlady emerita, ready to advise and counsel. However, I've a new interest now. Do you remember the line from 'Ulysses'?" She recited:

> "'Some work of noble note, may yet be done
> Not unbecoming men that strove with gods.'"

Dolly wondered what noble work Mrs. DeWitt planned to undertake, but the ancient housemother ended her suspense the next instant.

"The fact is," she confided, "after years of immersing myself in the great poets, I long to make my own feeble attempt at versification. My doctors have encouraged my ambition—Dr. Steinmetz, especially, thinks a creative outlet would be a great boon."

Dolly's thoughts were laboring in her head like Tennyson's mariners struggling up the laboring wave. Mrs. DeWitt's proposal would mean curtailing her acting career—maybe giving it up for good. Examining her emotions, the substitute landlady found only a sense of anticipation and an eager impulse to update her to-do list.

The ex-actress asked, "Mrs. DeWitt—Harriet, I mean—do you ever miss your stage career?"

"I do not," Mrs. DeWitt replied at once. "Don't misunderstand me—those gay, mad years at Die Schwarze Katz and later with the Bay City Shakespeare Society were delightful. But after twenty years in the life, so to speak, I was happy to put my hand to another plow. The tawdry glamour had worn thin, and I recognized the truth of the poet's words:

> 'Let not ambition mock their useful toil,
> Their homely joys and destiny obscure;
> Nor grandeur hear with a disdainful smile
> The short and simple annals of the poor.' "

Several women in the sunroom looked up, startled, as Mrs. DeWitt's voice gained in volume and feeling until the very windows rattled. In a more conversational tone, the old lady added, "The paths of glory lead but to the grave, you know!"

Riding the bus back to the city, Dolly repeated Mrs. DeWitt's apt quotation to herself: *The paths of glory lead but to the grave.* She'd been clinging to the acting life out of some silly notion that its glamour was superior to a landlady's useful toil. But the fact was, she'd enjoyed these past weeks thoroughly. She didn't regret her thirty-some years in showbiz, but right now a houseful of real, live girls was more interesting to Dolly than the coma victims and philanderers of her old soap opera!

As luck would have it, Miss Watkins was in the lobby when Dolly returned, saying good-bye to mousy Margie, as she put her coat over the tweed jumper and stylish ruffled blouse she wore.

"Miss Watkins!" Dolly stamped the snow off her feet and seized the career counselor like a long-lost friend. "I was just thinking I could use a little guidance! Would it be a big mistake for me to give up acting and take over for Mrs. DeWitt as permanent housemother here at the Arms?"

Miss Watkins regarded her thoughtfully. "Why, Dolly, I'd need to assess you a little more thoroughly before I could give you sound advice on such a sudden change. Are you free to take the PPA now?" She consulted her watch. "I've just finished administering one to Margie, but I have a little time before I'm due back at the office."

After her session with Miss Watkins, Dolly headed upstairs, humming "Have Yourself a Merry Little Christmas." The test hadn't been bad, she realized, relieved. Not at all like the ones she'd taken in her youth, during her sporadic schooling.

Dolly put away her coat and fluffed up her hair. Her head was bubbling with home improvement projects as she headed to the washroom to freshen up. Maybe some sort of coat closet downstairs—

Inside the tiled bathroom she stopped short, a muffled exclamation of horror escaping her lips.

Phyllis, who should have been at her job, was standing over the sink, razor blade in hand, apparently intending to slit her wrist!

Chapter 22

The Torch Goes Out

"Phyllis!" Dolly's voice rang out, and the girl started and inadvertently slashed herself. "Oh!" said the statistician, as if surprised by the blood that quickly welled up. Her face turned pale as she contemplated her wound with queasy fascination. "I forgot—the sight of blood makes me sick!" she said faintly.

Dolly rushed to the wan girl's side just as Phyllis's knees began to buckle. "What on earth do you think you're doing?" she asked, anger and concern mixed in equal measure.

"I didn't want to make a mess in my room." Phyllis's voice faded then came back. "So unpleasant for someone else to clean up . . ."

Dolly thanked heavens that the self-effacing statistician had planned her suicide attempt to spare her friends' sensibilities. Her selfless impulse had probably saved her!

"But why would you do such a thing in the first place?" Dolly harangued her white-faced friend as she hauled her out of the bathroom and down the hall to her own room. She laid the groggy girl on her bed, wrapped her arm in the towel she'd snatched from a hook on the bathroom wall, and then dashed across the hall to

Netta's room. Netta knew first aid and kept a kit in her room. "Netta! Netta!" She pounded on the door.

The exasperating idealist *would* be away during this current crisis!

Ramona's door swung open and the brown-haired girl blinked sleepily at Dolly as a haze of blue smoke drifted into the hallway from her room. "What's all the ruckus?"

Dolly sniffed the smoke suspiciously. "Ramona, you've been smoking tea again!"

Ramona hastily closed the door behind her. "No one calls it *tea* nowadays. And like I keep telling you, it's no different than a cocktail."

Dolly didn't have time to split hairs over Ramona's illicit habit. "Never mind! Phyllis slit her wrist, and I need Netta's first aid kit—and someone who knows first aid!"

Ramona shook off her sleepiness. "I'm certified in first aid! Give me your keys and I'll get the kit!"

Dolly thrust the key ring at Ramona and hurried back to Phyllis's room. The girl lay on her bed, awake but in a kind of stupor. Dolly noticed a picture of Miss Ware pasted over the desk. It looked like it had been cut out from the newspaper; Miss Ware, posed with a pair of scissors, was evidently participating in some ribbon cutting ceremony.

In fact, the walls of Phyllis's room were peppered with pictures of Miss Ware at a variety of public functions. The head of human services peered at Dolly from all sides, wearing a newspaper-ready smile.

"Did something happen at the Beautification Committee Christmas Party last night? Did you get some bad news?"

The girl on the bed turned her face away weakly. "Bad news! I guess you could call it that."

Phyllis was still wearing her red dress, Dolly realized. And come to think of it, she couldn't remember hearing the social scientist come in the other evening—Phyllis had stayed out all night!

"Where did you go last night, Phyllis?" Dolly quizzed the prone girl. "Who were you with?"

Phyllis pressed her lips together. "I won't tell you!"

Ramona came in, carrying the blue and white metal box with the red cross on the lid. She took Dolly's place on the edge of the bed and unwrapped the bloodstained towel. "This doesn't look *too* bad," she pronounced, peering closely at the wound. "I saw much worse at Metamora—we had a whole rash of wrist slitting one fall."

"You were with a woman," Dolly probed relentlessly. "Was it Miss Ware? Did something happen to her?"

The social scientist laughed a little hysterically. "Oh, Miss Ware is peachy!" she cackled. "Only I call her Winifred now—Winnie is in the pink!"

Dolly reeled, unable to believe the statistician's crush on the head of human services had at last been reciprocated. Apparently Ramona's mind was traveling down a similar path. "I know," guessed the street-smart girl. "You finally made your move, and Miss Ware turned you down." To Dolly she muttered, "That's the problem with these one-girl gals—they get no experience, good *or* bad." She swabbed some ointment on Phyllis's wrist as she spoke, and the girl winced.

"You're wrong!" she informed her listeners indignantly. "Winifred did *not* reject me. In fact, we've been an item for precisely twenty-six days!"

Dolly and Ramona exchanged mystified looks. Shouldn't the consummation of Phyllis's fondest dreams have sent the social scientist soaring, instead of plunging her into self-destructive despair?

Or was it just that after so many years of celibacy, the abrupt uncorking of their friend's libido had tipped the unbalanced girl over the edge?

"How did it start?" Dolly asked, trying to keep the suicidal girl talking. "And why was it such a big secret?"

"It was the week after Miss Watkins gave me my questionnaire results and warned me not to be so consumed by my career. I'd been feeling out of sorts anyway, so I accepted an invitation to attend the opening of a new warming hut that's part of the Parks Improvement Program."

Dolly couldn't help thinking that Phyllis's idea of cutting loose needed some work.

"Miss Ware was there. Something possessed me, and for the first time I told her how much working with her on the Dockside Commission had meant to me, and how I missed her pithy insights into Bay City politics. She said we ought to do something about that. She said she'd like to see more of me too!"

Phyllis's eyes took on a dreamy look. "The next few weeks were like nothing I'd ever known before. We met almost every night at a little chop suey place downtown. She suggested I join the Beautification Committee so we could see more of each other, since they'd made her honorary chairman of the Christmas party—"

"Did you go all the way?" interrupted Ramona eagerly.

Phyllis put her hand over her eyes as if to shield a memory too precious to share. "We used her assistant's apartment," the statistician said with some difficulty. "She said it was more convenient than her place in the suburbs, and she didn't want to come here for fear of people finding out about us. I thought at first she was just worried about what the mayor might think, discovering the head of human services in bed with zoning, but then she admitted . . ." Phyllis gulped. "I can't go on!"

"She had a girlfriend!" her more experienced friends chorused.

Phyllis looked at them wide-eyed, astonishment drying her tears. "How did you guess?"

"Never mind, finish your story," Dolly urged.

"I can't!" Tears began leaking from Phyllis's eyes again. "It's too awful!"

"I'm your housemother, Phyllis, you can tell me anything!" Dolly encouraged the heartbroken girl.

"It's better not to bottle it up," chimed in Ramona.

"She told me there was nothing between her and Fran, and that they hadn't loved each other in years!" The words came out in a rush. "She promised that after the holidays she'd break it off for good, and we could finally be together, in the open, and I could tell everyone! Then at the Beautification Christmas party, a human services secretary named Miss Olsen buttonholed me by the punch bowl and gave me an earful, all about how Miss Ware has made these promises before, and how she'll never leave Fran, and how I'm just the latest in a long— line." Phyllis's voice began to quaver. "Long line of girls who—Miss Ware keeps—stringing along—on—nothing but—empty promises!"

As soon as she'd squeezed out the last words, Phyllis turned on her side and sobbed as if her heart would break.

"That departmental Don Juana isn't worth the time of day, much less your tears," Dolly declared, full of wrath on behalf of her heartbroken friend.

Ramona added vengefully, "Winifred wants to keep your affair under wraps, huh? That's all the ammunition I need to make her sorry she ever tried to string you along!"

"You'll never understand, either of you!" cried the tormented bureaucrat. "It's not what she did that drove me to this, but the utter emptiness of my life! For a few weeks I really lived, for the first time—and now I don't even have the dream of Miss Ware to sustain me through the long days of statistical analysis!"

Dolly had an inkling of what her friend was going through. Phyllis hadn't just discovered her idol had feet of clay, but that she was made of Silly Putty through and through! Miss Ware had bounced off that pedestal never to return.

"You'll find someone worthier than Miss Ware," she comforted the sobbing statistician.

"I doubt it." Tears oozed from Phyllis's eyes and slid down the side of her face to soak the pillow. "I want to die!"

Ramona produced a pill and a glass of water. "Take this," she ordered the heartbroken girl.

Dolly recalled a scene from *A Single Candle*, when Dr. Dwight has to tell matriarch Olivia Kane that her dead husband has another family on the other side of town. "Even the most unbearable pain will pass," she quoted Dr. Dwight. "And in the end, you've only lost a false idol. The hollow in your heart will soon be filled by a real love!"

Phyllis swallowed the pill and lay back down as if she'd hardly heard her housemother. Dolly was disappointed—on the show, Dr. Dwight's advice had a more immediate effect. But perhaps Phyllis needed rest more than counsel right now.

The two girls left the sedated statistician lying on her bed and conferred in the hallway. "I hate to leave her alone in this state," Ramona fretted. "But I have to get to my job at the club soon."

"I'll ask Angelo to keep an eye on her," Dolly decided. "He's got a soothing presence." Maybe it would be breaking a bylaw or two, but this was an emergency! *Those pesky regulations!* Dolly mentally moved them to the top of her to-do list.

Ramona softly opened the door to Phyllis's room. "I'll sit with her until then."

Dolly peeked at her friend over Ramona's shoulder. The pallid girl lay with her eyes closed, as still as a corpse.

Thank heavens she's not one yet! thought Dolly. *Thank heavens I stopped her in time.* She murmured again the lines she'd heard Mrs. DeWitt quote earlier that afternoon:

> " *'Some noble work may yet be done,*
> *Not unbecoming something something something!'* "

Chapter 23

New Telephones

It was Friday morning, the day before Christmas Eve and the all-important benefit. In the kitchen, Dolly was doing the dishes and listening to the chatter of the girls in the dining room. For many of them, the holiday weekend had begun.

Phyllis came in, carrying her breakfast plate, with Angelo following her like a faithful sheepdog. Dolly noticed she hadn't finished her slice of egg and potato pie.

"Didn't you like the new dish?" Dolly asked, disappointed. "Angelo gave me the recipe."

"It was my grandmother's," Angelo added.

"It was delicious," said Phyllis dutifully. "I just don't have much of an appetite."

A week after the wrist-slashing incident, Phyllis was still down in the dumps. She'd assured her friends that her suicidal impulse was gone, but she was wan, low-spirited, and uninterested in life. Worst of all was her new cynicism. "What's the point of putting together pie charts?" she responded when Dolly asked her hesitantly when she planned to return to work. "Bay City bureaucrats are too busy bed-hopping to pay attention!"

Dolly and Ramona had removed all the pictures of

Miss Ware from the statistician's room while the girl was sedated. If only they could banish her from Phyllis's heart as easily!

"Do you want me to give you a manicure?" Angelo suggested. His solution to Phyllis's depression had been a series of beauty treatments, which Angelo believed could literally make a "new you" of the social scientist.

A ghost of a smile crossed Phyllis's face, as she answered, "You've polished my nails so often they're going to wear through."

Dolly tried to think of some occupational therapy for the dispirited girl. "Maybe you should check the costumes and props for tomorrow," she suggested. "See if there are any threads to clip or bell clappers to replace."

"All right," agreed Phyllis in her new, lackluster way.

Dolly watched her exit, Angelo hovering over her, and wished there was something more she could do. As the pair left, Beverly put her head through the doorway. "My friend Laura is here," she told Dolly.

Beverly had approached the landlady the other evening and said with a challenging air, "I have a friend interested in a room at the Arms."

"Why, that's great." Dolly had wondered at Beverly's attitude. "A nurse friend?"

"No, I met her through my church. She's a Negro girl, like me." Beverly had waited for Dolly's reaction.

"Did you think I would mind?" Dolly had asked, puzzled.

Beverly unbent. "Even progressive places like the Arms usually set quotas," she had told Dolly wisely. "So's they don't get 'overrun' with my kind of people."

"There's no quota here," Dolly had told her heartily, hoping this was true. She really had to work on those by-laws. "Bring on your friend!"

This would put the Arms at almost full occupancy.

That would be a feather in her cap at the trustees' meeting in January!

Now, Dolly undid her apron. She'd been about to start the gingerbread for tomorrow's reception, but first she'd get the new girl settled. It was shaping up to be another busy day!

She was still making mental lists and wondering if she needed more eggs for the eggnog when Beverly introduced her to the petite girl waiting in the lobby. "Dolly, this is Laura. I already wrote her a recommendation letter, and I've got presents to wrap before I go on duty, so I'll see you both later."

Dolly greeted the new girl warmly. "Glad to know you, Laura." Beverly's friend was an assured, attractive girl, and she looked around the lobby with a delighted expression. "What a lovely place!"

Dolly felt a little lift of pride. The lobby did look nice, especially since she'd redone the gold leafing on the doors. "Thanks," the landlady said modestly. "I intend to make over the individual rooms in the new year."

"I'm just happy to find something so convenient to my job, *and* affordable." Laura smiled as she pulled a sheaf of papers from her purse. "Here's my residency application."

"I see you're going to Bay City College," Dolly said, quickly scanning the meticulously filled out application. Laura was a few years older than Beverly and Jackie, and projected a mature confidence. In addition to the recommendation letter from Beverly, there was the requisite one from her minister.

"Just part time, at night," Laura replied. As Dolly began the tour, she explained that she worked for the Bay City Branch of the Federal Housing Authority as a clerk-typist during the day.

"It's a pretty heavy schedule," she confided. "And the

commute to the east side was just about killing me! I've started wondering if I can keep it up."

"You can do it," encouraged the housemother. "We had another girl here who got her law degree at Bay City College while working part time." It was ingrained habit, bragging about Janet and her academic success, but it gave Dolly a sudden pang of missing her old crowd.

When Dolly showed the new girl the dining room and explained about the breakfast included in the rent, Laura told her the Arms was "a dream come true." With a deprecatory smile, she added that her protective mother insisted on a respectable residence with proper supervision. "I don't know what trouble she thinks I can get up to." She laughed vivaciously as they climbed the stairs back to the lobby. "Busy as I am!"

Dolly led her to the repurposed visitors' parlor-cum-beauty salon. "You can entertain your visitors here or in the lounge," the landlady told her new tenant. "Angelo, our visitor, is available for free hair care Thursday afternoons."

"What a savings that would be!" exclaimed Laura. "Does he have a hot comb? Does he know how to relax and straighten hair?"

"If he doesn't, I'm sure he can learn," Dolly promised. "And this is the lounge."

The big room was, as usual, full of chaotic activity. Margie was rehearsing the dancing telephones, in costume at last. A group of girls were spray-painting pine cones silver, and Angelo was on his knees pinning the hem of Jackie's severe black gown while Phyllis stood by listlessly holding the pincushion.

Dolly introduced Laura to the sewing trio, nearly drowned out by Margie's exasperated, "Girls, girls, I *know* the phone costumes are heavy. That's why we're practicing in them!"

Laura was looking at Phyllis starry-eyed. "You're

Phyllis Densher? *The* Phyllis Densher, who wrote the policy paper on Dockside demographics?" She clasped her hands together almost prayerfully. "Why, you're my idol! We studied your paper in my sociology class!"

For the first time in days, a spark of interest kindled in Phyllis's face, as she contemplated the pretty girl looking at her with glowing eyes. "Are you interested in zoning regulations?" she asked.

Laura explained again about her job and night school, adding that she aspired to a career in public policy. "I'd love to ask you about your experience sometime, if you're not too busy," she said shyly.

Phyllis could never say no to a request for aid. "Of course," she said instantly. "I'm happy to share what I know."

Dolly decided not to interrupt this promising conversation. "I just remembered, I left something in the oven," she fibbed. "Here's your key, Laura. Phyllis, will you show Laura her room?"

She left the lounge, more than satisfied with her new tenant. Dolly didn't need a minister's recommendation to convince her that Laura was going to fit in just fine!

The sight of Netta coming down the stairs cast a damper on the landlady's cheerful mood. Dolly was fed to the teeth with the progressive teacher, especially after Netta's reaction to Phyllis's "accident" as they were calling it. Netta had lectured the depressed statistician on the perils of paying too much attention to petty personal problems, and then tried to persuade the distraught girl to join her in the "Experiment in Living." "It'll be just the thing to shake you out of yourself!" she'd assured her.

Now, as Dolly turned away, Netta called her back. "I'd like my deposit, please. I've moved everything and cleaned out my room."

"I'll write you a check now," retorted Dolly.

But after she gave Netta the check, the teacher put a placating hand on Dolly's arm. "I don't want to leave on bad terms," she told the landlady earnestly.

Dolly looked at her friend of almost ten years and something in her softened. In a surge of holiday sentiment, she asked, "Why do you have to leave at all, Netta?" She pretended to adjust the tinsel on the Christmas tree as she spoke. "What have you got against the Arms, besides Ramona moving in?"

Netta gestured impatiently. "It's not really Ramona, or any one thing. I just want to escape a world where everyone's so bent on material things and pushing ahead in life, always worrying about promotions and finding the perfect girlfriend. I don't belong here anymore—I couldn't care less if the lounge television gets a better picture, or if the doors get gold leafed, or more telephones are installed!" Netta's voice rose. "There must be more to life!"

Dolly listened attentively to this heartfelt cry, which echoed in many ways the struggle she'd undergone since her soap opera character was strangled.

"Listen, I get you," the landlady said earnestly. "It's like that poem about noble purposes—"

But before she could quote the appropriate verse, a blast of cold air made them both turn. It was a deliveryman, with a handcart full of boxes.

"Delivery for Ramona Rukeyser," he said.

Dolly signed his clipboard, examining the stack of boxes out of the corner of her eye.

"What on earth are they?" asked Netta suspiciously.

"Telephones," the deliveryman replied. "Merry Christmas!"

"Noble purpose!" sniffed Netta. "I'll see you later, Dolly."

The idealistic schoolteacher almost bumped into Miss Watkins, who entered the lobby as Netta exited.

"Merry Christmas," the career counselor called after Netta. "Merry Christmas, Dolly," she greeted the landlady gaily, shaking the snow off her fur-trimmed boots. "I have the results of your PPA, and there are some most interesting indications!"

"Just a sec, Miss Watkins," Dolly excused herself. "I've got to ask Ramona what she thinks she's doing with all these phones!"

Too impatient to wait for the elevator, Dolly ran up the stairs, taking them two at a time like a teenage girl. She'd never get to her gingerbread at the rate things were going!

She paused for breath on the fourth-floor landing and glanced automatically down the corridor. Kay was coming out of her room. "Hi, Dolly," the clarinetist greeted her casually. At that moment, Arlene's door opened and the sleek scenic designer emerged. "Hello, Dolly!" she said warmly. "I was just coming to look for you!"

Kay stiffened perceptibly, and Arlene shot a covert glance at the clarinetist.

Dolly looked at the two girls, so different from each other. Kay's red head and freckled face made her weak in the knees and melted her stomach; she felt like an underdone pancake with a liquid center every time she looked at the clarinet player.

But Arlene was so lovely and troubled, the housemother side of Dolly couldn't bear to hurt her. Her polished sheen reminded the landlady of an out-of-season peach you purchased at the supermarket; you couldn't believe something that looked so perfect wouldn't taste good, and you wondered if it just needed time to ripen.

Each was so attractive, in her own way, to Dolly. She

didn't want to hurt either of them; and she hated to see the growing animosity between them.

It was a doozy of a dilemma, and Dolly decided to duck it, darting up the stairs. "Can't stop, gals. I've got to find Ramona and ask her about some phones!"

She pounded on the jazz club hostess's door. "Ramona," she called, "wake up! Did you order twenty-five phones?"

The door behind her opened. Dolly turned to find Ramona framed in Jackie's doorway, wearing a pink satin dressing gown that belonged to Maxie. "They're here already?" the extravagant girl yawned. "Darn it, I meant them for a Christmas surprise."

"Pretty expensive surprise!" said Dolly.

"I took the money out of that little tin box." Ramona laughed merrily. "No kidding, I counted up the cash and I realized that we can cover the taxes and get our telephones too!"

"Ramona!" Dolly scolded. "You can't go spending that money just because you feel like it! It's not your decision to make. Give me the rest of it right now, so I can deposit it in the bank where it belongs."

"I'm sorry." Ramona was repentant. "I guess I just went a little crazy the other day, when I counted up the moola we'd collected."

She went past Dolly and pulled out the drawer of her nightstand. "Wait till you see all that green, you'll get giddy too!" she gloated as she unlocked the money box and opened the lid.

Dolly looked inside. The box was empty.

Chapter 24

Criminal Behavior

"It's gone!" Ramona stared down at the box in disbelief. "Where'd it go? It was all there last night!"

"Did you take it out of the box for safekeeping?" Dolly asked, trying to be practical as prickles of panic crawled over her like ants at a picnic.

"Did I?" Ramona opened her bureau drawer and pushed the piles of frilly lingerie around anxiously. Dolly joined her in the search, digging through drawers, looking inside shoes, even shaking out the sprigged sheets on the bed. Each time they came up empty the landlady felt a screw turn in her stomach, tightening her tense nerves. Ramona kept repeating, "It's *got* to be here somewhere!" opening and closing drawers aimlessly, feeling under her mattress, and even climbing on a chair to look in the light fixture.

Finally, as Ramona rummaged through her nightstand for the third time, Dolly ordered her to stop. "Let's use our heads," she suggested tersely. "When did you last see the money?"

Ramona sat on the edge of her torn-up bed, the mattress askew on the box spring. "Late last night at Club Lucky. I spotted a horn player, a friend of Kay's who'd promised to buy a pair of tickets. I reminded him, and he gave me a ten-spot and told me to keep the change. I remember putting the money in the box."

"And that was the last time?" Dolly prodded.

"Wait! Come to think of it—" Ramona flushed and bit her lip.

"Well?"

"I opened the box again a little later—not for money but something else," the girl said reluctantly.

"Something else?" Dolly was bewildered. "What else were you keeping in the box?"

"Cigarettes." Ramona tried to look innocent. "You know how cigar stores keep their stogies in special boxes? Well—"

All at once, Dolly understood. "You've been pushing tea at Club Lucky! Oh, Ramona! Why can't you keep away from that filthy weed?"

Ramona wilted. "This is the last time, I swear!" she wailed. "It's only because I'd invested my last dime on a shipment in San Francisco, and then when those bozos threatened me and I had to scram—"

The sordid story poured out. Tired of cocktailing in San Francisco, Ramona had reentered the reefer racket, only to run into trouble when a rival turned territorial. The frightened girl had gone on the lam, heading for the only refuge she could think of. The remorseful drug peddler told Dolly that she'd resolved to turn over a new leaf after a counseling session with Miss Watkins, only to succumb to the temptation of easy money once more.

"It wasn't just for me—it was for the Arms, too!" Ramona defended herself. "When you told me about that trustee's threat, I couldn't sit on my stash any longer! Besides," she reasoned, "I had to get rid of the stuff somehow—was I supposed to just hand it out for free?"

Dolly controlled her anger and disappointment with a

superhuman effort. "Are you sure that was the last time you opened the box? Selling someone a reefer cigarette?"

"Yes, I'm sure," declared Ramona. "Then I came back here, but I didn't go right to my room, I went to the kitchen, to find something to eat."

Dolly's lips tightened. Ramona probably needed a snack after sampling her own wares. Who knew where the fuzzy-headed pusher might have put the money?

"In fact." Ramona put a hand over her mouth. "Oh, Dolly, I forgot the box on the kitchen counter, and I had to come back down for it!"

"Wasn't the box locked?"

"I *think* so." Ramona's reply did not inspire Dolly with confidence. She remembered that just a little while ago when Ramona had crossed the corridor to her own room, she hadn't needed her key. An unlocked door wasn't unusual for the Arms. But a money box holding several hundred dollars!

"Where do you keep the key?" questioned Dolly.

"In my purse." They both looked at the purse sitting on Ramona's nightstand. Dolly felt something crumble inside her. Anyone, anyone in the Arms could have taken the money without even exerting any effort!

"Wait!" Ramona jumped up and went to the closet. "My hidey-hole." Her voice was muffled as she knelt on the floor and pushed shoes aside. Dolly felt her hopes rise as she watched Ramona pry up a loose floorboard with her nail file, revealing a secret storage space. Ramona felt around, and her face fell. "I thought for sure—" she muttered.

Something snapped inside Dolly. She seized Ramona and dragged her from the closet. "How could you have been so careless?" she cried, shaking her like a Raggedy Ann doll. "Don't you see what this means? Now we have no money to pay the taxes! I'll be fired, the Arms will be razed to the ground, and Mrs. Putney-Potter will put up some antiseptic housing project in its place!"

"I can take back the phones," gasped Ramona, her teeth rattling in her head.

"You've ruined everything!" Dolly dropped the shaken girl on her bed. "Feeding Mrs. DeWitt the gin, driving Netta away—why, I could go to jail!" Slamming out of Ramona's room, Dolly ran down the stairs hardly knowing where she was going.

In the lobby Miss Watkins was chatting to Kay as the Sisterhood of Swing carried their music stands into the lounge. Beverly was rearranging the presents under the tree. The door to the lounge opened, and Jackie came out. "What do you think of my dress?" she asked, twirling around.

"You look like you're going to a funeral," Dolly told her brusquely, and the young girl's face fell. At the sound of the tinkling piano and the voices of the girls practicing Angelo's "Bells Medley," the landlady ground her teeth. "Haven't they learned that stupid song yet?"

"Why, Dolly!" Miss Watkins looked at her closely. "Aren't you feeling well?"

"Didn't my PPA reveal a penchant for foul tempers?" Dolly snarled.

"Dolly, the kids are doing their best. Don't take your bad mood out on them." Kay's voice was disapproving.

"We all know the holidays can be full of headaches, especially for a housemother," Miss Watkins began gently.

Beverly looked up from under the tree, where she was placing her present. "And all the holiday drinking doesn't help," she put in her two cents. "I hope you don't put any liquor in the eggnog tomorrow."

"Can't you leave off your preaching for a single second?" Dolly's voice was loud in the suddenly quiet room. "Or fine, you want everyone on the wagon? Is that what

you want for Christmas? Okay, your highness! After all,
I'm just the old housemother, with nothing better to do
than kowtow to your convictions! I'll play Carrie Na-
tion, if it'll make you happy!"

Under the appalled gaze of the girls, Dolly tore
through the pile of presents under the tree until she found
the package she wanted. Ripping off the gaily striped red
and green wrapping paper and the card that said "To Ramona, from Dolly—stick to cocktails!" she took the bottle of gin from its gold box and smashed it against the
front desk as if she were christening an ocean liner.

The smell of alcohol and juniper berries filled the room,
and Dolly became aware of the circle of appalled and
frightened faces around her.

"I need some air," she muttered, and ran out the front
door.

Chapter 25

Mrs. Putney-Potter's Stooge

Dolly walked through the slushy streets of Bay City, hardly caring where she went. She barely noticed the cold that penetrated her heavy sweater and the icy puddles that soaked her loafers. She tried to slow the mad merry-go-round of doom-laden thoughts circling her brain. If only she could think straight! There had to be some solution to this wretched situation!

Everywhere were signs of holiday cheer. Gold and silver garlands wired in the shape of bells or stars hung from the light posts. The grocery store windows were plastered with red-lettered signs: GET YOUR CHRISTMAS TURKEY 41C/LB AND CRANBERRY JELLY ON SPECIAL. The streets were crowded with shoppers coming out of the stores clutching bulky bags and exchanging holiday greetings. On every corner were those ubiquitous Salvation Army Santas with their bright red collection buckets, ringing bells, endlessly ringing bells—

Dolly put her hands over her ears in impotent rage, wishing she could silence that insistent jangling. It wasn't fair! It wasn't fair! She'd worked so hard and had gotten so close! She wasn't asking for much—just a room in an old building and an unglamorous job no one else wanted. Why must even this simple dream be snatched away?

She fled the ringing bells and turned blindly up a quiet, tree-lined street. She shivered as the cold wind whistled through her inadequate clothing. Common sense told her she couldn't wander the icy streets of Bay City all afternoon. But neither could she bear to return to the Arms and announce to her girls that the benefit money was gone and the Christmas Capers a farce.

She passed a vacant lot surrounded by a chain-link fence. A large sign proclaimed ANOTHER PUTNEY PROJECTS DEVELOPMENT. Dolly stopped and stared at it.

I should pay a visit to Mrs. Putney-Potter—maybe if I tell her everything before she finds out about the missing money . . . The idea was born of desperation, but Dolly pounced on it. *Sure,* she told herself, pulling together the shreds of Ramona's old blackmailing scheme. *And after I've confessed the shortfall, I'll drop a few hints about the glove hoarding, and the cardsharping too—remind her we all have sins we need forgiven!*

As she headed for the bus stop with driven determination, a tiny voice inside her said, *And if worst comes to worst, I'll just throw myself on her mercy and hope the Christmas season is good for something!* Distasteful as the idea was, Dolly was willing to do anything to avert disaster.

The beleaguered landlady boarded a bus for Lakeside, grateful for the warmth. She dropped into the nearest seat and tried to pull herself together, wishing she'd run out of the Arms in more dressed-up duds. She smoothed her hair, grateful for Angelo's recent trim and tint, then pinched her colorless cheeks and bit her blue lips. It would never do to look forlorn and desperate!

Snatches of poetry and dialogue floated through her head as she got closer to Linden Lane. *Once more into the breach, dear girls!* ... *Better to have loved and lost than* ... *The paths of glory lead but to the* ... *'tis a far, far better thing I do* ... *You must pay the rent! But I can't pay the rent!*

None of this was any good. What would frighten or touch the real estate tycoon? What was Mrs. Putney-Potter's weak or soft spot?

Dolly rang the doorbell to the Putney-Potter mansion, dread and hope mixing queasily in the pit of her stomach. The maid ushered her into the elaborate entry hall, where the simpering mermaid still spouted her stream of water. Just like before, the maid disappeared down the corridor and then returned to tell Dolly that Mrs. Putney-Potter would see her in the study.

The real estate mogul was alone in the luxurious, leather-lined room, seated at an elaborate oak desk, writing busily. As Dolly approached, she saw that her nemesis was addressing Christmas cards.

"Sit down, Dolly." Mrs. Putney-Potter's voice was genial as she signed her name with a flourish. "What can I do for you?"

Dolly sat gingerly in the low chair. Mrs. Putney-Potter's desk was on a dais, forcing her visitors to look up at the woman behind the desk.

"I'm in a terrible bind, Mrs. Putney-Potter." Dolly's voice was low and humble. "The benefit tomorrow—you know about the Christmas Capers we're putting on over at the Arms?"

"Oh, yes, indeed." Mrs. Putney-Potter smiled, showing all her teeth. "I have my ticket and I'm looking forward to it."

Dolly's weak hope grew a muscle. "We—I've just discovered the money from the ticket sales is—is missing." The landlady swallowed. "Misplaced—maybe stolen, it doesn't really matter. The money's gone!"

Mrs. Putney-Potter remarked, "That was rather careless of you, Dolly." She licked an envelope and sealed it. "But all it means is you'll be without phones, just as you were before."

Dolly gulped again. This was the hard part. "No—not exactly. You see, the money was really to replace the tax money, which I used for some wood rot removal." There, the secret she'd kept from the trustee for so long was out. "I couldn't risk letting someone crash through the kitchen floor! You can see that, can't you?"

Mrs. Putney-Potter made a steeple of her fingers and looked at Dolly through half-closed eyes. "This is very serious, Dolly. You acted beyond your authority when you decided to use the tax money for repairs."

"I know, and I'm awfully sorry," Dolly said desperately. "I just—I just didn't want the board to shut down the Arms prematurely. All we need is a little time, and I know we'll make up the money! The rooms are almost all occupied now, and everything's finally spick-and-span—it would mean so much to so many girls if—"

Mrs. Putney-Potter was pitiless. "These details are beside the point. Financial malfeasance is a serious crime."

Dolly licked her lips nervously. "Well, we've all made mistakes—I mean, when you were a girl at the Arms, I'm sure you made a few boo-boos—at the card table, for instance—"

It was no good. Her weak threat missed its mark entirely.

"Yes, I made mistakes at the Arms." Mrs. Putney-Potter's voice was measured. "My biggest mistake was trying to fit in with those namby-pamby girls in the first place—them and their sentimental notions of sisterhood!"

Dolly saw that her hint had uncovered a hitherto hidden streak of resentment in the hard-hearted trustee!

"Even if I didn't stand to make a sizeable profit on the new housing project, my opinion would be the same. The Arms must go! It has no place in the modern world!"

Her voice rose vindictively, and Dolly listened with a kind of stunned sickness.

"It's actually quite comical, your coming to me like this." Mrs. Putney-Potter calmed down and leaned back in her leather chair, playing idly with her pen. "Did you really think that I, as a responsible trustee, would overlook the way you looted the tax account? And that's only the latest of your many mistakes. I've been watching you very closely, Dolly Dingle. You've perverted Mrs. Payne-Putney's original purpose—she never intended the Arms to be a refuge for the scum of society, yet you've welcomed both Puerto Rican hairdressers and tea-smoking criminals! You've even exceeded the Negro quota, which as the bylaws clearly state, limits the number of Negro tenants to five percent of the residence's population. And that's not all!"

The trustee rose to her feet, her face flushed with spiteful triumph. "There are reports of excessive drinking; late-night refrigerator raids; and rampant in-room eating, which everyone knows attracts vermin! The room inspection requirement has been disregarded, the curfew hour trampled, and girls have been counseled in deviance rather than moral rectitude!"

Mrs. Putney-Potter leaned over her desk toward Dolly, every word dripping with venom. "Oh, yes, there's plenty of evidence to convince the other trustees that the biggest mistake they ever made was letting you take Mrs. DeWitt's place! It's difficult to believe that anyone could be more incompetent than that gin-soaked, senile old woman, but you've risen admirably to the challenge!"

Mrs. Putney-Potter's every word was a lash, cutting into Dolly's very soul. "Someone's been twisting the truth and giving you a false impression of life at the Arms," she gasped. "Who's told you these lies?"

Mrs. Putney-Potter pressed a button on her desk, and when the maid appeared, she told her, "Ask Miss Sutton to step in."

Miss Sutton—did Mrs. Putney-Potter mean Arlene? Had the sensitive girl complained again about the cooking smell in 405? But if Arlene was unhappy, why hadn't she come to her housemother directly?

One glance at Arlene's guilty face and Dolly realized this was worse than a tenant complaint. "You're Mrs. Putney-Potter's stooge!" The horrified housemother could hardly speak. "You've been feeding her information all along!"

Arlene avoided Dolly's beseeching eyes. "Is this necessary?" she snapped at Mrs. Putney-Potter.

Dolly rose from her chair without realizing it. "You told Mrs. Putney-Potter about the disorganized paperwork! You took the phone off the hook! And you ratted on Angelo too! You skipped breakfast that morning to tell your tale here, without realizing that the girls had voted him in as a visitor! But why?"

Arlene threw herself on a leather club chair in mutinous silence.

"Arlene is actually an up-and-coming architect," Mrs. Putney-Potter told the duped landlady triumphantly.

"But every architect needs a patron if they want to see their plans realized!"

More pieces fell into place, snowballing into an avalanche of betrayal that crushed the hoaxed housemother. "You gave Mrs. DeWitt that gin! It *wasn't* Ramona, it was you, after you overheard Beverly warning me gin was poison for someone in her shape! You faked that television offer to try to get me out of town! Then you forgot all about it when you found out there was wood rot in the storeroom!"

As an architect, Arlene must have quickly put together the clues Dolly had dropped during her drunken discussion at Francine's. How could Dolly have believed that Arlene really wanted to share a bungalow with her in Hollywood? It was the kind of sentimental tripe she'd seen so much of in scripts from her old show. Suddenly the devastated landlady was struck by the most sickening revelation of all.

"You never had an insane girlfriend," Dolly whispered, heartsick. "I know now why it all sounded so familiar! It was a subplot from my old soap opera! Why— you've just been pretending to be interested in me!"

"She asked me more than once how much longer she'd have to play the love-struck tenant." Mrs. Putney-Potter twisted the serrated knife she'd plunged in Dolly's heart. "I'm afraid she didn't find it much fun."

What had Ramona once suggested about the twisted trustee? That she'd spent her childhood pulling the wings off flies?

"Stop it, Dora," Arlene said. "Isn't it enough that you've gotten your way?"

"And you must have taken the doll," Dolly continued dully. "But why? What was so important about it?"

Arlene shot Mrs. Putney-Potter a questioning glance,

and Dolly saw a shadow cross the unpleasant mogul's face. "Never mind that now." She pressed the button for the maid. "Go on back to the Arms and enjoy those telephones you've paid so dearly for. I suggest you make your first call to a lawyer!"

The maid came in. "Show Miss Dingle out," Mrs. Putney-Potter ordered.

Chapter 26

Christmas at Francine's

Dolly pushed open the door to Francine's and was greeted by the tinny sounds of "Silver Bells" playing on the jukebox. The music was almost drowned out by the rumble of chatter punctuated by raucous bursts of laughter, the clink of toasts, and the thump of drained glasses landing empty on the bar.

It was the season to be jolly at Francine's too. There was no escaping the holiday cheer. An artificial tree of silvery white stood by the jukebox, its plastic boughs draped with a few garlands. Overhead, a gold foil star hung from the light fixture, turning slowly in the smoky haze.

And the bar was packed. The twilight crowd had crowded in, this winter twilight, to swallow a little liquid courage before tucking their secret selves under their heavy winter coats and heading home for the obligatory holiday visit. "I wish we could spend Christmas together," Dolly overheard one girl say to another, as she squeezed through the crowd on her way to the bar, "but my family expects me."

Dolly glimpsed Sylvia at a table with a younger girl, and hastily changed direction, wedging herself into a spot at the other end of the bar. "HappyholidaysDollythe usual?" Jessie was pouring as fast as she spoke.

"Make mine whiskey," said Dolly. "A double." She tried to ignore the couple exchanging gift-wrapped boxes inches away from her. "Don't open it now," one cautioned the other. "I'll call you Christmas morning, and we'll open them together!"

One advantage to having a pushy stage mother with a gambling habit, now estranged: There were no inconvenient demands for holiday visits. What had she done last year? Dolly tried to remember, as she waited for her whiskey.

Oh yes; she and Mrs. DeWitt had shared a turkey breast from the deli with one or two other strays, eating in the kitchen, the radio tuned to carols. Later they'd moved to the lounge, drinking Dolly's homemade eggnog (well-laced with brandy) and putting together a jigsaw puzzle while the yule log flickered on the television. Tipsily, they'd taken off their socks, filled them with nuts and hard candies, and batted them about the floor like hockey pucks.

Dolly ducked her head to hide the sudden tears that pushed into her eyes, just as Jessie slid the glass of whiskey in front of her. There was no use getting maudlin about this whole mess.

She lifted her glass. "Here's to you, Ma!" she muttered.

"Silver Bells" had finally ended and the chattering voices sounded loud in the pause before the next tune began. It was "Jingle Bell Rock," and there was a whoop from the crowd. In her rush to the dance floor, one girl stumbled against Dolly, knocking the unhappy landlady off-balance so that her drink slopped over.

"Sorry," giggled the girl, before disappearing into the whirling crowd.

Dolly set down her glass, resisting the impulse to clap her hands over her ears. "That—goddamned—song!" she snarled instead. "I'd rather listen to nails on a chalkboard!"

A girl in a leather jacket turned and glared at Dolly. "You got a problem with Brenda Lee, Scrooge?"

"Why?" Dolly drew herself to her full height and sneered down at the biker girl. "Is she your best buddy, shortstop?"

The would-be tough girl glowered up at the hardpressed housemother. "Just because I'm not an overgrown lummox, like you, doesn't mean I'm not ready for a roughhouse!"

"Cool your tiny engine," Dolly ordered wearily. "As it happens, I like Brenda Lee fine—*I JUST CAN'T STAND THAT SONG!*"

"Then you must have a problem with Christmas!" The little leather girl was frothing with rage by this time. "No one knocks Christmas on my watch!"

She threw a punch at Dolly that did no real damage, except that another girl, backing away from the brawl, elbowed Dolly's glass of whiskey off the bar and sent it smashing to the floor.

"Enough!" Jill put down her tray to bounce the belligerent girl, grabbing the toughie's leather collar and hustling her through the crowd. "She insulted Christmas!" shouted the girl as Jill pushed her up the stairs.

Could this day get any worse? Dolly covered her ears, but she could still hear the endless idiotic refrain—*jingle bells, jingle bells, jingle bells!* It was as if some malevolent elf was pounding a kettledrum in her head.

"Sorry, Dolly." Jessie set another glass of whiskey in front of her. Dolly lifted the glass and swallowed its contents in one gulp. "Another!" she ordered.

A hand gripped her shoulder. "Dolly, I've been looking all over for you."

It was Miss Watkins, the persistent personnel professional. "I must talk to you about your Personality Penchant Assessment," she said earnestly.

"Not now, Miss Watkins," Dolly pleaded. *Where is that drink?*

"I could see you were upset earlier." Gently the professional advice-giver pried the unhappy landlady from the bar and led her to a table occupied by two girls. "I'm sorry, girls. I need this table for a little emergency counseling."

"Of course, Miss Watkins!" The two girls rose instantly and vanished. Miss Watkins sat down, and Dolly sullenly followed suit.

"I've sensed from the start that your reluctance to take the PPA stemmed from a common fear many women your age have—that it's too late to make any real changes in their life."

"No, I just thought it was a bunch of hooey!" Dolly hoped her rudeness would drive the dogged woman away. But Miss Watkins was impervious.

"Look—" Impatiently the career counselor swept aside the empty glasses and crumpled cocktail napkins, pulled a file folder from her leather satchel, and opened it up. "Subject is an independent thinker who requires no direction to accomplish an amount of work that often seems little short of miraculous." She looked up from the closely typed page to add with an air of suppressed excitement, "Mrs. Janska has just started grouping people with such characteristics under the label 'self-starter.' We think there's going to be a huge demand for them in the future."

The waitress deposited Dolly's whiskey and arched an

inquiring eyebrow at the counselor. "Nothing, thanks," she told Jill.

Jill retreated, and Miss Watkins went on. "Subject displays a unique combination of fine motor skills and sensitivity to social dynamics. A real people person. Retentive memory, eagerness to please, and uncertain ethics indicate success in the hospitality field. However, marked signs of selflessness and compassion—"

"Compassion?" Dolly interrupted in amazement, setting her whiskey down. "Your results have gone off the rails! I'll go along with social dynamics—I like a party as well as the next person—but I'm no bleeding heart like Phyllis and Netta!"

"Compassion," repeated Miss Watkins firmly. "Suggest subject should seek out an occupation with scope for caregiving. Subject should do well as concierge, occupational therapist, emergency shelter architect, or—listen to this, Dolly!—sorority housemother with carpentry as a sideline. So you see," the career counselor finished jubilantly, "your new position at the Magdalena Arms is one that you're peculiarly suited for!"

"Oh leave me alone!" Dolly was driven beyond all endurance. Every word Miss Watkins uttered was like salt in her wounds. "Don't you realize it's all over? I've messed up everything! Mrs. Putney-Potter is going to shut us down and build a project in our place. What does it matter if I've got this special self-starting ability when all I've started is the Magdalena Arms down the road to destruction?!"

"Surely it's not that dire, Dolly," Miss Watkins tried to stem the flood of self-reproach. "Come now, where's the cheery optimism and penchant for problem solving indicated here?" She tapped the sheets of paper.

But Dolly was beyond the reach of such appeals. She

swallowed the rest of the whiskey and coughed as the fiery liquid ran down her throat.

"I should have taken that job as Honey Bear on the General Jiggs kiddie show." She groaned. "At least I wouldn't have done so much damage!"

"Now, Dolly," the career counselor began, patiently persistent.

"Stop, Miss Watkins, just stop!" Dolly's voice rang out, and people turned to look at the two women curiously. "Can't you see this is no longer a case for counseling?" She turned away from the competent career woman and signaled for another drink. "I wish I'd never moved into the Arms!"

Miss Watkins stood up. "Do you really mean that?" she asked, her soft voice holding a hint of steel. "Have you even considered what that would mean?"

Dolly ignored her. She signaled for another drink, interested only in alcohol's easy escape into oblivion.

The landlady didn't see Miss Watkins depart. The hopeless wish repeated itself like a regretful refrain with each sip of whiskey. *If only I'd never moved to the Arms! If only I'd never moved to the Arms!*

At last the oblivion she sought climbed out of her glass and swallowed her whole.

Chapter 27

The Long Walk Home

Dolly lifted her head slowly. She must have fallen into a kind of stupor, her cheek pillowed on the table in a puddle of whiskey. She'd been drinking on an empty stomach again.

She sat up, feeling weary and aching in every joint. What to do now? She still couldn't face going back to the Arms. She ought to get something to eat, but she was so tired.

Her eyes traveled over the crowd at Francine's. The jovial holiday mood had dissipated and the women remaining were hard-featured and humorless, drinking with a businesslike efficiency that had nothing to do with pleasure.

Dolly spied Sylvia, at another table, still talking to her new friend. The mixed-up matron wanted it both ways, one foot in the twilight world, one foot in the suburbs. Dolly rubbed her temples. Who was she to criticize? Right now she needed a favor from Francine's weekend barfly.

She got up, lurching a little. The whiskey had left her heavy-footed and slightly dizzy. She stumbled past the unsmiling patrons to Sylvia's side.

"Sylvia, can I use your room at the Prescott? I can't go back to the Arms—and I need to lie down so badly—figure out what to do—"

Slowly, Sylvia turned her predatory, hooded eyes from the young girl opposite her to Dolly. The object of Sylvia's pursuit was fresh-faced and dewy beyond belief. Dolly was surprised Jill had allowed this obviously underage girl into the bar. The teenager was mesmerized by Sylvia, like a bunny before a cobra.

"Please, Sylvia," Dolly begged.

"Sorry, sweetheart," drawled Sylvia, flicking her eyes over Dolly indifferently. "I have a date."

Baffled and hurt, Dolly turned away. It wasn't like Sylvia to be so dismissive. Usually she was eager to introduce acquaintances to her latest discoveries, parading before them her familiarity with the gay world.

Dolly caught a glimpse of a group of girls heading up the steps to the street. Was that Pam? Was she out with Lois and Janet? Instinctively Dolly hurried after them, but when she reached the street, they were gone. She shivered in the icy wind, unable to decide what to do next. Maybe a hot dog from the little bean wagon down the block would help her think.

"Help!" came a shrill scream. "Help, help!"

It was all strangely familiar. Dolly pounded down the block toward two struggling figures. Her hand curled around the switchblade in her pocket, but her feet were like lead, and despite her hurry, the block stretched interminably before her. She was a few feet away from the pair, when one of them plunged a knife into the other with an underhand thrust. "I told you not to make fun of Christmas!"

The attacker was the leather-clad toughie from Francine's. "No!" Dolly gasped. The leather girl pulled out her knife and let the limp body fall to the ground. Her running footsteps faded away as Dolly fell to her knees beside the stabbed girl. "Jackie!" She gasped. "Oh, no!" With shaking hands she smoothed the girl's dark hair back from her forehead. Her young friend stared at her for a second with unseeing eyes, and then slowly her eyelids closed.

"Hang on, Jackie," Dolly begged. "I'll get help!"

The pool of blood pouring from the gaping wound in Jackie's side stained the knees of Dolly's ski pants. She pulled herself to her feet. Where was Nurse Beverly? Or Netta with her first aid kit?

Careening around the corner, the frantic housemother spied a police car, lights flashing. Dolly ran up to the uniformed patrolman. "There's a girl—over on Forty-eighth, stabbed!" she panted, trying to pull the policeman back to Jackie.

"I'll radio for an ambulance," he said. "But I can't leave my prisoner. We just caught a big league pusher!"

He pointed at the backseat of the squad car. Ramona sat there, dyed brown hair disheveled, handcuffs on her wrists.

Dolly banged impetuously on the glass window. "You know first aid!" she cried. "Get out! Get out!" Ramona turned her head. She was as high as a kite. Her pupils were like tiny pinpoints in her eyes as she stared at Dolly blankly. The landlady felt herself lifted up, her feet dangling in the air. It was the policeman, hoisting her away from the squad car. He deposited her a few yards away.

"Stop your overacting," he admonished sternly. "That punk isn't worth your worry!"

Dolly ran back to the street where Jackie lay bleeding. Angelo was standing on the corner in a pair of tight pants, but just as Dolly opened her mouth to call his name, he looked around furtively and then climbed swiftly into a blue sedan that had stopped at the curb.

"Angelo!" Dolly called helplessly, as the car pulled away.

But where was Jackie? Her body was gone. Had Dolly confused 47th with 48th Street? The unhinged landlady turned in a bewildered circle. When she saw the flashing red lights of an ambulance at the end of the block, she felt relieved. Two men were loading a stretcher into the back. The patrolman *had* radioed as he'd promised.

I'm so tired, Dolly realized, loping wearily to the ambulance. *I'll ride to the hospital with Jackie and maybe I can lie down while they work on her.* "Wait!" The medic was about to close the ambulance doors. "She's my friend. I'm coming too," she said.

But when she started to climb into the ambulance she saw that the girl on the stretcher wasn't Jackie but Phyllis—Phyllis, white and lifeless.

"But—I stopped her suicide attempt last week!" Dolly clutched at the ambulance driver's sleeve. "What happened?"

"Third time's the charm." He spat his chewing gum on the curb. "We're taking this one to the morgue—no ride alongs." He hopped into the cab, and they squealed away.

No sirens, Dolly thought numbly. *Because it's not a matter of life and death anymore.*

Miss Watkins stood up from a tenement stoop. "Don't you see, Dolly?" she said in her maddeningly reasonable way. "Jackie's dead because you weren't there to save her, or Phyllis either. Ramona never got her old room back, and Angelo did what he needed to survive, even if it meant putting on those uncomfortably tight trousers."

"I'm not his tailor," Dolly argued. "You—you put something in my whiskey that's got me hallucinating! What was it? Dexamyl? Benzedrine? A Miltown?"

Miss Watkins just smiled enigmatically. "When you're ready to discuss your PPA results, I'll be in my office." She walked briskly away.

Suddenly, the landlady wanted desperately to be back at the Arms. She forgot that she'd slammed out of it in a fury and shunned it all day. It was her haven again. She hurried through the dark streets, the looming tenements peopled with shadowy, half-threatening figures. The leather girl was out there, Dolly knew, maybe hunting the unhappy housemother.

Mrs. Putney-Potter passed her, pushing the old baby carriage and singing "Jingle Bells." Dolly wanted to see what was inside the carriage, but she had to get to the Arms. She was possessed by a gnawing anxiety that only the sight of the old building would soothe.

As she turned the corner, she heard a thunderous crack and saw the wrecking ball swing back from the hole it had smashed in the Magdalena Arms' brick facade. The crane swiveled, readying itself for another blow.

Crane operators and demolition crews don't work at night! Dolly was confused. Didn't their union rules make it prohibitively expensive? Phyllis would explain it to them—she knew the labor laws—

But Phyllis was dead. Phyllis would never explain labor laws or zoning regulations to anyone again.

A figure was walking away from the Arms, coming toward Dolly. She carried her suitcase in one hand and her clarinet case in the other. "Kay," breathed Dolly. It was a relief to find her dependable old friend, still standing in the midst of these inexplicable horrors. "What on earth is happening? Where are you going?"

Kay looked at Dolly in irritation. "It's obvious, isn't it?

The Magdalena Arms is being destroyed. I can't afford to stay in Bay City on what I make with music, so I'm going home to the farm. I'll give the neighbor kids piano lessons and help with the hoeing."

"You can't leave, Kay!" Dolly cried. "I love you!"

"Love me?" A strange smile twisted Kay's lips. "You don't even know me, sister."

Chapter 28

An Old Friend

"That's not true!" Dolly sat bolt upright in bed. Sun was streaming through the curtains, and someone was singing in the shower.

It had all been a dream! Dolly had never felt so relieved in her life. "No one is dead," she said aloud. The Magdalena Arms was still standing. *And it will keep on standing*, the landlady vowed, *if I have to hold back the wrecking ball with my bare hands!*

She'd wasted precious time, wallowing in self-pity and drinking herself into a stupor. Dolly remembered now the look Mrs. Putney-Potter and Arlene had exchanged the other night, when she'd accused Arlene of stealing the doll. That doll was the vicious trustee's weak spot. If she could just figure out what Mrs. Putney-Potter had been doing with that doll!

In her dream, the trustee had been pushing a baby carriage. Dolly shuddered, just thinking of the strange nightmare. Beverly was right about the health risks of hard liquor! She was never, ever going to drink on an empty stomach again. The disappearing money and the discovery of Arlene's duplicity had knocked Dolly for a loop, but she'd certainly given that depraved duo a hand, trying to drown herself in booze, and then sleeping it off here in . . .

Where was she, anyway? Dolly looked around. The twin bed next to hers had been slept in, the bureau had a purse on it, and there was a picture of a windmill and two cows on the wall. Clothes were strewn on the straight-backed chair, and the fire exit diagram on the back of the door looked oddly familiar.

Of course! Dolly snapped her fingers triumphantly. She was in the Prescott Hotel, and that meant—

The bathroom door opened, and Sylvia came out, toweling her hair. "Dolly, darling, you're awake," she greeted her guest. "How do you feel? You've been making the most horrible noises the last half hour!"

"Sylvia!" Dolly felt a wave of fondness for her fellow old-timer. In the bright light of this winter day, Sylvia looked herself again—an ordinary, attractive, older housewife, not some hooded cobra woman. "You're a sight for sore eyes," Dolly couldn't help complimenting her.

"Why, thanks." Sylvia combed her hair in front of the mirror looking pleased. "Maybe it's love!"

Dolly was preoccupied with the piece of her life that had gone missing between the whiskey at Francine's and this bed in the Prescott. "I'm awfully glad you took me in, but how did I get here?"

"You don't remember?" Sylvia was plucking her eyebrows now, with a pair of silver tweezers. "After you stumbled over to our table, practically falling and asking if you could lie down somewhere, we thought we'd better take you with us. We practically carried you!"

So it wasn't all a dream. "Who's we?" Dolly asked. She realized that the shower in the bathroom was still going. Someone turned the water off, whistling "Jingle Bells." Dolly looked at the clothes on the chair. Under a pair of blue jeans, a leather jacket peeped out.

"Why, me and Terry," Sylvia told her. "Do you know Terry?"

Terry came out of the bathroom wearing only a white T-shirt. She turned red when she saw Dolly sitting up in bed and hastily pulled on her blue jeans.

She was the leather-clad girl who had defended Christmas, punching Dolly in Francine's the previous night.

Now she strode over to the bemused landlady and stuck her hand out. With Dolly sitting in bed, Terry was a trifle taller. "Sorry about yesterday," she said gruffly. "I get a little carried away with the holiday spirit sometimes."

"That's all right." Dolly clasped the pocket butch's hand in both of hers. "I was acting like a real Scrooge!"

"I've ordered us all breakfast," Sylvia announced. "I hope everyone's hungry!"

Dolly was starving. "If the bathroom's free, I'll freshen up." She jumped out of bed, suiting action to word.

It was funny how her subconscious had twisted and distorted people into a nightmare version of their real selves. Dolly pondered the queer dream as she splashed her face and finger combed her short hair. It had turned Terry into a thug and transformed the fun-loving crowd at Francine's into a bunch of sullen, unhappy women who drank alone.

Thank heavens my friends aren't really pushers and hustlers. Dolly dabbed fruitlessly at the whiskey stain on her sweater. *Or at least,* she amended, remembering Ramona, *they're good eggs at bottom.* Not like the sinister types who had populated her bad dream.

The only thing real about that nightmarish world was the confession she'd made to Kay. *I am in love with Kay!* Dolly felt stunned anew by this earth-shattering realization. *I think I've been in love with her for quite a while!*

How could she have been so oblivious? Why hadn't

she understood what the irresistible pull she always felt in the presence of the carefree clarinetist really meant? Just because Kay didn't fit the pattern she'd planned for her life, she'd wasted all these weeks in her misguided pursuit of Arlene—Arlene! That girl was a liar and a cheat, not even a real scenic designer! All this time Dolly had been chasing a figment of her own imagination.

"Breakfast, Dolly," Sylvia called.

Dolly returned to the bedroom, where Sylvia and Terry were already gathered cozily around a wheeled cart covered with food. The hungry landlady fell on her eggs and bacon, barely remembering to use silverware. Fortunately, Sylvia had ordered lots. In addition to the eggs and bacon, there were sausages, pancakes, fried potatoes, toast, oatmeal, and a lone English muffin, which Sylvia claimed for herself. There was orange juice and coffee; Sylvia sipped a cup of tea. Terry handed her a packet of sugar, and they smiled at each other adoringly.

"How did you two meet?" Dolly asked curiously. Terry wasn't Sylvia's usual type. "Was it just last night, or—I mean, how long have you known each other?" She tried to backpedal from her tactless inquiry, but the two lovebirds just laughed.

"We met last week at Gruneman's department store," Sylvia told her. "Can you believe it? After all these years of haunting Francine's!"

"It was meant to be, baby." Terry leaned over and kissed the tip of Sylvia's nose.

"I was in the toy department, shopping for a doll for my daughter," Sylvia explained. "She's really too old for dolls, but I love the toy department."

"And I've been working at Gruneman's as a stocker," Terry took up the story. "Christmas help, hired for the rush. I was pushing a loaded cart—"

"And she ran straight into me!" Sylvia laughed gaily. "Of course she had to stop and apologize."

"Of course!" Terry grinned.

"And we got to talking..."

"I told her that her kid might like roller skates better than a doll."

"And we made a date to meet at Francine's on Friday. She wouldn't let me take her to lunch."

"I hated having her see me in that Gruneman's smock I had to wear," Terry confessed.

"And tonight"—Sylvia reached for Terry's hand—"we're coming to the Christmas Capers." She turned to Terry. "You'll get to meet my daughter, Patricia. I know you two will love each other!"

Dolly's fork full of eggs froze on the way to her mouth. The benefit! She'd completely forgotten!

"Cripes, what time is it?" She pushed back her chair. "I've still got the gingerbread to make and the eggnog to brew!"

Chapter 29
Christmas Surprise

When Dolly ran up the cracked marble steps, pulled open the Magdalena Arms' burnished brass doors, and burst into the lobby, the grand hallway was beginning its transformation into a theater. Angelo was on top of a stepladder, a length of black drapery tucked under one arm. Sue, Margie, and Ilsa were setting up folding chairs for the expected audience. "Closer," Ramona instructed them, clipboard in hand. "We're expecting over a hundred." Then she spied Dolly and the clipboard clattered to the floor.

"We've been so worried—"

"I'm so sorry I snapped—"

"*I'm* the one who's sorry—"

The two friends embraced as Angelo called excitedly, "Dolly's back!"

Suddenly, girls were pouring out of the lounge and pounding down the stairway, emerging from every crevice, crack, and cranny to surround their prodigal landlady in an excited, chattering crowd.

"Ilsa—Margie—Sue!" Dolly wanted to touch them all. "Jackie!" She hugged her young protégée. "You look so—so wonderfully healthy!"

Jackie extricated herself, laughing. "Careful! I have a little cold, and I don't want you to catch it!"

"Netta! You're still here!"

The progressive teacher was part of the beaming circle of tenants. "I came back when I heard you were missing," she confessed, with one of her rare, sweet smiles.

"Phyllis!" Dolly nearly strangled the suicidal social scientist in a fierce embrace. "Oh, Phyllis!"

"Where have you been?" Phyllis scolded. "We were all worried sick!"

"She had us calling all the hospitals and even the jail," Laura chimed in.

"I've been to hell and back, and yet never more than a few blocks away," confessed Dolly. "And I've learned that money doesn't matter so long as a girl has good friends! Where's Ramona?" The stage manager had disappeared, to Dolly's disappointment. She especially wanted to share her new insight with Ramona.

The group around her was snickering and guffawing. "Money doesn't matter!" Sue elbowed Angelo. "Get a load of that!"

Dolly couldn't interpret the winks and nudges and general air of suppressed excitement until Ramona returned, carrying the metal money box. "Look!" She opened the lid, and Dolly's eyes popped out of her head. The box was stuffed to overflowing with cash.

"You found the misplaced money!"

"No, no," chorused a half dozen girls. "It's all come in since yesterday—everyone contributed," Margie told her. "Once Ramona explained—"

"Everyone!" echoed Ramona. "Not just the girls here, but people in the neighborhood like Luigi—"

"I put the deposit check in," Netta told her. "I'm not moving after all. I think the Magdalena Arms is an even more interesting experiment in living than the place the DTs are putting together."

Ramona patted her ex fondly on the shoulder, and Dolly realized that in the course of the crisis her two old friends had finally made their peace.

Phyllis smiled. "I quit the Bay City Beautification Committee and put in my January dues."

"It wasn't much, but I put in what I'll save on carfare this week," Laura added a little shyly.

Happy tears pushed into Dolly's eyes. A verse of Tennyson came into her mind:

> *Ring out the grief that saps the mind*
> *For those that something something something*
> *Ring out the feud of rich and poor*
> *Ring in redress to all mankind.*

She could barely follow Ilsa and Margie, who were chattering excitedly about how as secret Santas they'd bought unsuitable presents for each other. "I got her a flowered ponytail holder and then she had Angelo cut her hair!" mousy Margie was bubbling over.

"And I got her a new wristwatch strap, but turns out she lost her watch!"

"And so we decided to take the presents back to Gruneman's and give the refund money to Ramona!" they chorused.

A gust of cold air announced another group of girls. "Are we too late?" asked Pamela anxiously.

Lois added, "We had to stop by the bank on the way here." She looked around the lobby in surprised admiration. "Dolly, you've done wonders with the old place!"

Janet and Rhoda were right behind them. Janet announced, "Rhoda had quite an interesting inmate yesterday—an accountant at Putney Projects."

Rhoda took up the tale. "She was arrested for being drunk and disorderly, and directing traffic in a Santa suit. Before she sobered up, she let slip some interesting items about how Putney Projects pushes its bids."

Janet finished, "I'd say there's a distinct possibility Putney will withdraw the bid for the housing project, rather than face a corruption scandal!"

"Ohhh!" cried the girls.

"Listen to this." Ramona turned away from a Western Union delivery boy who'd followed the former tenants in. She was holding up a slip of paper. "It's a telegram from Paris!"

"Shhh," Jackie quieted the crowd.

In the ensuing silence, Ramona read, "'Buffalo Gals Western restaurant huge success. Stop. Why didn't you say you needed money sooner? Stop. Am instructing Della to turn over Knock Knock receipts for December through May. Stop. Yee-haw. Stop. À bientôt. Stop. Maxie, Lon and Stella.'"

"Ahhh!" The girls burst into spontaneous applause, and Dolly had to wipe her eyes again as Ramona exulted, "Do you realize how much money that will be? Holidays are boom times for bars like the Knock Knock!"

Her vision blurred, Dolly saw the double doors of Mrs. DeWitt's suite open, and to her surprise, Beverly emerged, pushing a wheelchair. "Ring out the old, ring in the new," intoned a familiar voice.

> "'Ring happy bells across the snow;
> The year is going, let him go;
> Ring out the false, ring in the true.'"

Dolly fell to her knees as Mrs. DeWitt rolled up next to her. "Harriet," she said in a voice choked with feeling. "Harriet, you're home!"

Mrs. DeWitt beamed at her fondly. "Yes, Dolly, but you're still in charge! I intend to concentrate on my poetic compositions."

Dolly looked up at Beverly. "I'm awfully sorry I lost my temper. You're dead right about alcohol's ill effects!"

The crusading nurse met her halfway. "Sometimes I push people too hard," she admitted. "I get impatient with how slow things change."

Ramona clapped her hands. "Okay, kids, back to work! We still have a show to put on." She thrust the money box at Netta. "You be in charge of this," she said, with a slight shudder. "You're the responsible type."

Dolly looked around. Where was Kay? Why hadn't she been part of this festive gathering? Despite her happiness, the full-fledged landlady had an unfinished feeling. Her return would be incomplete until she told her fourth-floor friend how she really felt. "Have you seen Kay?" she asked Ramona.

"Not since breakfast," Ramona answered absentmindedly, her eyes on her crew. "Angelo! Get someone to help you!"

Dolly rose to her feet irresolutely. "I ought to start the gingerbread," she murmured.

"I'll take care of the baked goods," Lois proposed, rolling up her sleeves.

And Beverly added eagerly, "I'll mix up the eggnog."

Pam and Rhoda were helping with the chairs, and Janet was steadying the stepladder for Angelo. Phyllis and Laura were whispering together by the Christmas tree, as they hung the lower boughs with bells. Mrs. DeWitt had rolled herself into the curve of the staircase nearby, taken out a pen, and opened a new, leather-bound notebook. She looked into the distance with an air of concentration.

Dolly put her foot on the stairs, but Phyllis stopped her. "I wanted to tell you—" she began.

"Have you seen Kay?" Dolly interrupted anxiously.

"Not since breakfast. But I wanted to explain—"

Suddenly Mrs. DeWitt put her pen down and rolled forward. "Dolly, my dear, I remembered something more about Dora Potter," she said in her reminiscing way.

Dolly despaired of ever being free to find her beloved.

"It was seeing dear Beverly that reminded me, and the poor woman at Happy Valley whose children used to come on visiting day."

"What did they remind you of?" Dolly asked patiently as Phyllis waited politely.

"Why, that Dora didn't want to borrow just *any* babies, she was only interested in"—here Mrs. DeWitt lowered her voice to say delicately—"*black* babies—Negroes, you know. And she wanted their mothers too."

Dolly looked at her old housemother in complete bewilderment. "But what for?"

Phyllis's face, however, lit up with comprehension. She turned to her new friend. "Laura—are you thinking what I'm thinking?"

Laura's eyes snapped indignantly. "I certainly am!"

"What are you thinking?" Dolly demanded.

"Blockbusting!" chorused the housing experts. "Remember, Dolly, how I told you to keep the Magdalena Arms' predicament to yourself so as not to start a panic?" Phyllis reminded the landlady. "Well, that's what blockbusters do! They're real estate agents who start a panic on purpose in order to make a profit!"

"And they play the race card to do it," Laura put in. "Start rumors that Negroes are moving in—"

"They send out postcards saying they'll pay cash, put up big 'sold' signs—"

"Like the ones we found in the basement," Dolly said. She was beginning to get the picture.

"And some low-down vultures hire Negro women to walk around a block with their kids, like they've already moved in!" Laura fumed. "All for money! They'll buy a house for less than it's worth from the white folks, sell it for more than it's worth to the black folks, and make money financing too!"

"Dora would be too cheap to pay for a live baby, if she could get the same effect with a doll," Mrs. DeWitt remarked. "I suppose the stagecraft that permeated the Arms in those days must have rubbed off on her!" She picked up her pen again. "Ode to . . . ode to . . ." she murmured.

"If only we still had that doll," mourned Dolly.

"But we do." Phyllis looked a little embarrassed. "I took that doll."

Chapter 30

The Missing Doll

Dolly gaped at the self-conscious statistician. "You took the doll!"

"That's what I've been trying to tell you. I wanted to show it to Win—to Miss Ware," Phyllis explained haltingly. "And then, what with—with everything that happened afterward—" She glanced nervously at Laura.

"You forgot," Dolly helped her out.

Phyllis nodded gratefully and hurried on. "She—Miss Ware—sent it back yesterday."

Dolly heaved a sigh of relief. "So long as you've got it now." She started up the stairs.

"Actually, Arlene has it," Phyllis told her.

"Arlene!" Dolly wailed in despair. "How did she get it?"

Phyllis was taken aback. "I was bringing the doll downstairs when I saw Arlene packing her things. I asked where she was going, and she told me the Arms wasn't going to be around much longer and I should get out too. I was reassuring her that the Arms was in no danger, when she noticed the doll and said wouldn't it be fun to wrap it up for you and put it under the tree." The statistician bent to survey the pile of gifts. "I don't see it, though."

"Phyllis." Dolly was trying to be patient. "When did all this happen?"

"Right before I came down to help with the setup—right before your return." Phyllis remembered, "I haven't seen Arlene come down, so she must still be in her room!"

"Arlene is Mrs. Putney-Potter's stooge," Dolly said over her shoulder as she bounded up the stairs. "If you see her, stop her!"

"Arlene!" She pounded on room 402's door furiously. "Arlene!" She pushed open the unlocked door. The room was empty, the closet had been cleaned out, and the bureau was bare except for a brand-new telephone. Her expensive suitcase stood at the foot of the bed. Dolly undid the clasps and rummaged through the contents rapidly, thinking, *I bet you never gave up that swank Lakeside address!*

No doll. Where had the duplicitous designer taken the stolen toy?

As she stood thinking, Dolly became aware of muffled thumping noises. It was as if someone were practicing prizefighting moves on a punching bag. She went out into the corridor and listened as hard as she could. The noises seemed to be coming from Kay's room.

When Dolly yanked the door open, she almost banged Kay's head. The clarinetist was on the floor, bound and gagged, her ankles tied to her bed!

The thumping noise came as the persevering musician inched across the floor, dragging the bed behind her.

Dolly tore away the gag and set to work on the knotted cord that bound the gasping girl's wrists. The knots were impossibly tight. *Thank heavens for that switchblade,* Dolly thought gratefully, taking the weapon from her pocket and flicking it open.

"Arlene stole the money!" Kay said hoarsely as soon as she'd caught her breath.

"Wha-a-a-t?" Dolly sat back on her heels for a split second. *Of course,* she thought. *It made complete sense.* She resumed sawing away at Kay's bindings. The nefarious trustee needed to prove that Dolly was unfit and the Arms a failure. If the show was a success, and Dolly replaced the missing tax money, her case was gone. Undoubtedly Mrs. Putney-Potter had instructed her stooge to sabotage the show by stealing the ticket money!

Kay misinterpreted Dolly's silence as she put the pieces together. "I know you think she hung the moon." The words came pouring out as fast as a series of triple-tongued triplets. "But I've been suspicious of my no-good neighbor for quite a while. When Ramona told us about misplacing the money from the ticket sales, I suddenly remembered the noises I'd heard the night the money disappeared. I was lying awake, brooding about—well, it's not important. But I was awake when Ramona came in, and I heard her climb upstairs, and then downstairs and then upstairs and the doors opening and closing—hers and then Jackie's right overhead. Then I heard Arlene's door across the hall open. And *she* went upstairs. It was like Grand Central. After a little while, she came back down and went back into her room. Naturally, I thought at the time—I mean, I just assumed—" Kay stopped.

Dolly couldn't let the clarinetist labor under her mistaken impression any longer. "Oh, Kay," she said, tenderly chafing the girl's raw wrists. "There was nothing between me and Arlene, nothing that mattered, even before I found out she was Mrs. Putney-Potter's stooge. I've been awfully slow, but this morning I finally figured out why I was never really gone on Arlene—it's because *you're* the girl for me!"

Kay's whole face lit up, and she made good use of her

newly freed hands. "I tried to convince myself my growing fondness was just a flicker from that old crush I'd had," the clarinetist confessed. "But instead of fading, my feelings just kept getting stronger!"

As she and Kay kissed, Dolly realized that at last she'd found the perfect tenant for her heart, a heart that had been vacant until Kay had quietly moved in, clarinet case and all, while the misguided landlady flitted about, trying to rent out the already occupied organ.

Kay's tongue touched hers, and Dolly's happiness was augmented by a sudden surge of desire, like the gushing of water through the pipes when she turned the shutoff valve from off to on. Then she was lying next to Kay, kissing her deeply as she untucked Kay's T-shirt and slid her hands over the clarinetist's smooth flesh. Her lust almost blinded her to the fact that they were on the floor and Kay was still tied to her bedpost. Reluctantly, she called a halt to this seductive madness.

"Wait, stop!" Dolly extricated herself from Kay's grasp. "We don't have time for this just now!"

"Are you sure?" Kay pleaded. "We've worked under tight deadlines before!"

"Arlene's on the loose somewhere in the Arms, wreaking who knows what havoc, and your legs are still tied." With difficulty, Dolly pulled away from the carnally minded carrottop and set to work again with her switchblade. "Was it Arlene who tied you up? What happened?"

"I found your keys this morning when I was pinchhitting as a dishwasher," Kay began. "You'd left them on the shelf above the sink. I knew Arlene was out, so I went up to her room to see what I could turn up. And sure enough, there was a pile of bills underneath her underwear. It didn't really *prove* anything, but I guess Arlene panicked when she saw me poking in her bureau, because she snuck up behind me and conked me on the head with my own clarinet!" Ruefully she added, "It'll never sound the same, I'm sure."

Dolly saw red as she thought of her precious Kay, beaned by amoral Arlene. With a final savage thrust, she freed Kay's ankles.

"Ahhh! That feels better!" Kay climbed to her feet, holding on to Dolly. "While I was still groggy, she dragged me in here and tied me up, gagging me with my handker-chief. Are you sure she hasn't skedaddled? Why would she hang around?"

"She has to figure a way to sneak the doll out of the Arms, past everyone in the lobby, and she can't use her suitcases because she thinks Phyllis thinks she persuaded her to stay," Dolly explained rapidly as they clattered down the stairs. "If I were her, I'd go to the sub-basement storeroom and look for a box—in this hullabaloo no one in the lobby would notice her. Or maybe she'll try to call Mrs. Putney-Potter since she's the real mastermind of this pernicious plot. But that would be hard, because the only phone . . ." Dolly stopped so abruptly Kay bumped into her. "Oh no! I forgot, there are phones in every room now!"

When they reached the bottom of the stairs, they found a curtain blocking their path. Kay and Dolly pawed at the heavy velvet, looking for the opening. At last Dolly found the gap and they emerged into the lobby. All the seats were set up, and Laura and Phyllis were tak-ing tickets from some early audience members. There were Sylvia and Terry, a bored girl between them who must be Sylvia's daughter. *Where is Sylvia's husband?* Dolly couldn't help wondering, even in the midst of her distraction. Mrs. Pryce and Miss Craybill were chatting with Mrs. DeWitt, and Dolly even glimpsed Miss Barnes sitting in the back row taking a catnap.

Phyllis waved a handful of programs to get Dolly's attention. "Your Mrs. Putney-Potter is here," she said breathlessly. "She told Mrs. Pryce she was going to the sub-basement storeroom to inspect the new joist!"

Dolly dodged Mrs. Pryce, who wanted to compliment her on the lobby's paint job, and rejoined Kay. "We better hurry," she said, an uneasy feeling growing in the pit of her stomach. "Mrs. Putney-Potter's gone down to the sub-basement storeroom, and I've got a funny feeling it's not on a tour of inspection!"

They clattered down the uncarpeted steps to the dining room, already set for the reception with piles of silver and stacks of plates and napkins, and passed on to the kitchen. Lois was taking a pan of gingerbread out of the oven, while Beverly whirred the eggbeater in a big bowl, peering at the *Woman's Companion Cookbook* open before her.

"Did you see Mrs. Putney-Potter?" Dolly demanded.

Beverly stopped beating the eggs long enough to answer, "That crabby-looking lady in the fancy fur coat? She went downstairs without a by-your-leave, like she owned the place."

As soon as they opened the door to the sub-basement storeroom, Dolly's nose told her something was amiss. The next instant Mrs. Putney-Potter and Arlene came into view. They were both bent over a kind of miniature funeral pyre, like members of some secret cult of Satan worshipers.

"We need more newspaper," Mrs. Putney-Potter snapped.

They're trying to burn the evidence, Dolly deduced. But so far they'd only succeeded in melting the poor doll's plastic face and making a big stink.

"Leave that innocent doll alone!" ordered the landlady.

Arlene made an instinctive attempt to hide behind an old trunk. "It wasn't my idea," she cried. "None of it!"

Mrs. Putney-Potter ignored the two girls, flicking her lighter as fast as she could in a desperate attempt to incinerate the incriminating doll.

"For heaven's sake," said Dolly impatiently. "Don't you know when it's over? The Magdalena Arms account is flush! The physical plant is in the pink! The rent rolls are full! Meanwhile, Putney Projects' bid for the housing project is being scrutinized, and your blockbusting past is all the buzz upstairs in the lobby! Go home and get ready for the expected audit!"

Arlene turned on Mrs. Putney-Potter like a threatened rat. "Is this true? You promised me I could design the new project! I've been preparing my streamlined modern housing plans all this time I've done your dirty work—and now they'll never be built?"

"Stop your whining and fetch me something flammable," ordered Mrs. Putney-Potter.

"Find another flunky!" cried the disenchanted stooge. "I'm through with you and your crazy vendetta!" She ran up the stairs, pushing past Dolly and Kay.

Kay went after the girl who'd sapped her. "You're not going anywhere with that money you stole," she vowed.

Alone in the storeroom with Mrs. Putney-Potter, Dolly felt almost sorry for the soon to be dethroned real estate mogul, who'd never learned the art of getting along with others. "Even your henchwoman has deserted you, Mrs. Putney-Potter! Give up, before you set fire to the storeroom in your silly attempt to destroy that doll!"

Mrs. Putney-Potter looked up for the first time. Her proud profile was twisted by a crazed determination that had nothing to do with a desire to dominate the real estate market. "That's not a bad idea," she said, a not-quite-sane expression on her sharp-featured face. "If I can't bulldoze the Arms, I'll burn it!"

She kicked the doll aside and gingerly pushed the pile of smoldering newspaper toward the tall stack of cardboard boxes that stood against the wall, as she ranted:

"Let them go up in flames, those self-satisfied, supposedly superior sapphics! Pushing me out of this Podunk place all because a couple girls lost at cards and I wouldn't loan out my gloves! Who did they think they were dealing with? No one does Dora Potter dirt! I'll evict *them* this time, if I burn up myself!"

The flames began to singe the bottommost box, and Dolly knew she had to act fast to stop the fire from spreading.

Fortunately, the conscientious landlady had recently replaced the regulation fire extinguishers. It was the work of a moment, to vault down the remaining stairs, whisk the red canister off the hook on the wall, and douse the flames in fire-retardant foam. Mrs. Putney-Potter, who was kneeling by her bonfire, was covered as well.

"I think you'd better resign as trustee," Dolly advised the thwarted woman, whose face under the foam was purple with frustrated rage. "If the blockbusting doesn't make you ineligible for such a responsibility, attempted arson certainly will!"

Chapter 31

Angelo Sings

By the time the police had taken the enraged trustee away, along with her cowering stooge, the audience had arrived and settled into their seats, some of them catching the end of this unexpected preshow entertainment. Mrs. Pryce was delighted at Dolly's hasty account of Dora Putney-Potter's misdeeds. "You'll have a free hand at the Magdalena Arms now," she promised. "I'm so glad you're staying on as our new landlady!"

Miss Barnes, next to the trustee, hushed her sharply. "The show is about to start. There's going to be clog dancing!"

Dolly faded to the back of the room, where she could look out over the audience whispering and pointing and rustling their programs. The lights went down, and Jackie emerged from behind the curtains that hid the lounge door. She wore one of the mod striped shift dresses that Phyllis had sewed. An offstage piano began to tinkle a familiar tune, and Jackie sang,

> *I can't be home for Christmas,*
> *Sure wish that I could call*
> *To hear them tell*

Of all the—hell,
I'll have to miss it all!

Laughter rolled through the room as a cardboard cutout of a telephone was lowered jerkily down, stopping just out of Jackie's reach.

Dolly applauded vigorously at the end of the number. Jackie took her bow and was replaced by a trio of long-haired girls equipped with a banjo, guitar, and mandolin.

As the mournful voices twined in poignant harmony with the twanging instruments, the curtain covering the front door was pushed aside. Dolly turned to pass the latecomer a program, and then grasped her by both arms. "Miss Watkins!"

The career counselor smiled at her. "I'm glad to see you back where you belong, Dolly," she said softly.

In the dimness, the personnel woman's smile had an almost otherworldly quality. Dolly peered closely at the placid face and shivered. Had Miss Watkins put something in her whiskey at Francine's? Or was it simply that her career wisdom had penetrated Dolly's brain, lying dormant in the landlady's subconscious, to bloom into the lesson of that horrible nightmare?

Dolly would never know. But she would always be grateful. "Thank you," she said simply.

Miss Watkins nodded, as if she knew exactly what Dolly was thinking. "Did I miss Jackie's Pinter monologue?" she whispered. "I'd better find a seat."

As the enigmatic career counselor crept away, Dolly looked around for Kay. Arlene had remained mute about the missing money, but Kay was sure she'd hidden it on the fourth floor and was determined to find it. The clog dancing, comic impersonations, and still no clarinet player. Finally, as Jackie appeared again and announced,

"Scene, an old house in North London," Kay material-
ized on Dolly's right.

"I've got it!"

"Really? Where was it?"

Onstage, Jackie was talking about the family being all
together, but Dolly was more interested in Kay's news.

"She stuffed it in my bashed-in clarinet! She must have
thought it would be the one place I wouldn't think to
look. She probably planned to go back and collect the
cash while I was playing my spare in the second act.
Look!"

Kay held out the broken instrument. Dolly could see
the tightly wadded bills poking out of the bell. "If I'd
played the trumpet, or something with a bigger bell, I
might not have spotted it."

"So now we have twice as much money," the landlady
realized, her eyes alight with improvement schemes.
What a windfall! She began making a mental list.

New room for Angelo.
Revise the bylaws! Consult Janet.
Revamp rooms.
Singles into suites?
Tuck-pointing—see if enough in the bank now.
New couch for the lounge—or reupholster?

Jackie finished her monologue, and the applause was
followed by a lively murmur of comment. "Frankly, I
didn't understand that at all," muttered one audience member to her neighbor. "There was nothing about phones *or*
Christmas."

Kay nudged the landlady. "What are you scheming?"
she asked softly.

Dolly replied sotto voce, "What do you think of a suite on the fourth floor? With Arlene gone, we could move Ilsa from 404 to 402, and then you and I—"

Kay's teeth gleamed white in the darkness. "Sounds homier than a house with a picket fence!"

And much better than a bungalow in the Hollywood Hills, thought Dolly.

"In fact, I don't mind if we stay until we're as old as Mrs. DeWitt!" Kay finished. A woman in the audience turned and said, "Shhh!" Kay pulled Dolly away, back to the corner by the visitors' parlor.

"That's good," whispered Dolly. "Because I have to look after my girls!"

She could see them, a stream of girls trooping toward the Arms from small towns across the country. Generation after generation of girls, of every color and creed, some not even born yet, all arriving at the venerable boardinghouse, suitcases in hand, in search of cheap housing, a filling breakfast, and fast friends.

"You can leave them to look after themselves for a few weeks, can't you?" Kay asked, still holding Dolly's hand. "Maxie wants the Sisterhood of Swing to play at her restaurant in Paris."

"Paris in springtime!" Dolly caught her breath.

"In February," corrected Kay. "Want to come? We'll have a ball!" She slid her arm around Dolly and nuzzled the housemother's neck. "In fact, why don't we get a head start now?"

Dolly wrapped her arms around the clarinet player's waist. "I *have* seen the show a half dozen times already," she murmured. She hadn't the faintest idea what was happening up onstage anyway. "But don't you have to play?"

"Not until after intermission," Kay reminded her, her lips and hands setting the landlady buzzing like a kazoo. "We've managed with time limits before, and there's a couch in the visitors' parlor."

It would be quite a caper, slipping off with Kay in the middle of the Christmas Capers. Was this the kind of example of moral rectitude she wanted to set for her girls?

Dolly was trying to open the visitors' parlor door as quietly as possible, with Kay close behind, when Jackie came edging along the wall, a somber sprite, still in the black dress she'd worn for the Pinter monologue.

"There you are!" she pounced. The audience was applauding the operatic number, and under cover of the noise, Jackie told them, "Ramona's tearing her hair out backstage in the lounge! The girls say those phones are too heavy for the big finale. They can't sing and dance in them—they're refusing to wear them!"

There would always be some crisis, the housemother realized as she tried to focus on Jackie's story. This time it was the problematic props, constructed by an undercover architect who knew nothing about stage design.

"Forget the heavy phones." Dolly didn't want to spend too much time on this. "Grab some of the new ones from the second floor at intermission and have the girls hold them while they dance."

A jingling noise on stage attracted her attention. The chorus was coming out, and one of the singers bumped a bough on the Christmas tree and set the bell that hung from it jingling. "Or have them take the bells off the trees and shake them like castanets," the ex-actress suggested.

She turned back to the visitors' parlor. Kay was holding open the door. "Come on, Dolly," the clarinetist urged. "There're only three more acts before intermission."

Jackie protested, "Where are you going? Angelo's going to sing!"

"We know," said Dolly, closing the door behind her. "We'll hear him just fine in here."

And in fact, Angelo's soulful rendition of "Bei Mir Bistu Shein" only added to Dolly and Kay's pleasure.

Author's Note

Thanks are owed first and foremost to my editor, John Scognamiglio, for suggesting I write a Christmas book. Thanks also to Julie Ann Yuen and Bethany Qualls for their feedback requested, as always, at the last minute; and to Kathy Hennig for answering a clarinet question. All errors and inaccuracies are mine.

In this book, Bay City is even more ahead of the times than usual. Dolly enjoys the televised yule log in 1965, a year before it debuted in New York; and Jackie's monologue from Harold Pinter's *The Homecoming* was performed a year before that play crossed the ocean from England to America. Mrs. Putney-Potter's methods as a blockbuster are only slightly exaggerated.